MW00579158

ASP

GUARDIAN SHADOW WORLD, BOOK TWO

KRIS MICHAELS

CHAPTER 1

*A*sp meandered up the gravel trail from the cafeteria at Guardian's South Dakota training complex to the temporary Shadow Headquarters. The core of the Guardian hierarchy had flown out to attend a wedding, leaving an unnatural hush over the normally bustling area. Anubis, or rather Kaeden, had been left in charge. Asp popped one of the half-dozen peanut butter cookies he'd carried out of the cafeteria into his mouth. They were good, but not as good as Mrs. Henshaw's. He'd grown attached to that old lady and not just for her cooking. She lived in the heart of D.C. in a cruddy little apartment she could barely afford. She was lonely, and she was a sweetheart. Asp longed to pay her kids a visit and teach them to value their mom, but he figured most of Guardian would have a problem if he did. Dammit.

He trudged up to the door and went through the gyrations necessary to enter the facility, all while trying to keep his cookies from crumbling into a scattered pile on the fingerprint scanner. The damn thing red-lighted him...again. He punched the intercom and waited.

"Seriously?"

Asp flipped his middle finger in front of the camera. His fellow assassin laughed before the buzzer sounded, and he was permitted into the entrapment area. Asp waited for Anubis to make it from his office to the holding cell. Well, that was what he called it. Sooner or later the Shadows would have a permanent building, the majority of which would be underground. Literally. A set of twins had been working to get the facility built.

Asp popped another peanut butter cookie into his mouth and munched on it. All things considered, the idea of a base where the Shadows could come to rehab, train and just fucking relax—hell, that was an awesome idea. Asp loved the South Dakota ranch. He could wander down to watch the horses, which were cool as shit, or he could go sit on a high hill overlooking thousands of acres of ranchland. The peacefulness recharged him each time he came back, and he'd chosen to return more and more lately. This time, however, the choice to return had not been his. He'd been recalled. He was to report directly to Anubis as soon as he stepped off the plane. Asp smiled and bit a cookie in half. Not likely. If he had to go through a briefing after forty hours of non-stop travel, he was going to do it with something in his stomach. The door in front of him buzzed, clicked and then swung open.

"I see that, once again, you followed reporting instructions."

With a snort, Asp elbowed the door open and followed Anubis down the short, vacant hall.

"I did. Without sounding weird, you're looking good." Asp marveled at the change in his friend since he'd stopped working the field. Anubis had a major issue with food which Asp wholeheartedly understood. Hell, when your primary weapon of assassination is poison, Asp could see how a phobia could develop. But, obviously Anubis's wife Sky had convinced him to eat her cooking because the guy actually looked healthy.

"Between Sky, Keelee, and Amanda, I've been forced to stretch my boundaries on my food issues." Anubis flashed his card in front of a lock, hit a six-digit number, and lowered his eye to a retinal scanner. Asp followed him into his office. "Hit the comm shield." Anubis threw the order over his shoulder.

Asp reached up and hit it. The thing flashed yellow for about ten seconds before it turned a solid green. Whatever they were going to talk about, nobody else on the planet would be able to hear it.

"I thought you'd be at Bengal's wedding." Asp planted his ass in the big, comfy chair in front of Anubis's desk.

"Can't. Someone has to stay and man the fortress. Besides, they'll all be back this afternoon. Well, except for Zane and Jewell. They are doing the honeymoon thing." His friend took out a key and unlocked his desk.

Asp leaned over to see what he was pulling out and laughed when a can of nuts and a sealed bottle of water appeared. "Dude, you're still locking up your food?"

"Old habits." Anubis shrugged and popped the top off both containers. He grabbed a handful of pecans and leaned back in his chair. "I've got some news to relay."

Asp brushed his hands together getting rid of the crumbs the last cookie left in his palm. "Good news or bad?"

Anubis swallowed his mouthful of pecans and grabbed the bottle of water. He shook his head and took a long swig. "I don't know. I guess that depends on you."

Asp felt an unpleasant clutch in his gut, and it wasn't because of the dozen or so cookies he'd eaten. He leaned back and started raising his mental barriers. He recognized that tone in his friend's voice. There was something screwy with a new assignment or an assignment he'd completed. His mind scrolled through the year. He'd been injured while executing a kill and had roamed playing tourist while he recuperated. He'd had exactly one assignment since he'd been reinstated—the "Italian job" vetted by the Council.

According to rumors, the Council consisted of a permanent member of each of the FBI, CIA, Homeland, Guardian, Mossad, MI6, Interpol and three rotating members of other international security agencies. The Council examined the requests for "termination" on a case-by-case basis. If a unanimous vote was cast, the person indicted in the case was coded. The unanimous vote was mandated so that no country or entity would shoulder the responsibility of the action any more than any other country. It also worked as a failsafe in case a Shadow or an asset from another organization or country were ever captured, tortured and broken.

He slid his gaze up to meet Anubis'. "Am I going to have to play twenty questions?"

Anubis pursed his lips and shook his head. "No, I'm afraid that's my job today."

"What the fuck are you talking about?" Every nerve in Asp's body stood ready for fight or flight. His usually straight-shooting friend had keyed his biological response tighter with his hedging.

"There is a case currently in front of the Council." Anubis dropped his eyes to a folder on his desk.

Asp waited for a full three minutes. "Again, am I going to have to guess?" Asp uncrossed his legs and leaned forward. "Spit it out, man."

"The subject in this file is the individual being reviewed."

Asp lifted an eyebrow and reached for the folder. He leaned back in his chair and gave Anubis a hard stare. "Why do I get the feeling if I open this folder, my life will never be the same?"

"Because you have some of the best instincts in the business." Anubis nodded toward the file. "Archangel and Alpha cleared me to approach you. If this case is coded, and that is a *big* if, it is yours."

Asp cocked his head. He glanced at the folder and then back at Anubis. "Why are you telling me this?"

"Open it and see for yourself."

Asp studied the folder on his lap. The standard red cardboard gave no hint of its contents. He drew a breath and flipped the folder open. Male, Caucasian, late forties/early fifties. He appeared to be in shape, not overweight. The guy glared at the camera with cold, hard eyes. He didn't recognize the picture. He glanced up to find Anubis staring at him like he was a bug under a microscope. Asp flipped the page and noted the name. Jarvis Cavanaugh. Huh...still didn't mean anything. The man's address and work information were also listed. Asp stopped reading, flipped closed the cover of the file and threw it on Anubis' desk. "He's CIA, Shadows don't work on American soil and we don't do friendlies. I won't violate those directives." Never again. Not for anyone.

"Right. This guy is ex-CIA, a real notorious son of a bitch. He is currently somewhere in Colombia. His whereabouts vary whenever the wind changes direction, but according to what our friends in the CIA are telling us, his current nest is the area formerly controlled by the Fuerza Alternativa Revolutionaria del Comun."

"We have *friends* in the CIA?" He'd rather Guardian and the CIA never communicated. He harbored a deep distrust of the Central Intelligence Agency. In his experience, the agency operatives worked harder at political grandstanding and ruthless backstabbing to gain power within the agency than they did gathering intelligence. The CIA was the antithesis of Guardian. Guardian had strict rules of conduct, ethics, and integrity. In his experience, the hallowed halls of the CIA lacked all three.

"*We* don't have any friends." Anubis flicked his fingers between himself and Asp. "But our liaison, also known as Alpha's wife, has numerous contacts embedded throughout the agency, and as far as I know, they've never fed her any bullshit."

"You know I hate the CIA, and you have an idea why."

"I do." Anubis stared at him from across the desk trying to do that silent ninja, mind-meld thing again as if Asp had ever been able to read anything in the assassin's blank stare. Asp shook his head and lifted his hands in defeat. "I give. I can't read your mind. Why am I getting advance intel on this guy?" To be honest, he felt pretty fucking stupid at the moment. He wasn't following whatever conversation Anubis thought they were having.

Anubis reached for the folder, flipped it open and turned over the last piece of paper. Printed on a label affixed to the back of the folder was a call sign Asp would never forget. Equal measures of hatred, guilt, and shame had seared it into his brain. Halo One-One.

Asp leaned back in his chair and stared not really seeing his friend. *Halo One-One.* His former CIA handler. The motherfucker who'd sent him to stalk and kill an innocuous university professor. Asp shook his head as his mind slammed him back in time to the briefing Halo had given him on his target.

The man had a wife and two sons. He was no more a threat to national security than baseball and apple pie, but Halo had cooked the dossier and forged the authentications needed for a hit. When the professor traveled overseas for a conference, Asp followed. A simple mission on an unsuspecting and blameless man.

As soon as Asp had been given the folio, the guy was as

good as dead, but the days of surveillance had made Asp wary. The professor's behavior didn't support the accusation alleged in the dossier—that he was accessing or selling national secrets. Asp had been so doubtful, he had broken procedure and questioned Halo, his handler. He could remember staring at Halo's email. He could still see the cursor blinking after the words "terminate as directed."

Before that case, Asp had never violated agency protocol. Before that night, he'd never made a copy of a dossier or of an email dead drop communication. But his gut told him the man wasn't what Halo suspected. He'd emailed Halo's superior with a coded request to have the mission reviewed, and for days afterward, there was no response. Asp dragged his feet until he received the one sentence response from Halo's superior. It simply read, "proceed with mission."

The next morning Asp killed a fifty-four-year-old, American, professor of economics. He returned to the states and went to CIA headquarters, an act that violated every cannon he'd agreed to when he signed on with the agency. When Asp scanned his credentials, every alarm and warning system in the building activated. He got everyone's attention, and that was exactly what he needed. He demanded to speak to his department section chief and refused to buy into their stall and mitigation tactics. When he finally met face-to-face with the deputy director, his superior accessed the dossier and the dead-drop email communications. The man was livid. But not at Halo One-One. No, the man was steamed at *him*, for breaching protocol. After the director tore him a new one, the man took the information Asp provided and left. He gave no indication why Halo wanted the professor dead or if the man had been a legitimate target. If he was wrong and the professor was a traitor selling information to the enemy, Asp would be washed up and would probably end up dead. But he didn't care. His gut told him the man was innocent. He should have fucking listened to his gut. The man was innocent. He'd found that out from a contact within the CIA. Without a word, he walked away from the agency.

"Yo, man. You still with me?"

The question from Anubis snapped Asp out of his memories but did little to quell the sickness of his soul awakened by ghosts of the past. He shot a look across the desk and nodded. Once. "When will I know?"

"The Council will reconvene next week." Anubis nodded at the folder. "You know his background up until the time you left the agency." Anubis pulled out another folder. "This is the information being presented to the Council. Archangel doesn't know which way this will go. The likelihood of him being able to accomplish what he's attempting is slim, but if Cavanaugh gets the remnants of the FARC stirred up in Colombia, it will be impossible to calculate the cost in human lives."

The FARC was a militant entity. From what Asp recalled, the United States, using the tried and true process of having the CIA 'train' local civilians, had successfully crushed the civil disobedience. "I thought the FARC disbanded last year. They are a legitimate political party now." Asp tossed that softball at Anubis. He needed information, and it was obvious Anubis knew more than he was sharing.

"They did, and they are, but if Cavanaugh stirs up the malcontents and rallies the members who didn't agree to the cease-fire and peace accord, well then he's the fuse in a powder keg. The FARC were, and quite possibly still are, recruiting from local villages. They aren't asking nicely. They take able-bodied men and young boys anywhere from twelve on up."

"I thought that practice had been abandoned." In an effort to get a solid understanding of what he'd be diving into, Asp stirred what information he had around his brain for a moment..

"Why change something that works?" Anubis dropped another folder on the desk. "The latest intel on the FARC movements according to Guardian."

He grabbed the file and read words that spelled out the ugly, undisguised truth of both the government of Colombia's abuse of its citizens and the FARC's deadly grab for power.

Anubis shook a few pecans into his hand. "We want to know why he's down there."

Asp slowly lifted one eyebrow at his friend. "There isn't a question as to why he's down there. The FARC was making money hand over fist by guarding illegal drug channels and charging a tax to the growers and manufacturers to keep their shipments safe. If that revenue source is lying dormant, then my money is on that bastard trying to set up his own system."

"Drugs?" Anubis rubbed his chin and gazed off into space.

"Money, power, and yes, drugs. You know he was excommunicated from the agency after I exposed what he did, right?" Asp wasn't sure how far Anubis's knowledge of the situation went.

"I know he was arrested, but he wasn't prosecuted. The file doesn't indicate why."

Asp leaned forward and placed his elbows on his knees, linked his fingers together and fixed his friend with an intent stare. "He had dirt on everyone in that organization. If they had tried him, he would have exposed them. It was how he operated. I didn't fear any repercussions when I exposed him because my parents died earlier that year."

Anubis cocked his head and stared at Asp. "I don't understand."

"I know, in my gut, the man would have gone after me by

targeting my folks, somehow he would have hurt them, or worse. Believe me, it is extremely simple and completely convoluted at the same time. Did you know I was recruited into the agency out of the Marines?"

The assassin across the desk shook his head. "I have access to the information, but I didn't feel it was necessary for me to look into your past. Whatever happened back then was what made you who you are today. I trust today's version to let me know anything that is pertinent."

Asp internalized the gratitude he felt. Anubis could know every detail of his life, but he chose to respect his privacy. He cleared his throat to block the sudden rise of emotion and leaned forward as he spoke, "I was a sniper. My spotter and I were in country after leave before we returned to our duties. We'd just processed back into Iraq and were bunking down in the Green Zone until we had transport out toward our new forward operating base. That was August 2010. There were twenty-three rocket attacks on the Green Zone that month. One of those motherfuckers brought our barracks down around our ears. My spotter died of his injuries, I was evacuated to Landstuhl Army Hospital in Germany."

"Landstuhl, shit." Anubis shook his head.

"Yeah, you don't get a free ride to there without having some serious injuries. I'll admit, I was pretty fucked up. They kept me doped up, the military's standard response." Asp ran his hand through his hair and stared at the wall past Anubis's shoulder. "Whoever was in charge of notifying next of kin screwed up. They told my folks that I'd died in the attack." Asp chuckled although it sounded bitter even to his ears. "The CIA showed up and made me an offer. They showed me pictures of my family burying what they thought were my remains. I have no idea who was in that casket. After I got back to the States, I visited my spotter's grave, so at least his parents got the closure they deserved...I guess...anyway those bastards in the CIA played me like I was a fucking violin."

Asp let out a bitter string of cuss words before he stood and started pacing Anubis' office. "Imagine it, man, there I was hopped up on drugs, staring at pictures of my mom and dad all tore up and grieving and all these 'recruiters' are telling me that because I'm a sniper it was just a matter of time before my folks would have to live through that pain again. They offered me a way to take care of them financially and still serve my country." Asp stopped behind the chair he'd been sitting in and grabbed the padded leather backrest. He dropped his head down between his shoulders and stared at his feet, embarrassed by his display of emotion.

"They brought you into the black ops side of the house. You were dead, and you were used as a weapon for the CIA."

Asp nodded his head without looking up. He shrugged and studied his fucking boots for a moment before he spoke again. "I was used, all right." He lifted his head and stared straight at the folder on Anubis's desk. "Cavanaugh used me, and because of him I'll never know if the others I killed while employed by the CIA were legitimate hits." He lifted his eyes to Anubis's face. "I'll *never* know."

Anubis stared back at him, and Asp knew to the very core of his soul, that Anubis got it. Anubis understood the need to know what he was doing was for the greater good. His friend had lost sight of that once, and Asp had helped him remember why they did what they did.

"If the Council codes him, is it your desire to take this case?"

"He's mine." Ice filled his veins. He would take pleasure in finding Halo One-One and killing him.

"I'll let Archangel and Alpha know. Are you staying here or floating until a decision comes down the pipe?"

A shit-eating grin spread across his face. Anubis had just

told him where the motherfucker was. He had a picture to go with the name. Hell, he was booking it to Colombia the second his foot reached the exit door. Furthermore, Anubis knew it.

"Right, that was a stupid question, wasn't it?" Anubis rubbed the back of his neck and shrugged.

"We are all authorized one or two in a lifetime." Asp spun and grabbed the door handle but paused, halted by a sudden need to acknowledge what his friend had done for him. He'd learned never to ignore his gut. He turned around and waited until Anubis looked up. "Thank you, Kaeden. For everything."

Anubis froze. "This isn't goodbye." He stood and walked to the door, extending his hand.

"It isn't my intention, but..." Asp took the proffered hand and shook it.

Anubis pulled him in for a tight and unexpected hug. "Don't you fucking do anything stupid out there."

Asp swallowed back a deluge of emotion normally nonexistent in his day-to-day life. "Shit, now you're asking for miracles." He gave his friend a smile he didn't feel and spun on his heel. He had a plane to catch.

CHAPTER 2

*A*sp glanced at his watch as his four-wheel drive vehicle lurched up another steep incline, the transmission grinding and the wheels slipping on the loose gravel. The road trip from Suriname, through Guyana, crossing the northeastern tip of Brazil, through the lower portion of Venezuela and into Colombia had taken three days, the equivalent of several thousands of dollars in bribes to border guards, and one hell of a lot of patience. The patience was not an issue. If there was anything Asp possessed in spades, it was patience.

He couldn't risk flying into either Colombia or one of the neighboring countries. He had no idea how far Jarvis Cavanaugh's reach extended, and as of this moment, he didn't have clearance to go after the bastard. So, Asp spent his long hours behind the wheel formulating a plan to stalk the son of a bitch.

He mentally ran through the list of what he did know from the briefing Anubis had given him. One, Cavanaugh's connection to the FARC organization ran deep. Whether he'd made the connections when he was employed by the

CIA, or after, was irrelevant. The man had a network to keep him informed. Two, the people who worked for Jarvis were not likely to flip sides for cash so Asp would have to either assume a role as a friend to Cavanaugh, or he'd have to ghost his way through the central foothills of Colombia. The first option might expedite finding his quarry, but undoubtedly, it would also expose him to detection.

Asp ground his teeth together and gripped the steering wheel hard enough to leave impressions. Just because *he* hadn't known what his handler looked like, he couldn't assume that Halo One-One didn't know what *he* looked like. If he made such a stupid leap of logic it would probably get him killed. No, he'd have to ghost through the foothills. Halo One-One was a diabolical son of a bitch. Asp glanced in his rearview mirror and then to his side view. A black four-by-four had been following him for over thirty minutes. He pushed his foot down on the accelerator and glanced at the GPS he'd checked out from the complex before leaving South Dakota. The device used government satellites and rarely if ever lost reception. He'd just crossed the border where the Buenaventura Transverse highway connected Colombia's largest port with the Venezuelan border in Puerto Carreño. The road was abysmal, but it was a road. The road signs that did exist on the Transverse Highway were sparse and helped little in navigating the vastness of the country. Asp glanced at his gas gauge. A half a tank of petrol could get him a couple hundred kilometers, but he'd need to stop. Sooner, rather than later, it seemed. He noticed the black four-wheel-drive vehicle had met his speed and was cruising back there. Not threatening, not demanding...just following.

Asp dropped his hand to the GPS. He pinched and spread his fingers bringing the secondary roads into sharp relief on the display. He glanced up at the road and back down at the GPS. A small spur to his left would be his first chance to make a *desviacion*, or detour. He glanced at his rearview and discarded the idea. He'd wait until he had a hill in between him and his new best friend. Until then, he'd play. He let off the accelerator and watched as the SUV behind him similarly slowed. The fucktard following him was either stupid or naive. Asp grunted and slapped his hand against the steering wheel, unless... The driver could be playing with him. His eyes flew to the horizon. He could be being forced into a trap ahead of him, too worried about who or what was behind him to be proactive about what could be waiting ahead.

His decision was made as he approached the *desviacion*. He whipped the vehicle onto the dirt road and flew over a small rise. His foot damn near shoved through the floor of the vehicle as he stomped on the brake and jerked the gear shift into park. He exited, palmed his .45s and took aim. A roil of red dust indicated his friend had followed. As the vehicle crested the top of the hill, Asp spread his legs and found where his target would be behind the black tinted glass of the windshield.

The car skidded to a stop. Asp's fingers twitched when the vehicle's engine turned off. He held the position for several seconds before the driver's side door opened. Every muscle in his body relaxed at the familiar figure that unfolded from the SUV.

"Thanatos?" Asp returned the weapons to his twin shoulder holsters and braced his hands on his hips. "Why the ever loving fuck are you following me?" He gave the man a once over. It was the first time he'd ever seen Thanatos in anything but a suit. The jeans, cowboy boots, t-shirt, and baseball hat screamed American. Unlike Asp's tan slacks, ankle high boots, button down and lightweight jacket. Asp's clothing screamed European.

"Well, that seems to be the question of the day." The slow Texas drawl sounded foreign coming from Thanatos. The man's natural-born Irish brogue was nowhere to be found. Although every last one of the Shadows were chameleons, Thanatos had never before displayed this ability—at least not to him.

Asp crossed his arms over his chest and leaned on the used-to-be-black back of the vehicle he'd driven across three countries. "Well if that is the question of the day, why don't you tell me the answer?"

Thanatos crossed his arms and leaned against the front of his black four-wheel drive. "Halo has been officially coded. Additionally, it would appear that Archangel thinks Colombia is a damn big country and finding your mark will be like finding a needle in a haystack." A wide, slow smile spread across Thanatos's face. "So I'm here to be visible and to keep that fucker guessing.

Asp understood immediately, and he didn't like it. Not one bit. "I'm not going to let you be a target for that bastard. Granted, we don't know where he is, but setting you up to take a bullet in my place is bullshit."

"I don't plan on taking a bullet, my friend." Thanatos took off his ball cap and scrubbed his hand through his hair. "Hot in this fucking place."

"It is. It is going to get hotter if Halo One-One has you in his sights. I don't need help. I have a plan." Asp took off his jacket. This close to the equator the outer garment was ridiculous. "Were you given a direct order to perform as the pony in this one-horse circus?"

"No. Just given a suggestion and told I wasn't going to be needed until after this mission." Thanatos put his ball cap back on and glanced up at the sun. "Makes you long for the green pastures of home, don't it now?" The Irish brogue Asp had grown used to snapped back into place.

"I don't have a home any longer. Unless you count South Dakota." He locked gazes with Thanatos, who smiled.

"Those were the pastures I was speaking of, for certain. Seems those rolling hills have taken up a place in my DNA." Thanatos gestured toward the main road. "What is your plan, and how can I help?"

"Meet me in Villavicencio. There are about five hundred thousand people in the city. It is big enough for us to get lost for a while. There is a small restaurant, not far from Bolera Parque de La Vida Cofrem near the corner of Calle 25 and Carrera 19."

"When?" Thanatos lifted off the front of his vehicle and went back to open the driver's side door.

Asp glanced at his watch and did a mental calculation. "Tomorrow night. Seven thirty. Also, lose the cowboy attire. What I need you to do will not require painting a target on your back."

"So much the better," Thanatos said as he got behind the wheel. He executed a three-point turn and headed back to the main road. Asp swiped away the sweat and dust from his face. It was good to have Thanatos available. The country was huge, and the likelihood of finding Halo on his turf anytime soon was small. But...Asp glanced at the sun and rolled his shoulders. There was always a chance they would go unnoticed. He opened the driver's side door and smiled at the blast of cold air that greeted him. He might as well enjoy the comfort while he could.

CHAPTER 3

*T*he little restaurant where he'd agreed to meet Thanatos hadn't changed in the years since his last visit. The small wooden tables still formed two straight lines with the back, right-hand table standing alone due to a jut out in the wall. It wasn't impressive, but the food was good, and the cerveza was cold. Asp moved to the back of the dining area, near the kitchen door. It was a short five strides through that kitchen to the back alley. He stretched out in the corner and ordered a local micro-brew cerveza, preferring the hoppy tang to a bottle of water. He watched the cars fly by on the busy street out front. People moved at the same speed in central Colombia as they did in New York City. The only difference was the backdrop.

Asp accepted his beer and observed the condensation on the glass with satisfaction. Nothing better than a cold beer. He leaned back in his chair and waived off the menu. He'd order when Thanatos arrived. He was tired and in need of a few hours sleep. From the moment he'd driven into the heart of Villavicencio, he'd been working the streets, and his time had been productive.

Like any major city, the outcasts of this society wandered the streets like ghosts, unseen and ignored. If you wanted to know the true pulse of a city, talk to the homeless and the destitute. They knew what happened in the underbelly of humanity, and most times they knew why it was happening. He'd spent the night in el barrio bajo—skid row. He went armed with a backpack full of cheap alcohol, cigarettes, several packages of new socks, a handful of toothbrushes and several tubes of toothpaste. The alcohol was to loosen tongues, the rest, well that was just doing the right thing.

Thanatos walked past the restaurant. The casual observer would think the man was heading to a business meeting like the people on the sidewalk with him. He knew better. Thanatos would circle the block and make sure they weren't being followed. The last to arrive at a meeting always surfed their six and made sure no one was lying in wait. The wait for Thanatos was minimal, as he expected. Asp had watched the restaurant for over an hour before he approached.

When Thanatos entered the darkened interior, he took off his sunglasses and made his way to Asp's corner table at the back. Asp motioned for the waiter and listened as Thanatos ordered a cerveza in fluent Spanish.

"Our friend at the Complex was briefed on your desire to change the flow of activities. He agreed that you were lead and he'll deal with his bosses. He told me to tell you that you better make sure to get back in time for a certain young lady's birthday party." Thanatos had a smirk on his face the entire time he relayed the message.

"Not like *you'd* miss her birthday either." Asp threw the taunt back at his friend. Thanatos was wrapped around the finger of Anubis' daughter just as tightly as he was. "I seem to recall a doll that made its way back from France not too long ago."

"You are imagining things again. You see, this is why they

send me after you. You're going soft in the head." Thanatos hid his smile behind his beer. He chuckled and lifted it further in a toast. "To a successful venture and a speedy return."

Asp lifted his glass, clanked the heavy mug and drank half the contents. He motioned to the waiter, bringing him closer, and ordered tamales wrapped in banana leaves and two orders of lechona blimense—a slowly roasted pork dish that was normally served during celebrations.

Thanatos glanced around the little dining area before he leaned forward and cradled his beer.

Asp mirrored his actions and murmured, "Halo is gathering support in the foothills southwest of here. The population on skid row is flush with men coming from the smaller cities where the new version of the FARC is looking for volunteers. Willing or not."

"You know for a fact Halo is with them?" Thanatos lifted his beer and took a drink.

"They described the man giving the orders. Everything I heard leads me to believe Halo is actively working the dissatisfied and disenfranchised. Several of the young men who escaped being pushed into service stated there were five to ten Americans. Two always with Halo and the others came and went. One young man described the weapons. I believe they have at least two snipers."

Thanatos nodded, absorbing his information. Asp watched as the waiter made his way to their table with steaming platters of food.

After the waiter left, Thanatos asked, "What is your plan?"

"I'm going to ghost into the foothills. The young men I spoke with last night indicated Halo was working his way through the smaller villages. One said he overheard several of the men discussing a ready pool of potential men. Farmers."

"Fuck me. History repeating itself?"

"Sounds like it. But, we aren't here to stop the FARC from forming." Asp unwrapped a tamale and forked a huge bite into his mouth. The rich masa and seasoned meats floated across his taste buds and reminded his stomach that he hadn't eaten in almost twenty-four hours.

"What do you need me to do?" Thanatos dipped a fork into the gravy-soaked rice under the lechona blimense and took a bite, rolling his eyes and groaning in appreciation.

Asp smiled at his friend's reaction to one of his favorite local dishes. He finished eating the last of his tamale while Thanatos devoured his pork. Finally, Asp switched plates and started on his main course. He stalled his fork only long enough to inform his friend, "I'm traveling tonight. Southwest to the small farming communities nestled at the foothills. If my information is correct, Halo will target those areas, not only for able-bodied men but to pressure the local farmers to start planting coca again. The information Guardian provided indicated that most farmers have switched to other crops the co-ops are selling."

Asp put his fork down and waited for Thanatos to meet his gaze. "You go south, beyond the foothills. Monitor the areas on the plains for any indication of FARC presence. Cavanaugh's a cagey son of a bitch. I could be wrong. He could head south. If he does, double tap him and get the hell out of Dodge." Thanatos was a good marksman, he wasn't Asp's caliber, but he was more than capable of a long shot.

"I thought this kill was personal." Thanatos pushed his empty plate away and grabbed his half-full cerveza.

"It is. It most definitely is, but getting this bastard is the mission. Would I like to be the one to end him? Fuck, yes. Am I going to let others suffer so I can be that person? No. The bastard has destroyed too many lives. He needs to meet his end." When he considered the damage Halo had done, Asp pushed away his plate, half eaten.

Thanatos swung his attention to his plate long enough to pull it back and scrape up another meager mouthful of rice and then glanced back to Asp. "How do we communicate?"

"Routine check-ins." Asp pulled a small map from his pocket. He dropped his fingertip on the first meeting point. "One week from today, midnight, at the westernmost edge of this village." He pointed again. "Two weeks, same time, this location." They'd find each other. Asp leaned back, and Thanatos looked from the map to him. Neither one of them would ever place a mark on a map. No evidence of anything they talked about existed. They both knew if a third meeting was required they'd discuss it at the second.

"Then this is farewell. May the road rise up to meet you." Thanatos quoted the first line of the old Irish blessing they'd used many times before.

"May the wind be always at your back. Whatever it takes," Asp replied.

Thanatos pegged him with a stare. "As long as it takes, my friend."

～

Asp hunkered down just shy of the top of the highest rise overlooking the valley. His weapon and tripod were camouflaged, as was he. He pulled out another damn protein bar and slowly unwrapped it. Five weeks of this tasteless birdseed shit. He could barely stomach another one, but he needed the calories. That bastard Halo had led him on a hell of a merry chase, but between him and Thanatos, they'd found the son of a bitch's camp. Now all he needed to do was to wait.

Wait and think. The ability to block out everything while

lying prone for hours, or days on end, was an acquired talent...and he hadn't quite perfected that skill set yet. He balanced the need to stay sharp against his thoughts that shuffled through his past like a well-worn deck of cards. He'd been dealt a shit hand by the CIA. He called their bluff, and he won, after he lost...everything.

His parents had died without knowing he was still alive. The corrosive guilt that ate at him for allowing himself to be manipulated never took a break. He'd carry that one to the grave. When he agreed to the CIA's terms, he'd become hollow. He cut all tethers to the life he knew and worked. He did missions for his handler, and up until the end, he believed he was serving his country, was making the world a better place. He drew a deep breath and let it out, resetting his heart rate. He had been manipulated, so why did he feel guilty? Because there was no way of knowing how many innocent lives he'd taken. He had no illusions about what he did. He killed people. Strip away the membrane-thin belief he was working to make the world better and he was no more than a thug, a murderer—no better than Cavanaugh. *That* was the torment he'd carried for so long after he'd left the CIA. He'd expected to spend the rest of his life disenfranchised, drifting and alone. Instead, he had a tight group of people he would gladly die for—Anubis, Bengal, Thanatos, Lycos, Moriah and now Anubis' family. That little girl looked at him like he was a hero. Her big smile and tight hugs made him feel twenty-feet tall and indestructible. Seeing Anubis, Bengal, and even Fury happy and starting families, well, for a moment he wondered if *he* could have a family life.

In the FARC camp, a group of people moved from one structure to the other. Asp followed their movement with his scope. None of them were Halo. He moved his shoulder in a slow, deliberate stretch and breathed a sigh when the joint popped—his body's protest against his long hours in one position.

It was only a matter of time. He'd get *the* shot, and the motherfucker's evil would end. Until then, he'd wait, be still and think. He longed for bygone days when he had a spotter with him. His mind shuffled again, and he played the memories of missions when he and Billy served together. His spotter and friend, Billy Pearson, was an excellent marksman, almost as good as he was, but they both knew who would be the one to take the money shot when the time came.

They'd shared a hell of a lot during those long ass hours. Whispered truths about life and the mistakes they'd made. Now Billy was gone, and Asp? Well, he'd started to feel like he was living again. Until five weeks ago when he read the name Halo One-One. Bitterness, resentment, and anger filled the places where he thought some light had seeped into his life. He had a chance now to right the scale and remove the man who'd betrayed him and so many others.

Asp moved with deliberate slowness. He took another bite of the horrid protein bar and glanced through his scope again. He avoided eye fatigue and took breaks from his observation of the area and camp. He'd been in his position for almost two days. When prone, he lay behind his match-grade M-21. The weapon had been crafted by the highest caliber gunsmiths to ensure its finite accuracy. His weapon, coupled with match-grade ammo, resulted in the seldom-found consistency Asp required.

During the last two days, he'd already calculated the distances by using static markers located in the camp. The only thing he'd need to adjust for was altitude, leading his target and wind conditions. His weapon was bolt fired, and he had to load a shell for each shot he took. He *could* fire it in semiautomatic mode, but he didn't. Personal preference. In the field, any movement could get you killed. If he used the weapon on semi-automatic, the brass ejecting out of the rifle could be what the enemy needed to zero in on his location, or for that matter, any movement he made after the shot could be used to tack a target on his ass.

The hair on the back of his neck rose and he froze. He surveyed the area around him in a strip and grid pattern, searching for whatever he'd sensed. He trusted his gut. Something or someone was out there.

It wouldn't be Thanatos. He was in the lower valley. Thanatos would take Halo out if he had a chance, but Asp was the primary. Asp swept the camp below him again and then used the scope tracing the ridgeline across from him. Thanatos had been warned to stay out of the hills. Any movement would be a target, and he didn't want to kill his friend by mistake. One shot, one kill. He continued to search the hills. He couldn't see the threat, but someone was out there. He knew it. He'd been trained to trust his instincts and every last fiber of his being told him he wasn't alone.

The sun reached its zenith. Sweat streamed from his brow down his face, and into his t-shirt. He was soaked, but he remained still except for the constant movement of his eyes. He looked for bulk at the base of formations he'd searched in the past two days, a clump of grass that wasn't there yesterday. Attention to detail was a requirement, and it had saved his life more than once.

The long low drone of vehicle motors approaching the encampment set his nerves on fire, but within seconds, a self-imposed blanket of calm floated over him. Asp slipped forward two inches bringing his shoulder snug against the weapon. He glanced at his scope and noted the wind before he adjusted his weapon to compensate for the breeze. He rested his cheek against the stock of his rifle and waited. The vehicles rumbled into the clearing and stopped. Asp focused on the middle vehicle. Training and experience said Halo would want a lead and trail vehicle to protect his worthless ass.

His target exited on the far side of the Jeep. *Fuck, yes!* That bastard was going down. Asp drew a quick, shallow breath and held it, pushing his immediate excitement down and away from his thoughts. He could rejoice after the son of a bitch met his maker.

Halo moved quickly to the back seat and pulled something out. Asp drew a breath and released it in a slow exhale. The natural figure eight motion of his rifle barrel was minuscule due to the tripod, but it was there. Breathing moved his body. His body moved the weapon. He stopped breathing after exhaling. That moment of calm provided for the smallest amount of movement and optimum precision. His crosshairs found their mark. Asp squeezed the trigger in one, slow, steady movement.

Time slowed as Asp followed the trajectory of the bullet. He watched through the scope as Halo's head exploded, spraying his brains back and out. Asp didn't move. Training and instinct froze him to the spot. He continued to watch the encampment through the scope and what he saw in the camp confirmed what he'd known earlier. A man dropped behind the jeep. He had a radio held to his mouth and was looking up at the hills across from where Asp was positioned. He motioned with his arm and then turned in Asp's direction and pointed to the ridgeline where he was located. If he so much as twitched right now, he'd be dead. Asp closed his eyes for a brief moment and calculated the hours until dark. Too much time. He'd never manage the absolute stillness required for that number of hours. In less than a minute, he'd gone from predator to prey.

CHAPTER 4

*A*sp watched, using his peripheral vision to stretch his field of sight. Someone positioned in the opposite hills searched for him at the same time as he was scoured the terrain for them. Asp was at a disadvantage. He needed to reload. He waited as the sun moved across the sky dropping his position into a shadow. With infinite care, he moved millimeter by millimeter until his hand reached the bolt of his weapon and retracted it. The small sound of the well-oiled mechanics echoed in the silence. He held a bullet in his hand and slowly exchanged the spent casing for a fresh round of ammunition before he started to move the bolt forward again.

He'd stopped sweating, a sign of dehydration from baking in the hot Colombian sun. His muscles shook from the rigors of the insanely slow movement he was forced to use. For a minute or two, extending your arms parallel to the ground wasn't hard, but after thirty minutes, preventing any betraying shake wandered into the territory of exquisite torture. Asp chanted the same word over and over in his mind as his eyes scraped the distance across from him.

*Steady...steady...*his eye caught a flash of movement. He reacted.

Asp cowboy'd his weapon and shot at the movement a split second before he rolled. It was that movement that saved his life. Two shots rang out. Searing pain detonated in an explosion of acid-based lightning bolts that tore down his left hip and leg. He didn't know if he'd hit the motherfucker who shot at him. He rolled down the small embankment and earned a few precious seconds. Asp whipped his belt off and pulled the waistband of his woodland camouflage pants down. The bullet had entered at top of his thigh and exited lower about six inches above his knee. He glanced at the amount of blood flowing and said a silent prayer of thanks. No spurting arterial bleeds, but he could still bleed to death if he didn't find a safe place and get his shit stitched up. Asp oriented himself, grabbed a dressing from his cargo pockets and tied it to his hip with his belt. He used a torn piece of his uniform shirt to bind another clump of gauze over the wound on his inner thigh. The triage and self-aid took far longer than he would have liked, but bleeding to death wasn't on his agenda. Then again, neither was getting shot. He pushed up to his good leg and did the only thing he could do. He put one foot in front of the other and moved—until he couldn't.

Asp grabbed a small tree and sucked in ragged breaths trying to clear his mind enough to find a place to hold up. He swept the area where he was and glanced up at the dark sky. Fuck, he had no idea which way he'd gone or how far he'd moved away from the camp. He leaned against the tree and ground his teeth to stop a guttural growl at the agonizing pain searing through his hip and thigh. Blood saturated his pant leg. The way his mind fogged over, he had no doubt he'd lost too much. Asp slid down the tree trunk, extending his injured leg.

With difficulty, he pulled his canteen from his web belt and unscrewed the top. His hand shook wildly, forcing him to grab the cool plastic with both hands. He managed to drink several large gulps without spilling it, which given his condition was no easy feat. Asp carefully resealed the container and tried to reinsert it into its carrier only to drop it. It tumbled down an embankment. Embankment? No, that was a steep-ass ridge. Asp dropped his head back against the tree. *Of fucking course, the motherfucker fucking dropped farther than he could fucking reach. He should just fucking sit here and go to fucking sleep. Fucking son of a bitch canteen.* Asp snorted a laugh at his fuck spewing diva moment and blinked back to the problem at hand. The easiest way down the ridge was on his ass, so he scooted forward, trying to keep his injured leg from being jarred unnecessarily as he slid down on the loose dirt that covered the slope. He snagged the canteen as he passed, out of control and gaining momentum down the steep grade. He landed at the bottom with little fanfare and writhing in pain. *Fucking canteen.*

He dropped his head and rested on his back facing the dark sky. Instinct told him he needed to move, but dammit, he was tired. The motherfucking hill still trickled loose gravel down its slope, occasionally pelting him with small clots of dirt. He rolled his head to the left and took in the floor of the small valley he'd landed in. The trees and foliage indicated he hadn't descended as far as he'd believed. Dammit He needed to be farther down, closer to civilization. A breeze ruffled the leaves, and he blinked at the brief glimpse he was able to see when they moved. Drawing on strength that shouldn't be there, Asp lifted up to his elbows and craned his head to get a closer look. He didn't trust his eyes and his mind to interpret what he thought he saw, so he rolled onto his stomach, making sure his rifle and pack were still attached to his back. It was probably two hundred feet across the meadow. Child's play until he'd been shot. *Dammit.*

The short distance morphed into a gauntlet of pain. He ground his teeth together and drew the last vestiges of strength he had and low-crawled across the meadow. The breeze moved the leaves of the bushes again, and this time Asp knew he'd seen correctly. He pulled his body weight forward on his forearms and elbows, using his good leg to help kick himself forward. The mouth of a small cave was so close. It was exactly what he needed. That dark space, cleverly tucked behind several flowering bushes, was his sanctuary. A place he could rest. He pulled himself arm over arm toward the bushes, over the rock and then hopefully into the small cavern. Training told him he should have wiped out any indication of his trek, but he was too tired to give a shit if he left a blood trail to the cave's entrance. If the bastard was tracking him, well then, the son of a bitch could have him. He was done. Asp dug his fingers into the ground again and again. The desire to stay alive kept him going far longer than his energy should have lasted. He pulled himself into the cave, moved his rifle from his back into his hands, propped himself up against the wall, and shifted the weapon so it was pointed toward the door. He dropped his head back against the rock and closed his eyes, depleted and damaged—a condition he was unhappily familiar with. This shit never got easier.

CHAPTER 5

*L*yric Gadson pulled her thick brown hair up and off her neck and tried to catch a breeze, but the wooden wall of the shed behind her blocked what little air movement there might have been. Her muscles, stiff and sore from bending over the stone grinding wheel all afternoon, protested the movement, but the effort had been worth it. She'd finished sharpening all the implements she'd gathered and held the machete her father favored in her hand. She'd been especially careful to sharpen the blade he would use during the banana harvest next week. Testing the edge one more time, she chuckled to herself. The banana stalks didn't stand a chance.

Slowly standing to ease the tight, cramped pull of her back, she rolled her shoulders several times, forward first, and then backward. Vertebrae in her back cracked when she arched backward. The relief was instantaneous and delightful. Lyric lifted up on her toes several times as she gazed around her grandfather's farm, her gaze stopping on the herd of goats, the tilled fields with corn and the lines of banana trees—all with the backdrop of the towering, snow-capped,

Andes Mountains. A sudden movement caught her attention. Jo-Jo, the most cantankerous, mean and bull-headed donkey that ever lived, lunged after one of the milk goats, chasing it away from a lush patch of grass. The goat moved about two feet and lowered its head. The typical daily standoff between the two animals. The chickens cackled in their enclosure, scratching the ground in search of the feed she'd given them earlier. She glanced beyond the house to her garden. The tomatoes needed to be harvested again. She'd spend the weekend canning the bounty from the large plot. Everything was normal, as it was yesterday, and the day before.

She again wondered for the millionth time at the unlikely set of events that had uprooted a happy yet extremely irresponsible teenage girl from Jacksonville, Florida, US-of-A and deposited her in rural Colombia. Her gaze dropped to her chipped nails with ingrained dirt. No amount of scrubbing could remove the hard work from under her nails. She grimaced, remembering all her teen angst over her choice of nail color. Had her life really been that trivial? Yes. Still... what she wouldn't give...

She shook herself from her pointless mental ramblings and moved to put away the tools she'd sharpened. The sound of a motor drew her attention to the main road. She groaned and dropped her head, muttering swear words under her breath when she recognized the National Police vehicle that bounced down their gravel driveway. Ricardo Castro de la Mata.

The car pulled to a stop. Ricardo unfolded from the front of the vehicle and leered in her direction. Far from intimidated, she stood eye-level with Ricardo's less than macho, five-feet-nine-inches and returned his sneer. Ricardo faced her and gave her his full attention.

The hair on her arms rose in reaction to the man's predatory stare. As he took off his mirrored sunglasses and meandered over to where she stood, the sensation of being violated rippled through her. Lyric gripped the handle of the machete, taking comfort in the knowledge she held a keen blade.

By anyone's standards, Ricardo was handsome. He had dark hair, dark brown eyes, a square chin and a trim body. His uniform stretched tight around his well-muscled physique, but no number of attractive physical attributes could overcome the ugliness of his sadistic nature. Lyric had witnessed the way he treated his younger brothers and sisters. He was brutal and a bully, sending his siblings cowering with a look. The man had laughed and smiled when he kicked a small dog. The poor thing had simply been lying in the sunshine. Her stomach revolted at his attention. No, Ricardo would never be a welcome suitor.

She'd never seen any compassion from the man, not that she'd stuck around to watch him. He was toxic, and she avoided him. When he settled his attentions on her months ago, she steeled her resolve and rebuffed his every advance. The problem was, the man had an ego the size of Colombia. Being rebuffed angered him. He was vicious. He was evil, and he was unwelcome. Period.

His stare pinned her as he moved closer and leaned into her personal space. His eyes evaluated her much like a woman examined a piece of beef at the market. Lyric held her stance, tightened her grip on her machete, and waited.

"Why do you try to run from me, beautiful one?" Ricardo cupped a hand at her waist and tugged her toward him.

She grabbed his wrist, spun around and peeled it off her waist in a move her father showed her after Ricardo had made his intentions known. She threw his hand back at him. "I'm not running and you do not get to touch me. Whether you believe it or not, I *am not* interested in you."

Ricardo laughed at her. "You are interested." He stepped closer to her.

Lyric shook her head. "No, I am not. Do not come here again, Ricardo. I do not desire you, and I do not want you to return to this property." Lyric shook with raw anger.

"You *do* want me. Look at the way your chest heaves. Don't play hard to get with me or you will regret it. Besides, you cannot tell me to stay away. I am an officer of the National Police. I go where I want, when I want." Ricardo's words emerged low and dangerous.

"I've done nothing to warrant your presence here. I don't fear you or the police." She lifted the machete in her hand and put the blade between them. She didn't make the mistake of pointing it at Ricardo, but pulled the one and only trump card she had and metaphorically slapped it on the table. "If you insist on harassing me, I'll call Jesus Garcia, your district commander, and explain how you come out here in your uniform, with your official vehicle and harass us—how you press unwanted attentions on me." Her grandfather and the district commander were cousins. If she called and complained, Ricardo's career very well could be stalled.

Ricardo recoiled as if he'd been slapped. "You wouldn't dare." He sneered at the machete. "You don't want to start a war with me. You will not win."

She felt his anger grow as the implications of her comment manifested. She lifted a single eyebrow. "Oh, that is where you are wrong. I dare, and I am unlike any other woman you've ever met. Leave. Now."

Ricardo closed the space between them, and she held firm, refusing to flinch or back away from the rage she saw in his eyes. She trembled, but refused to lower the blade when he pushed closer.

He was so close his breath brushed across her cheek as he

hissed, "You will regret threatening me, and I will enjoy teaching you manners."

Lyric kept her eyes pinned to his. "I will never regret defending myself against an animal like you. You have no idea where I came from or what I'm capable of doing. Do not push me, or you will lose what you hold so precious." Lyric would lob his balls off.

Ricardo snapped his attention to the sound of another vehicle bouncing down the access road to the farm. "Don't threaten me about losing things that are precious, woman. This, what's between us, it won't be over until I say it is."

"You're a fool. There is nothing between us and never will be. I will make sure of that."

Ricardo grabbed the forearm of the hand holding the machete. He squeezed hard and snapped her arm down, forcing her to drop the knife. "You have no say, you never did." He pulled her in and smashed his lips against hers. Lyric gasped and felt his tongue invading her mouth. She bit down as hard as she could. Ricardo screamed and pushed Lyric away. She spit at his feet in fury. "That's it! You will pay for forcing yourself on me. District Commander Garcia will hear about this. My grandfather has connections. You will pay for this!"

"Don't make a mistake you won't live to regret." Ricardo's threat was ominous even though he had to mumble because of his injured tongue. He spun and got into his car. Gravel spit from the treads of his tires as he punched the accelerator and turned around. He gunned the vehicle past her father's truck as it pulled into the parking area in front of the shed.

Lyric bent down and picked up the machete. The skin on her arm was already turning red and swollen from his grip and jerk maneuver. *Jerk maneuver.* As if the man had any other kind. She grabbed the knife with her other arm and slipped her bruised forearm behind her back, trying to look casual. If her father noticed the bruise before she was able to cover it up, he'd...well, he would probably hunt down Ricardo and kill him. She'd never allow that.

"Does that bastard not understand the meaning of the word 'no'?" Her father pulled his purchases out of the old truck and glanced over his shoulder to watch the police car bounce down the washboards and potholes leading away from the farm. He'd always let her fight her own battles. She thanked him for that. It had made her strong and her own woman, but Ricardo's persistence, despite her numerous rebuffs, wore on both of their nerves.

His car hit a rut and bounced high, only to crash into another pothole in the road. A small smile tipped her lips. If he damaged his precious car, maybe he'd give showing up again a second thought. *As if.*

"He understands the word, but he doesn't want to believe it." She shook her head thinking back over their recent...conversation. If she didn't think he'd have used it against her, she would have put the point of the machete she carried into his groin and threatened him.

Her father walked up to stand beside her. At six feet tall, James Gadson towered over almost everyone he met. "That man is trouble." Her father's eyes followed the vehicle's departure.

"He is gone for good this time. I threatened to call Jesus." Lyric bent over and put the machete into a tray she'd been using to collect the items she'd sharpened.

"I'm sure that pissed him off." He put his hands on his hips and watched the vehicle disappear.

"Oh, yeah, it did." She straightened and motioned to the bags in her father's hand. "Did you get everything?"

"I think so." He sighed and walked with her into the small house. "I'm worried. He's never been late coming back before."

Lyric nodded. Her grandfather was due back two days ago from his annual pilgrimage to the shrine he'd built in the mountains memorializing his loved ones who had died in the civil unrest—his wife, his sons and most recently his daughter, Lyric's mom.

"I'll leave at first light." She motioned to the small white bag. "Antibiotics?"

Her dad nodded and tossed the bag to her. "Yup. Jo-Jo to the rescue again. One of these days our vet is going to demand to see this accident-prone donkey." He shrugged. "Though chances are he already knows half the medicines he prescribes don't go to animals." Her father looked down and seemed to shrink, suddenly showing the stress and worry of the past few days.

Lyric gave him a sad smile. "I'll find him, Dad. Grandfather always takes the same trails. I'm sure there is a logical reason for him to be late."

"Logical? I doubt that. The man is a stubborn old cuss." Her father's back was to her as he looked out the kitchen window towards the path that her grandfather should have emerged from days ago.

"Too stubborn to die. I'll find him." At least she hoped he was and that she could. Her grandfather was never late. Never.

"I should be going instead of you." Her dad ran his hands through his hair and spun from the window.

"I can't fix the tractor or handle the chores that need to be done before the harvest. It is best if I go. Besides, what would I do here alone if Ricardo came back?"

Her father turned back to look out the window. "Let's get the pack loaded." Her dad marched into the small living room, but not before Lyric saw the worry etched in his face.

She closed her eyes and said a quick prayer for her grandfather and for her father. The two men in her life depended on each other although neither would admit it.

Her father called from the back of the house. "Where did you put the bandages? And rubbing alcohol?" Doors slammed shut.

"I'm coming!" Lyric turned on her heel and headed to the back room before her father pulled everything out of the cupboards.

~

Lyric swung her braid off her shoulder as she moved along a trail that rose into the Andes. Every year at this time, Grandpa made this trip to the shrine he had erected to his beloved wife of twenty years. He'd also inscribed the names of his children as they died. Her mother had been the last of his children. If he wasn't back, something bad had happened. Lyric and her father had accompanied him, and she knew the way...basically. Did she regret not paying more attention to the route? Hell, yes. She grabbed the water bottle out of the side pouch of her heavy backpack and took a long drink. There was a stream near the small shrine. She could refill her bottle and use the water purification tablets she carried when she reached her destination. She mopped her face and throat with the small towel she used to protect the back of her neck while she walked.

Her father had insisted she take the pistol with her. It hung off her hip in its holster. She'd learned how to shoot out of necessity. Snakes, especially rattlesnakes, roamed the foothills as freely as the human predators that populated the Andes. Lyric learned to shoot so she could protect herself and had no problem carrying the weapon. Her concern was leaving her father with only a rifle. Normally when they were out harvesting, he carried the pistol and responded if the need arose. Unfortunately, until recently it had been necessary to remain armed in case factions of the FARC demanded taxation. Lyric stepped out from the shade of the tree she rested under and headed up the steep incline. She struggled up the loose dirt and gazed down the drop off. Her grandfather was part mountain goat, but still, she worried that he'd missed a step and fallen. She kept her eyes active as she headed further up into the foothills.

She would have to make camp soon. It took two days to reach the shrine, although with as far as she'd traveled today, she might reach her destination by early tomorrow afternoon. Without the assistance of the sun, gathering firewood for the night would be impossible, so she found a flat spot along the trail and set up camp. With the worry that assailed her, she dreaded the long hours of darkness and the sleepless night yet to come. She built her fire, cleared the area and set up her small camp. Living in Jacksonville, Florida had not equipped her for roughing it in Colombia. It was her grandfather who taught her how to survive. The ten years she'd spent with him had taught her many things—survival being the most important of those lessons. As a protection from the insects the fire would attract, she wrapped a lightweight shirt around herself and sat back against the trunk of a fallen tree. The music of the night floated around her. Exhaustion, both mental and physical, magnified the worry that floated unchecked through her mind. As much as she tried to block the thoughts, the worst-case scenarios played like a movie on repeat in her brain.

To combat the runaway doomsday thoughts, she pulled out a book she hadn't read. Her father had ordered it for her —reason enough to cherish it, whatever the story. Lyric hadn't been the best student while in school. Hell, *that* was an outright lie. She'd run wild and barely managed to pass her classes. It was after they moved to Colombia that her mother had taught her to love a good book. Her mother said even if her body was stuck in Colombia, there were no barriers to where a book could take her mind. Lyric opened the cover and caressed the clean linen pages. The simple act reminded her of her mom. Leaning next to the firelight, her mind fell into the marvelous world of words, because according to the first line, "*It was the best of times...*"

The terrain had changed since she'd last made this trek. Bushes that lined the path were larger, and the walkway wasn't as wide as Lyric remembered it. The trail crumbled into nothing, forcing her to leap over the breaks that punctuated the now treacherous way up the hill. She crested the ridge and gazed into the small valley below. Trees covered a vast portion of the valley, and there was no campfire evident. Lyric deflated. For some reason, she'd hoped she'd notice her grandfather's presence immediately. With each step she took down the steep slope, she reminded herself the trees could be hiding him.

She trudged straight across the meadow toward the face of granite where her grandfather had carved his love's name into the rock. Her grandparents had buried three sons, all lost to the FARC and then shipped away their only daughter, Lyric's mother, to America to keep her safe. After all the death and tragedy, this valley became their haven, the place where she, her father and her grandfather spent one week every year, the one place in the world where war, worries, and pain couldn't reach them. This valley was a sanctuary, and Lyric prayed it had kept her grandfather safe.

Saplings and flowering marmalade bushes populated the small meadow. The flowers, a mixture of yellow and shades of orange, blossomed almost year-round and provided an abundant natural habitat for butterflies and birds. Lyric noted them in passing, but she didn't have time to admire their beauty. Bent under the weighty and cumbersome backpack, she jogged across the meadow floor toward the shrine. When her father had helped her prepare the pack, they had no idea what she would find, and it was laden with medical supplies and some food in case her grandfather needed it. She gladly shouldered the heavy pack. Her breath caught in her chest as she hit the rock ledge leading to the shrine. Her leg muscles strained. The weight on her back was as heavy as the worry in her heart. Lyric dug down and found the strength to push herself harder.

She reached the small shrine, nothing more than carved words and a cross chiseled in the stone face of the mountain. There was recent evidence her grandfather had been there. Several days' worth of ashes remained in the small rock-ringed fire pit off to the side. Shouldering the heavy backpack, her center of gravity shifted when she bent down and threaded her fingers through the fine ash. The movement overbalanced her, and she barely caught herself from planting face first into the dirt.

No hot coals or lingering warmth remained in the feather soft ashes—only the faint smell of wood smoke. She clutched a handful of ashes and closed her eyes, as disappointment and despair fought for dominance. *Had she missed him?* She'd been careful, but fast. *Could she have missed where he went off the trail? Had he used the trail, or had he taken another route back? Where was he?* Her mind whirled as she pushed up and spun around, visually examining the area for any clue as to where her grandfather had gone.

"It took you long enough. If I were hurt or dying..."

CHAPTER 6

*A*t her grandfather's words, Lyric spun, made clumsy by the backpack. Immediate relief filled her heart as she lunged towards him with a shriek of happiness. "Why didn't you come back?"

His strong, able arms surrounded her and held her tight. "There were reasons. What have you brought?" He grabbed the top handle of her backpack and, after she unbuckled her waist strap, helped her free of the shoulder straps.

"Food, medicine, bandages, a little bit of everything. We didn't know what had happened to you." She waited until he had set down the pack before she caught his arm and made him look at her. "Tell me, why didn't you come back? You had to know we'd be worried."

"I did know you would worry. I was counting on it." His eyes searched the meadow before he picked up the pack. "Come with me."

Lyric sent a furtive glance around the area, the same way her grandfather had, only she had no idea what led him to look so worried. "Grandpa, is everything okay?" Horrible thoughts erupted again. The visceral sensation something was very wrong grabbed her and pinned her with unyielding tenacity.

He lifted his weathered hand and put his finger to his lips silencing her. He made a beckoning motion and disappeared behind a marmalade bush. Lyric hesitated for a microsecond before she pushed the branches aside and followed him.

A two-foot-wide clearing opened up, leading into what appeared to be a cave. She hated caves. Caves had spiders and snakes and animals. *And bats. Shit, shit, shit. She hated bats*. Not that she'd ever seen one, but she had memories of a horrible television show where bats had attacked a woman. No, she wanted nothing to do with bats. While she was more willing to face the animals, the ones that lived in caves could probably kill her. No, she really didn't want to meet them on their home ground, in a cave. In the dark.

Rather than follow her grandfather into the back hole in the rock, she squatted down and peered into the darkness. A small fire deeper in the cave threw a faint glow on the walls of stone a few steps into the opening. If there was a fire, where was the smoke? She popped up, no longer encumbered by the pack, and scanned the rock above the cave. There had to be a fissure which allowed the smoke to dissipate and escape. Well, fire meant no bats, or at least she assumed that's what it meant. *Right?*

Her grandfather put the backpack down and walked to his left and out of her view. *Dammit*. She gritted her teeth and stood, only to duck low through the entrance and remain bent as she moved deeper into the cave. The ceiling lifted as she approached the fire. Her eyes tracked her grandfather's movements. She gasped at the sight of her grandfather on his knees beside a huge man lying on her grandfather's blanket. His hair was dark brown, and he was unnaturally pale beneath his full beard. Lyric shuffled over as her grandfather took a cloth out of a square camp container and wrung it out, wiping a film of perspiration off the man's face and neck.

"I watched him." Her grandfather dipped the cloth again and wiped the man's parched lips. "He half fell, half slid down the slope near the trail's head. I could tell he'd been injured. I waited." He lifted his shoulders in a shrug. "He could have been FARC." His hand dipped in the water again, and he repeated the process. "He could have given up at the bottom of the hill. He did not. He pulled himself into the cave. Propped himself up and aimed his rifle out the opening. I watched for an hour, maybe more. I heard someone walking above. There were words. My ears aren't so good anymore. I don't know what was said. I came into the cave. This one, he's unconscious. His wound...filthy. He needed stitches." He shrugged again. "I could not leave him to die."

"This man is why you didn't come back?" Lyric sank to the ground beside her grandfather.

He nodded. "What else would you have me do?"

His eyes turned toward her, and she smiled and shook her head. "Nothing else, Grandpa." Turning, Lyric rose to her feet and walked to the fire. She dropped a small log from the substantial stack someone, probably her grandfather, had placed alongside the wall before she once again tugged the heavy pack onto her shoulder and carried it to her grandfather. "He needs fresh dressings. I can clean the wounds. Has he regained consciousness?"

"No." He shrugged again. "He mumbles. In English, in Spanish and in languages I don't know."

Lyric looked at the ashen pallor beneath the man's heavy beard. "Does he have any identification?" She glanced at the pack and weapon leaning against the wall. The rifle was unusual. A huge scope and tripod legs at the front of the weapon made it different from any she'd seen before. It wasn't like the automatic weapons the FARC had used. It was...more, somehow. Could he be from some branch of the military or maybe the National Police?

Her gaze returned to their patient and scanned his massive body. She thought he'd be taller than her father's six-feet and he was much more heavily built. Deep, puckered scars, some red, some pink, distorted the smooth skin of his arms. She could only guess at the cause. Her grandfather had cut the outside seam of the man's pant leg from ankle to hip and peeled it away from his body to expose the wound. One of his red and black checked shirts draped the man's genitals to keep his privacy. Small streaks of red radiated from both the entry and exit of the bullet. His thigh had puffed and was warm to the touch. Lyric glanced from his healthy leg to his injured one. Not too much swelling, at least that she could see with the other leg still clad in denim. She opened the backpack and pulled out the necessary supplies to clean and dress his wounds.

"He was shot."

Farmers tended to perform their own emergency medical treatment and Lyric had plenty of experience stitching cuts, cleaning wounds and warding off infection, but what she looked at now sent a deep sense of helplessness through her.

"Yes." Her grandfather moved to allow her access to the man's wounds.

"Who would have shot him?" She glanced at the weapon leaning on its tripod and facing away from them.

"That is a stupid question, even for a beautiful woman such as yourself."

Lyric snapped her head up and glared at her grandpa. His old school, chauvinistic upbringing still raised its head from time to time.

"Why is it a stupid question?" She opened a sterile pack of

gauze and sat it on the man's chest, still protected and kept clean by the bottom layer of wrapping.

"Who in this area shoots people?" Her grandfather reached for an elastic bandage and unwrapped it.

Lyric opened a bottle of rubbing alcohol and doused the gauze with the liquid before she glanced at her grandfather. "The FARC."

"Yes." He nodded as she cleansed the wounds. The unconscious man didn't move as she worked. Her grandfather continued to assist when needed. He would wipe the big man's brow when the perspiration beaded.

Lyric cut the stitches which her grandfather placed to close the lower wound. The infection inside his leg was putrid. She opened the suture and removed what infection she could without causing further injury. If he didn't get antibiotics, the infection could take his life.

"The infection is bad. Grab me the small bag on the outside pocket, please."

Her grandfather fished out the small white bag. "Jo-Jo?"

Lyric nodded. "We didn't know what had happened." She shook a pill out and sat on her heels. "How much do you think he weights?"

"Hmmm..." Her grandfather stroked the grey stubble at his chin. "One hundred twenty five, maybe one hundred thirty five kilograms?"

Lyric blinked at the guess. Two hundred eighty to three hundred pounds? Well, he was massive and so tall. She glanced at the pill in her hand. "Hand me your knife please, Grandpa?"

The man slid the knife out of his belt and handed it to her. She placed the pill on a rock and cut it in half. "I'll need some hot water to dissolve this in." Her grandfather moved toward the fire and a small kettle beside it. When he returned

Lyric poured a small amount into a cup and used the tip of the knife to help disintegrate pill.

"Would you lift his head?" Lyric waited until her grandfather had positioned the man's head and opened his mouth. She slowly trickled the liquid into his mouth. He gagged and choked on the mixture but kept the majority of the liquid down. She put the cup down and rested on her heels. "I've done everything I can, for now." Lyric sat back on her heels. She glanced from the injured man to her grandfather. There was no way they could carry this massive man over the rough terrain. "You need to go back to the farm, Grandpa. Dad will be coming up here if one of us doesn't head down the mountain." Once again, she examined the work she'd done and shook her head.

"I will stay. It is not good to leave you with him." Her grandfather stood and took the water he'd been using to clean the man's wounds to the front of the cave. Ahh...he'd been using water from the creek, and he probably hadn't used the purification tablets she'd packed in his supplies. That could be why the stranger's wounds were festering. But he'd done what he could.

"He's unconscious. He'll probably stay that way for days, or he could get worse..." She didn't finish the sentence. Her grandfather would know the man could die. Only God knew how much blood he'd lost. Add that to the fever and infection. He was in bad shape. "There is nothing he could do to hurt me and Dad really needs you for the banana harvest."

Her grandfather looked at the unconscious man on the floor of the cave for several long moments, before shrugging. "I'll leave at first light." He turned to go back into the cave. "But first, woman, I want a meal that my hands haven't prepared. Just don't burn it."

Lyric blew out a lungful of air and shook her head, exasperation at the old man replacing her worry for a brief moment. If she didn't love the old, grumpy, chauvinistic man so much... At least he was alive and well. She was happy, and even if her grandpa was from another era, she'd deal with his quirks. She smiled as she followed him back into the cave. Obviously, it was time for her to cook a meal.

CHAPTER 7

*L*yric worried her thumb nail with her teeth as she mulled over what else she could do. The stranger's fever had spiked yesterday afternoon. Determined to keep the man alive, she'd cut the rest of his clothes from his body and had carried countless small containers of cool water from the stream to bathe him. Her hands had traveled every inch of him. She'd leaned down and traced his scars. What could have caused the damage to his arms?

"You are so big. Your muscles look like a movie star, you know the ones in all the action flicks." She sat down beside him and ran her hand down his arm again. "I miss going to the theater on Saturday afternoon." She let her hand caress his arm. He seemed to calm when she touched and talked to him. "I bet I've missed some good ones? Do you like movies?" She glanced down at his unconscious form. "Everyone enjoys movies, right? Popcorn! Oh, god, I loved the smell of popcorn when you first go into a theater! There was this one place in Jacksonville. They had the world's best popcorn." She glanced down at her patient. "I used to live in Jacksonville, before we came here."

Lyric let her hand continue its mindless caress as she gazed unseeingly at the cave wall. "I wasn't a very good person then. I hung out with the wrong crowd. God, we got into some serious shit. When Mom and Dad told me we were moving to Colombia, I ran away. Ended up in some dive. There were drugs and, well it was really, really bad. My dad, he came, and he got me out of there. He saw...everything and he didn't care. I'd never seen my dad cry before." Unfortunately, she'd seen him cry since.

Lyric shifted off the uncomfortable ground and lay down on her side, still looking at her quiet companion. "You'd like my dad. He's an American. He and Mom came down here when he lost his job..." The man moaned, stilling her one-sided conversation.

He'd grabbed her hand. His eyes wide open, yet unseeing. "You have to take care of her." His English told her he was an American, so she answered him in English, "Who do you want me to take care of?"

"Mrs. Henshaw." His eyes closed, but his hand still grabbed her arm. His grip was tight, but not painful. "Alone. She's alone. Her kids won't...won't come. Promise." His expression displayed nothing but desperation and worry.

To still his fears, Lyric touched her other hand to his brow. He jolted at the contact. "Shh...I promise I'll take care of Mrs. Henshaw. She's safe. Don't worry. She's safe."

Lyric waited until he calmed a little before she glanced out of the cave. It was nearing dusk. He should probably have another dose of antibiotics. She rose and made her way to the bottle of medication sitting beside the fire next to her pack.

"KD's birthday. Gotta go. Gotta... present...no present."

Startled, Lyric twisted back to him. His eyes were closed. His body twitched, and his head tossed from side to side. She rose from the fire and knelt beside him. He became more agitated, so Lyric tried talking to him again, "You did get a present, remember? It's right here. Can't you see it?" Lyric dipped the cloth into the cool water again and started wiping down the man's fever-riddled body.

"Where?" He shivered and moaned. "Cold. So cold."

She pulled a blanket up over his chest. "This will help."

"KD?"

"KD isn't here right now."

"Need to get..."

"What do you need to get?"

"Birthday."

His words clicked into place. "You did get KD a birthday present. It's okay." He turned away from her and moaned when he moved his leg. The fever was spiking. She left his side long enough to make a powder of the medication and stir in just enough water to liquefy it. He was burning up. Lifting to her knees, Lyric lifted his head onto her lap. "You need to drink this." She touched the cup to his lips.

He made a weak attempt at batting the cup away. She grabbed his hand and lowered it onto his chest. "It's medicine. You have to drink it. I promise I won't let anyone hurt you." Lyric tried again and gave a mental scream of joy when he opened his mouth. He choked on it and spit up some, but she sent a prayer of thanks that at least some of the medication made its way into his body. She added a small amount of water to the cup and sloshed it up along the sides to make sure any medicine remaining in the cup incorporated in the water. She began to sing an old lullaby she remembered her mother singing to her. She wasn't sure if it was to calm him or her. Because right now, she was terrified. Terrified that the fever would take this man. She couldn't explain why the thought of this stranger's death sent a bone chilling fear through her, but it did.

Her hands repeated the task of dipping the cloth,

wringing it out and carefully wiping his skin to cool the fever that wracked his body. That done, she once again cleaned the bullet holes and coated the wounds with antibacterial cream. They were no worse than when she'd first examined them, and for that she was grateful. His breathing had leveled out, and he appeared to be sleeping more comfortably. She stood and rolled her shoulders and neck before she picked up the makeshift bucket and made her way to the mouth of the cave. Clouds darkened the afternoon skies. A low rumble of thunder hastened her steps to the creek not more than fifteen feet from the mouth of the cave. She emptied the water, rinsed out the cloth and refilled the container just in time to jog back to the cave and almost miss the deluge of water released from the skies.

As she sat next to her patient, she cocked her head and listened. *Water running?* The sound did not come from the mouth of the cave but from further into the interior. A shiver of apprehension brushed her. What did that mean? Were they about to be flooded out of the cave? She picked up the flashlight her father had loaded in her pack and flicked it on. Where was the source of that sound? She flicked the light beam over the ceiling and let out the breath she'd held. *No bats. Thank goodness.*

Her feet followed the sound of running water while her hand directed the flashlight toward the ceiling and her eyes searched for objects that hung upside down from the ceiling. She discovered the source of the sound. Rainwater trickled down the walls of the cave and landed in an expansive pool. The flashlight cast light through the pure water. Lyric could see the bottom of the pristine underground lake...well, pond, but it was impossible not to be impressed. She reached down with her free hand and rippled the surface with her fingers. Cool water trickled from her fingers as she lifted them. The rings left by the drips broadened outward and disappeared.

She flicked light through the cavern and noted a large elevated area off to the side. Lyric steadied the beam of the flashlight on the shelf. It held the remnants of a long-ago used fire ring. She moved the light and peered farther into the cave. Unwilling to go farther away from the entrance, she examined as far as her eyes could see. The darkness beyond would remain unexplored for now. Her sense of adventure was tapped out. She circled the small body of water and then headed back toward the cave entrance. She'd explore more tomorrow.

Her patient had stilled, his brow felt less hot. The slurry of medication seemed to have worked, to a degree. She went back to the fire, added another dry branch to the coals, and shook out another half tablet to crush so she'd be ready when his fever crested again.

She took up her position beside the man and leaned against the wall, her hands around her legs, with her head on her knees. Tired from a sleepless night, she closed her eyes. Her hands fell from around her legs and she startled awake. She had to get some rest. She glanced around the cave and at her patient. He lay quietly. Lyric stretched out on her side, cradled her head on her arm, closed her eyes and passed out.

"Get out. Now. Run!" The statement rang with such clarity that Lyric gasped and jolted backward, smacking her head into the cave wall. She raised her hand to the place a goose egg would no doubt form on the back of her head. She lifted her chin and narrowed her eyes at the man on the pallet.

"What did you say?" Lyric whispered the words. Had she dreamed it? His eyes were still closed, and she could see rapid movement behind the lids. His muscles spasmed as if he was dreaming. Lyric moved over to him and placed her hand on his brow. The fever had returned. There was no way to tell how long it had been since the last dose or how much he'd taken, but his fever was better with the medication, and he had seemed to rest. Grabbing the canteen cup from the niche she'd tucked it into, Lyric lifted his head and put the cup to his lips. "Here, you need to drink this. It's medicine. Drink it."

He lifted his arm again, but this time she was expecting it. She caught his arm and intertwined their fingers. "Please. For me." She offered him the cup again and managed to get the majority of the mixture down his throat.

He turned his head and mumbled something unintelligible. Lyric let out a huff of air and dropped her head into her hands. "You know you scared the shit out of me, right?"

The man's muscles twitched. She reached out and laced her fingers through his. He squeezed her hand. Somehow the random clenching of his muscles around her fingers made her feel better.

"So..." She gazed around the cave. Her eyes landed on her book. "Do you like to read? I didn't like it at all, until I came here." She gave a bitter laugh and leaned back against the wall while still holding his hand. "I told you that I wasn't a good student, right?" Lyric couldn't remember, she'd been rattling on, talking to him since she'd figured out the sound of her voice seemed to make him rest easier. "Well, if I didn't, I wasn't. Mom knew I didn't want to come to Colombia. She introduced me to reading." Lyric smiled at the memory. "She said that I could travel to the far reaches of the world or even to other worlds through words." She squeezed the man's hand. Her mind thrashing through the memories, good and bad, of her time in Colombia.

"Can I ask you a question? And I mean, be honest with me, but have you ever felt like you were trapped in the wrong life? That you were never meant to be where you ended up?" She glanced around the cave. "I've lived here for ten years. Colombia isn't my home. I feel like a stranger in my own home."

"My mom, she knew how miserable I was. We started selling our surplus vegetables from our garden. We were saving up for a ticket to take me back to the states. I had friends, no... not those friends," she glanced over at him and chuckled, "other friends that my parents actually approved of, thank you very much. Anyway, I wrote, and they agreed that I could stay with them until I got a job and got myself an apartment. Can you imagine? Nice people, right?"

Lyric brushed his hair off his forehead. He'd stopped twitching and his breathing was steady. "My mom was on her way back from the village market when the FARC attacked the bus she was on. Nineteen women and children killed that day." Lyric sniffed back the tears that threatened. "She died because I was selfish and wanted a different life." Lyric looked up at the ceiling of the cave. "Yeah, go me!" A bitter laugh followed. She glanced down at the man again. He was resting now and she needed to do something, anything, to get away from the memories. She grabbed the flashlight and headed back into the larger cavern. Bats were preferable to the guilt that swallowed her.

≈

"Well, that was successful." Extremely happy with the back entrance to the cave she found and the treasure that it led her to, she plopped down beside her patient. She touched his brow when she pushed his hair back. For the first time, it was cool, no indication of fever whatsoever.

"Well, look at you. Getting better, aren't you?" She glanced down his body. She knew ever bulge of muscle, every scar and every intimate detail of the man. She'd bathed him, cared for him and cleaned him. His hands had calluses that ridged just beyond the fingers on his palm. She wondered how he got them. Hard work? Driving? She glanced at his muscles and bobbled her head as she considered what else could have caused them. Weightlifting maybe? Lyric lifted his hand and lightly caressed them before she ran her palm up his arm to his biceps. Even relaxed in slumber, his muscles were defined and ... Lyric smirked, the man was a puzzle that intrigued her. She had pieces but didn't know if she was putting them together correctly.

Lyric held his hand as she gazed out to where sunbeams danced on the dirt at the front of the cave. "You know, I may be a little bit forward here, but since I've been bathing, cleaning, and making you drink so you wouldn't die on me for over a week now, I should probably tell you that you are very attractive, and I'd be lying if I didn't admit I've wondered what it would be like to be with you. You know, like *be* with you? Because, damn, all portions of you are so fine." She chuckled and glanced down at him.

She squeezed his hand and he squeezed it back. Lyric shifted to face him. His eyes blinked open, first one, then both. A smile spread across her face. He was conscious. Finally! He blinked up at her and squeezed her hand again before his eyes rolled back into his head and he convulsed.

CHAPTER 8

*A*sp fought through layers of heaviness that fell across him like wet blankets—clingy and suffocating. Wood smoke was the first thing he recognized. He clung to the odor and tried to think. The soft angelic voice that soothed him was now silent. His eyes were so heavy, the effort to open them was almost too much, but he managed to lift an eyelid. Nothing came into focus, but once he was able to open one eye, his brain seemed to engage, and it became easier to make his body work. He blinked, trying to bring the greyish-brown over him into focus.

Fuck, what he wouldn't give to separate his tongue from the roof of his mouth, but damn if he could get the industrial strength adhesive holding it up there it to separate. He lifted his arm, and that's when all hell exploded from the under-world and crash landed on top of his body. A direct fucking hit from Satan himself. Asp gasped, grabbed his hip and convulsed in a spasm of pain.

"Stop moving, please, you need to stop."

The soft-spoken words stilled him. He managed to peel his eyes open like the thin, hooked blade of a P-38 opened cans, slowly and with a concentrated effort. He blinked trying to focus. A pathetic, weak moan escaped. Shit. Fitting, because he felt like he'd been beaten by a gang of thugs wielding Louisville sluggers and then left to die.

He turned his head slightly and peered into the soft light. Hair. Long dark hair. A woman? Hell, his eyes closed again. He was too fucking tired to open them. If she was going to kill him, let her.

"Don't move or you will make your wounds bleed. I've worked too hard at keeping you alive to let you kill yourself now."

Well, that didn't sound like she wanted to cause him any harm. He swallowed, or at least he tried to make his throat work. It wasn't happening.

"Here, drink this."

Drink? Fuck, yeah. He felt her lift his head, and maybe he'd worry about being as weak as a two-day-old kitten later, but right now...he felt the cool rim of a cup at his lips. He opened his mouth and moaned as the liquid filled his mouth. The taste was cool, fresh, and most importantly, wet. The cup left. Asp tried to grab it.

"More..." The harsh grit of his voice shattered through the silence.

"Shhh...I'm getting you some more, but you have to let me help you."

He could hear her moving and heard the sound of water being poured into a cup. She was back and lifted his head again so he could drink. He allowed her to feed the water to him in slowly measured sips because he was too tired and too weak to do anything else. She lowered his head. Asp tried to speak, tried to move, but couldn't—just slipped into a state of semi-awareness. His mind grasped fragments of remembered sensations. Cool swipes, pain, shivering, cold...so damn cold...blessed water and the voice of an angel.

Asp woke in a panic. What had woken him? He remained still, for one, because he was too weak to move, but also because some instinct told him his environment had changed. He listened for his angel, but there was a distinct absence of sound, sound that he'd become accustomed to hearing. Her soft humming, the sound of her voice singing a lullaby, her talking to him as she...hell, he blinked and tried once again to focus on the ceiling above him.

"You're awake."

Her voice startled him. He shot his glance to her and blinked at the vision he witnessed. She was beautiful. Her huge, soft, brown eyes smiled at him. Her eyes. Asp could read a person by their eyes, and this woman was no exception. She watched him as he examined her from head to toe. He couldn't help but notice her. She was...all wrong. Why was she here? Where the fuck was here?

She tipped her head and narrowed her eyes. "You are not FARC?"

FARC. His mission. Fuck, he'd been shot. A fucking sniper across the ravine from the camp. Asp closed his eyes but gave his answer with a slight shake of his head. *Where the hell was he?* He shifted his eyes to take in what he could see. His gaze landed on his M-21 and backpack. He glanced from the weapon to woman only to see a smile spread across her face.

She pointed at Asp. "See, this fighting spirit, this is why you are still alive." She smiled down at him, and fuck him six ways to Sunday, the woman was as beautiful as she sounded. Asp closed his eyes and opened them again. No, he wasn't hallucinating.

"My grandfather found you. I took care of you. You've been very ill."

He glanced from the woman to his pack and weapon before forced himself to speak. "How long?" His voice was harsh, and fuck, just saying two words exhausted him.

"Eleven days since you fell into this valley." The woman stood, she was tall and fuck him if she wasn't curved in all the right places. Asp blinked his gaze back to his gun. There was no way he could lift the damn thing. "You are safe here. My grandfather hid us well. I will stay with you until you are strong enough to travel."

Asp closed his eyes because he couldn't keep them open any longer. The effort it took to think exhausted his limited capacity. He had no choice but to believe his unexpected benefactor.

"Thank you." It seemed too little, but he knew the woman had remained with him, in a cave for fuck's sake, and she'd probably saved his ass.

"Rest now. Your body still needs to heal." Her voice softened, and he nodded, without opening his eyes.

Asp slept and woke, slept and woke. His guardian angel was beside him every time he'd opened his eyes. She was humming over the fire this time. She stopped and chuckled to herself. "Well of course he has a girlfriend or a wife. The man is gorgeous. Get your head out of the clouds."

Asp kept his eyes closed but he couldn't help the small smile that pulled at the corners of his mouth. She thought he was gorgeous. *Well, right back at you, sweetheart.*

The sounds of her moving became background noise and Asp let himself drift to sleep again.

CHAPTER 9

*A*sp woke slowly. He was warm, but not hot. His body ached, and his wounded leg hurt, but it wasn't the intense burning it had once been. He blinked his eyes to focus on the woman sitting next to him. She leaned against the cave wall reading a book, unaware of him. It gave him the opportunity to study her. Her long brown hair trailed over one shoulder in a braid. The clothes she wore were different, so obviously he'd been asleep or out of it for a while. She drew her bottom lip into her mouth and held it while she read. She released it and smiled at the book. Her long eyelashes prevented him from seeing her eyes as she looked down at the pages. His gaze followed the long sweep of her neck.

She shifted, set the book down and regarded him with a soft smile. "Are you awake? Your fever broke yesterday." She moved closer and poured water into a tin cup. "Are you thirsty?"

Asp groaned and nodded. He could drink the Atlantic Ocean dry. She lifted his head for him, and he sipped at the cup until he drained it.

"I have some broth."

Asp blinked up at her and cleared his throat. "Thank you."

"You're welcome. I'll be right back."

She lowered his head and moved quietly away from him. Asp took the time to search for his weapon, which hadn't moved. His hands itched with the need to examine it, to clean it. He'd fired it almost two weeks ago. His weapon was their only protection and as soon as he had strength, he'd make sure it was operational.

He noticed her sleeping pallet against the wall. Three books lay on a flat rock along with a kerosene camp light, a flashlight and a bottle of water. He shifted and pushed himself up to his elbows. The world spun on its axis and didn't bother to tell him to hold on. He closed his eyes and fought through the dizzy spell.

"You shouldn't be sitting up yet." He blinked her back into focus as she sat beside him. "You were very sick."

"How long have I been here?" He accepted the cup of broth and fucking hated that his hand shook so badly she had to help him hold it steady as he took a sip. He moaned at the incredible flavor of simple broth. His stomach growled, making sure he was aware it was pissed with a capital P.

"Twelve days." She glanced back behind him. "Thirteen. The sun is coming up." She cocked her head and considered for a moment before she asked, "What is your name?"

"Cooper." He dropped his hand when she took the empty cup, and ungracefully lowered back down onto his pallet, his strength abandoning him.

"Is that your first or last name?" She put the cup down and pulled her knees toward her.

"Isaac Cooper."

"I'm Lyric Gadson. It is a pleasure to finally meet you."

Her soft laughter filled the cave, and he couldn't resist the pull of his lips upward. Lyric was the perfect name for a woman with the voice of an angel. "Thank you for..." he lifted his hand and made a feeble attempt at a gesture towards the cave opening, "everything." He closed his eyes, drained of any energy.

"It was the right thing to do."

"You're an American?"

She pushed her hand through his hair. He couldn't open his eyes to acknowledge the tender gesture. "Sleep, Isaac Cooper. It's what your body needs now."

~

Asp woke to the sound of pages turning. He opened his eyes and blinked Lyric into focus. The woman was beautiful from angle.

"Are you staring at me?" she asked without looking at him.

"I am." He wasn't going to lie and from her comment, she had seen him watching her.

She dropped her book and smiled at him. "I'm glad you're awake. The book was losing its appeal and having someone to talk to after all this time is pretty amazing."

"You're American?" She had spoken fluent Spanish to him earlier, yet there was no hesitancy in her American accent.

She blinked as if surprised and then smiled. "Yeah, I am. Sorry, I told you that before, but you weren't awake to hear me rambling on." She laughed and shook her head. "I talk when I'm nervous or scared, and with you, I was both for a while."

Asp scratched across his chest and noticed her eyes followed his hand. He held back a chuckle when her eyes flew up to his and then away almost immediately. "Why don't we try the conversation thing now that I'm awake?"

Lyric laughed, a beautiful melodic sound that filled him with happiness. "Where do you want me to start?"

Asp lifted his arm and dropped his head onto it, so it was elevated. Her eyes slid to his bicep before she grabbed at the canteen and unscrewed the top. "Thirsty?"

"Thank you." He struggled to sit up and the blanket fell to his lap. She lowered her eyes to his lap where the blanket bunched. She handed him the canteen and averted her gaze. "So, I was born in Jacksonville. I was a typical teenage girl..."

Asp took a drink and listened to her voice as she held an entirely one-sided conversation. He put the cap back on the canteen and lowered back onto the blanket listening to every word and logging every movement. Graceful and beautiful. They talked for hours. Correction, she talked, and Asp listened. She enthralled him with stories of her first days in Colombia, the things she missed about Jacksonville and her mother's death. The tears in her voice when she described the shrine her grandfather built for her family above them against the face of the mountain almost gutted him. Finally, she shrugged and looked at him. "I'm an open book Isaac Cooper. But, you're a mystery and that intrigues me."

"Is the mystery the only thing you find intriguing?" Asp lifted an eyebrow, because frankly it was the only thing he was capable of lifting, but it was nice to be alive and to be able to appreciate the woman in front of him. He appreciated, holy shit, did he appreciate her. Not just her looks, because the woman was beautiful, but she'd quite literally saved his life.

A low sexy laugh filled the cave. "I think you know better." She leaned against her backpack using it to pad the pallet she'd built next to him.

"I'd like to assume I do, but you know what they say about assumptions."

Lyric laughed again. The sound was magical because it

pushed away everything. Every scrap of worry, concern, anxiety and pain that lingered evaporated at the sound. "Are you implying I'm an ass?"

Asp blinked up at her. "No, why would you..."

Lyric pointed at him and rolled with laughter. "Oh, God, your face!" She laughed until she wiped tears from her eyes. Finally, between bouts of amusement, she pointed at him. "Assume. It makes an *ass* of *u* and *me*." She pointed to herself when she said the last word.

Asp shook his head slowly from side to side. "No, the saying I was referencing was assumptions are usually wrong."

Lyric's eye widened before she threw her head back and laughed again. "No wonder you looked like that!" She dropped a hand onto his arm and Asp moved his hand over hers. She stilled and turned her attention to the hand covering hers. "It is nice to feel your touch." Her eyes met his. "I'm intrigued by you, Isaac Cooper. The mystery of who you are. That is a very small portion of what draws me to you."

Asp lifted his hand to her face and she leaned into his touch. "You are beautiful."

Her eyes closed, and she sighed. "Beauty fades."

"Not the type of beauty you have. You are beautiful on the inside and it makes the outside that much more appealing." Asp used his thumb to caress her bottom lip and cheek.

She regarded him for several seconds before a slow smile crept across her expression. "You are a smooth talker. My momma warned me about men like you."

Asp lowered his hand and entwined their fingers. "Your momma was a very wise woman."

"She was. She also told me how to deal with men who use words to distract you." Lyric lifted an eyebrow in a silent challenge. One that he accepted immediately.

"And how do you deal with men like me?"

Lyric bent down and stopped a fraction of an inch from

his lips before she whispered, "I act." She pressed her lips to his and was gone. She grabbed her backpack and walked to the entrance of the small cave. Asp twisted, flinching from the stab of discomfort to watch her. She turned around and winked at him before she slipped out of the cave and left him there, completely dumbfounded.

Asp rolled onto his back and rubbed the hair on his chest as he gazed at the cave's ceiling. He was so screwed. Lyric ticked every box on the list of his requirements for his dream woman. He'd mentally built the lengthy list through a life of loneliness, and now that he'd found his unicorn, he'd have to leave her as soon as his wounds healed. He'd go back into the shadows, and she'd find someone else. That thought sent a spike of anger through him. The emotion was wasted, however, because *they* could never be, and she was too...Asp closed his eyes. She was too special to treat as a temporary solution to a permanent itch. He needed to remember that. He needed to protect her from his life, from his world, no matter how much he wanted more.

Asp woke and knew immediately Lyric was not beside him or in his general proximity. He felt better. Alive. He was still weak, but he no longer felt incapacitated. With considerable effort, he bent into a sitting position. The blanket covering him dropped, exposing his chest and abs and it was a damn good thing it stopped there, just in case Lyric walked back in, because he was buck-assed naked under the blanket. He gathered the material around him and examined the cavern. He noted everything, filing it away as he should have done two weeks ago. He listened carefully to make sure Lyric wasn't coming back and only then lifted his blanket to examine his wound. The thought she had to have seen him like this...and cleaned him...teased at his brain. Fuck, if in any other scenario. Asp shook his head and regretted it immediately as he tried to stop the dizziness that shattered his balance. Once he regained himself, he peeled the bandages away and grimaced at the extent of healing. Not that healing was a bad thing, but damn it, he'd been here for two weeks. His wounds were healing well, thanks to Lyric.

Thanatos had to believe him dead by now. He'd missed their arranged primary meeting, and the secondary rally point they set up in case shit went bad. Without contact of any kind, Thanatos would get to safety and check in with Anubis and Bengal back at Guardian. He closed his eyes and drew a deep breath before he pushed it out again. He was too fucking weak to get word to them, but they all knew the price of doing this job. More times than not, an assassin would meet his end via violent means. Asp chuckled. Hell, he hadn't heard of many old assassins. In fact, he couldn't name one. Nope, the odds weren't in his favor. He glanced around the cave. When his time came, the best he could hope for would be to die alone without endangering innocent lives.

Asp replaced the soft gauze that kept his almost healed wounds clean before he draped the blanket back over himself. He leaned back against the wall. The coolness felt good against his back.

"You're up." Lyric's voice startled Asp. He must have dozed off while sitting.

"Yeah. Trying to be at least." He straightened from the wall and stretched his shoulders slightly. Every move still ate at his reserves of strength.

"I'll get you something to eat." Lyric moved with effortless grace around the campfire as she prepared him food. He didn't have the energy to move, so he just sat there and watched. Like a creeper. Fuck, his eyes followed the curve of her breast and the way her jeans hugged her legs and ass. He closed his eyes and swallowed hard. Was he reprehensible? The woman had sacrificed to help him, and he was leering at her like she was food and he a starving hyena. Fuck, he *was* starving. Cookies would be amazing. He wondered how Mrs. Henshaw was doing. He chuckled at the thought. He was so fucking weak he couldn't even concentrate on one subject. His mind hopped from one thing to another. Did he have a concussion too, or was he brain damaged.? Who knew? Maybe he'd lost too much blood, and he would be like this permanently.

"What's so funny?"

Asp jumped, and his eyes flew open. She stood immediately in front of him. "You need to stop sneaking up on me. You're going to give me a heart attack." She laughed and extended a cup with a spoon in it. He took it and said a silent prayer of thanks. Stew, not broth. He emptied the cup in about three seconds flat. Okay, more like three minutes, but fuck, he was starving.

"I think it is safe to say your appetite has returned." Lyric stood from her seat across from him and went to refill the cup.

"The food is good. Thank you." He took the stew from her and tried to eat like a civilized person. He managed it...maybe.

"Would you like more?" Lyric held her hand out to him for the cup.

He glanced at the small pot over the fire and back at her. "Have you eaten?"

"I have. The stew is for you." She tipped her head toward the fire. "More?"

"Absolutely, thank you."

She filled the cup again and walked it back to him. "Are you feeling better today?"

"I am. I'm still weak, but I'm feeling better." He took the cup and waited until she sat down across from him. "How did your grandfather find me? Did you ever say?"

She looked at him and tipped her head as she considered

her answer. "I think I did, but it could have been while you were unconscious." She shrugged and began, "He travels to this valley once a year. He and my grandmother would come here when she was alive. It was something special between the two of them. He still comes. He watched you fall from the top of the ridge, then watched you struggle to get to the cave. The men that were looking for you passed by because he concealed your trail. He waited until they'd gone before he came into the cave. You'd passed out. He did what he could for you until we got worried about him. I came up to find him."

"We?" *Husband? Boyfriend?* Asp had a thousand questions, but for some reason knowing who '*we*' was seemed to be the most important. He held his cup and spoon suspended halfway to his mouth waiting for an answer.

"My father and me. We live on Grandpa's farm since we moved from America."

"Ah, that's right." Asp filtered through the conversation they'd had...or she'd had, whatever. The flare of jealousy died, and Asp stomped out the coals it left. He could not afford to get involved. He needed to remember that. "You were born in America?" He slipped into English.

"Damn straight." She returned in English, laughed and shrugged.

"Do you ever think about going back?" Asp scraped at the bottom of the cup as he spoke.

"It was all I thought about until my mom died. Now?" She shrugged her shoulders again. "Life has a way of sucking your dreams away from you."

Asp put his cup down and waited until she looked up at him. "I am sorry for your loss. Believe me, I understand your feelings better than you think." He cleared his throat and continued, "I've lost both of my parents. The hole that leaves in your soul never goes away. "

She nodded slowly. "That's true. Who shot you?"

"I don't know." Whoever was up on that ridge was damn good, though.

"Fair enough. *Why* did they shoot you?" She tipped her head to the side and studied him. "Who are you, Isaac Cooper, and what do you do that people want to kill you?"

"You don't want to know the answer to that question." He blanked all emotions from his response.

"I don't?"

"No." Asp held her stare as he spoke, "I am poison, Lyric. I am pure, unadulterated evil, and I have more enemies than you can possibly imagine. You endanger yourself and your family by helping me. Pack your belongings and go back to the farm with your family. Forget I exist. Leave before someone finds out you're helping me."

He watched as her eyes widened when his words registered, but she didn't get up and start packing. Instead, she reached over and grabbed his cup, went to the fire, filled it and handed it back to him. Her voice remained level and calm as she spoke, "Poison and evil? I don't believe it for a second. You are polite, well-mannered, and begged me to take care of Mrs. Henson, no wait...Mrs. Henshaw, because her children wouldn't. You wanted to buy KD a birthday gift and you felt guilt about missing the party. You're not evil, Isaac Cooper. You may have a dangerous job, but *you* are not evil. I don't scare easily so stop trying. Nobody should find you here. I have been very careful. In fact, if I suspect there are others in the area, there is no reason to leave this cave. I don't go out into that valley unless I'm sure it is safe. Now if you're done trying to protect me, finish your food and then lie back before you fall over."

She got up and went to the fire, keeping her back to him. Asp literally snapped his mouth shut. That beautiful, angelic woman had just handed him his ass. Politely. He blinked from her to the stew in his cup back to her. *Well shit.* His respect for the woman toggled up twenty notches.

"Stop thinking so hard and eat." Lyric's voice floated to him from the front of the cave.

Asp narrowed his eyes at her as he finished his stew in three bites, drank some water and lay flat on the pallet. He followed her directions because he was hungry and tired. No other reason.

CHAPTER 10

$\mathcal{L}$yric kept her eyes on the front of the cave listening to the soft roll of thunder. She'd spent the morning foraging the area over the ridge for bananas, mangos, guanabana and several shoots and roots to add to their very small stores, but the torrential afternoon rains should obscure any tracks she'd made. Isaac's appetite had returned, and she was glad she'd taken the time to gather her large backpack full of fresh food. She leaned against the side of the cave and watched the rain. She'd been cautious, but what if someone actually was looking for Isaac as he suggested earlier? She could handle the threat, but if she led his enemies back to her family? No, that wasn't acceptable. She wouldn't be the reason someone else in her family died. The guilt of her mother's death still hung over her. She couldn't be responsible for putting what was left of her family in danger.

She knew the FARC were reorganizing again. There were many who were unhappy about the way the government handled the disbanding of the group. No doubt anyone looking to gather malcontents would find more than enough willing to volunteer. She'd spent ten years in this country. She knew the horror stories, and yes, they put a healthy fear into her, with good reason. Many women had been abducted from their homes and brutalized. Lyric suddenly wished she'd kept the handgun with her instead of sending it back down to the farm with her grandfather. But, it was better the men had the protection while harvesting. She glanced at Isaac's rifle propped against the wall. He'd had her bring it to him as soon as he could sit up and had spent an hour cleaning and checking the weapon. She wouldn't even know how to begin to load it, let alone shoot the thing.

Isaac tried to scare her away this morning. His words alarmed her, but she wouldn't run away, not when he needed help, and despite his bluster, he did need her help. Her only hesitancy in throwing his words back in his face were thoughts her family might be put in danger by her helping him.

She narrowed her eyes and stared hard through the rain, seeing nothing as her mind tumbled over what might happen in the next two weeks. Two weeks was a long time to look for someone. Adding another two weeks, considering how fast he was healing, would make it a month since he'd been shot. Would the men that hunted Isaac still be looking by then? She shoved her hands into the back pockets of her jeans and drew a deep breath. She'd be more careful about leaving any indications she'd been harvesting fruit around the valley and make sure Isaac rested and regained his strength.

"Do I hear water running?" Isaac's voice behind her sent her catapulting into the wall of the cave.

She grabbed her shoulder where she slammed into the unforgiving rock and spun around. "That is the second time you've scared me enough to make me abuse myself." Her eyes flitted from his face, pale and drawn to his bare chest. He'd found his jeans and pulled them on over his injury. They were zipped but not buttoned. His muscles rippled under his skin as he lifted his arm to brace himself against the wall.

"Second time?" His drawn face held a quizzical expression.

"Once when I was asleep. You spoke loudly, and it jolted me. I bumped my head." She reached back and felt the still tender spot.

"I feel like I should apologize."

"For having a fever? No, you don't need to do that." She shook her head. "You shouldn't be up."

"I won't get stronger if I don't push myself."

"You push yourself too much and you'll set back your recovery." She pointed toward the pallet. "Go lie down."

He smiled and nodded outside. "Nature calls." Lyric felt the blood rush to her face. She'd taken care of him while he was unconscious, but of course, he wouldn't want...no...

"How strong do you feel?"

"I'm managing." She waved towards the back of the cave. "There is a way out of the cave toward the back. It is very secluded. I've dug a trench." She didn't wait for him to answer but went to her pack and pulled out the flashlight before she took the kerosene light and lit it. Her embarrassment at the memories of his body...his entire body, fueled her flurry of activity.

"If we walk slow, I should be able to make it." He limped from the wall towards her.

Lyric swore bitter words to herself. She was so lost in her own embarrassment she hadn't thought to offer him help. "Here, lean on me for support. I'll go at your pace."

His heavy arm draped over her shoulder though he wasn't leaning her much, more like using her for balance. She didn't care, as long as it assisted him. She wrapped her hand around his waist. The light of the flashlight in her hand bounced with his step sending weird illuminations against the wall and the small waterfall that fed the pool of water. The size of the cascade and the resulting pool had gotten considerably bigger with the recent afternoon rains. He stopped and scanned the inner chamber of the cave. She allowed him to take it in and catch his breath.

"Beautiful, isn't it?" She looked up at him and smiled. "You can see through the surface to the very bottom. It is clear, pure and beautiful."

His gaze fell to her, and he blinked before he spoke. "Yes, beautiful."

Lyric narrowed her eyes. Was he going to pass out? Why did he sound like that? She motioned toward the back of the cavern. "Can you make it?"

"I will."

She suspected his answer resulted more from determination than ability, but she helped him to the back of the cavern and a narrow walkway. "Use the walls for support, they are mostly smooth. The walkway is about ten feet and then two sharp turns to the right. At that point, the sun lights the interior of the cavern enough to see, even with the rain clouds. I'll be waiting here. Call me if you need me." She gave him the flashlight and sat the kerosene lamp down on the floor of the cavern near her feet.

He nodded, took the flashlight and braced himself against the walls of the narrow passage. He was shaking. The flashlight danced wildly as he shifted his hands and stepped forward. She watched with growing concern until he turned the corner and then lifted her light and quietly trailed after him, wanting to be closer if he needed her. She stood in the fissure and waited...and waited...just when she was ready to go out and check on him, she heard him coming back. She retreated to the main cavern before he reached the turn. He was soaking wet when he threw an arm over her. His hair was plastered to his head as if he'd wiped it back. His beard was soft and full, and he looked completely exhausted

"What happened? Why are you soaked?"

He leaned against her, heavier than before, giving her more of his weight, making her clothes wet from the contact. "I couldn't stand the smell of myself. There is another waterfall just outside your bathroom area. I took a shower. Well, that's not true. I stood under the water, clothes and all."

Lyric looked up at him. "Well, you know our bathrooms have all the modern conveniences. Next time I'll bring you soap and a towel."

"Deal." He leaned against her, and they slowly hobbled back to the front of the cave. He glanced at the bed and then at his wet jeans. He ran a hand over his face and sighed, "Fuck, didn't think that one through, did I?"

Lyric grabbed one of the blankets off his pallet. "No problem, here, hold this." She wrapped the material around his waist and waited for him to grab the gathered area. Before he could object, she reached in between the folds, unzipped his pants and slid her hands inside his waistband, pulling them down to his feet. She kept her eyes trained on his upper body in case he started to topple, even though she'd love to see the man standing...naked and standing. She flushed at the thought and tapped his ankle. "Lift your foot."

Isaac put his free hand out to the cave wall and leaned against it before he lifted one foot and then the other. Lyric pulled the wet and now sandy jeans out from under the blanket. She threw them on top of a rock where they wouldn't get dirtier and stood up. "Now, that is enough of an outing for you. Time for you to lie down."

Isaac stared at her for a moment before he nodded. "Okay, but only because I'm going to fall down if I don't."

She smiled. "Well, thank you for admitting that. Go ahead, lie down. I'll take your jeans over by the fire and get dinner started. You rest." She helped as best as she could during his controlled fall to the pallet and draped the other blanket over him. His eyes closed almost immediately. She was tempted to brush his wet hair from where it was plastered to his forehead. Her time of touching him because she wanted to give him comfort was coming to an end. She gave in to the urge and pushed his wet bangs away from his eyes. His eyes opened briefly, and a smile flitted across his face. Lyric stood and turned to the tasks at hand. He was healing, and she would be gone soon. There were only a handful of days until she walked away from him forever. An ache took up residence in her chest. So, she did what was right. She shoved those feelings down, grabbed his jeans, and went to work.

Two hours later he woke, silently. She'd have missed it if she hadn't been watching him. He was quiet as his eyes scanned the cave, finally settling on her.

"It's not freaky at all that you're watching me sleep." The chuckle from his chest rumbled through the cave.

"Sorry, the television didn't have anything interesting on. Hungry?"

He chuckled, "Always."

Lyric smiled at the honesty of that answer. She gathered his food and brought it to him.

"Have you eaten?"

She nodded and pointed to her own plate beside her pallet.

He glanced over as if making sure she'd actually eaten something before he picked up his food and consumed it. Quickly.

"Who's KD?" Lyric couldn't stop the curiosity. Isaac wore no wedding band. He had never mentioned anyone other than his dead parents. Of course, he'd been asleep most of the time, but he did mention Mrs. Henshaw and KD.

Asp kept his focus on his plate, but he didn't take another bite. "Why do you want to know?"

"You wanted to get whoever they are a birthday present. What would you get?" Lyric hoped she could determine his relationship with this KD by contextual clues. She knew it was wrong to be jealous. He wasn't her friend, let alone her lover, but after taking care of him, nursing him back to life, she had a vested interest. At least, that was what she told herself. When had she allowed herself to hope for much more?

Asp leaned back against the wall of the cave and stared at her for a moment before he shrugged. "I wanted to get her a pony. I figured her other...uncles wouldn't be able to top that."

"Uncles?" A flutter of happiness winged around her heart and took a perch there. She refused to examine the reason why.

He took a bite and nodded. "Kinda. I'm friends with her dad. He's the only one of us that has a family." He chewed his food and looked toward the front of the cave as if lost in thought.

"Her parents would be okay with you buying her a pony?" Growing up in Jacksonville she knew most kids went through a phase where they asked for a pony. The issue was where to keep a horse, in the backyard?

"Yeah. They live on a ranch out in the middle of nowhere. Her dad would be okay with it, but her mom, well, she hovers. Kadey was sick for a long time, but she's fine now. Her momma is protective."

She saw his eyes soften and a smile played on his lips. "You like being an uncle."

"I like having a family. It's been a long time."

"What do you do when you're not working?" Lyric grabbed several bananas and peeled one open, handing the fruit to him. His hand was huge against the size of the fruit. She marveled again at the sheer size of the man.

He ate the banana in three bites and took a drink of water. "I travel."

"Where?"

"What do you mean?"

"I mean, where have you been? I've lived in America, and we flew here. So, I've been to America and Colombia. Where have you been?"

He leaned back against the cave wall and smiled. "Listing the countries I haven't been to would take less time."

Wow, that was not the answer she expected. Her curiosity peaked. "Do you enjoy it? Traveling?" She'd never had the itch to travel, well except to go back to the US. Maybe she was a homebody. That was what her mom had called herself.

"I did when I was younger. Recently, I've been sticking around my friend's place." He reached for the other banana and stripped it of its peel.

"The one with the little girl?" Lyric wrapped her arms around her legs.

"Yeah. Either there, or I go to the east coast and check in on Mrs. Henshaw. She's a cool old lady. She makes great cookies." He smiled before he took the last bite of his banana.

"Cookies? Say it isn't so. Isaac Cooper has a sweet tooth?" She laughed when he blushed.

"Hey, I get enough sh ... uh, crap from my co-workers. I have a healthy appetite. They like to point out how much I eat." He examined his blanket and shrugged. "They are good people."

"I haven't seen you eat too much. You're hungry, but that is to be expected after being sick for so long." She couldn't imagine teasing someone because they were hungry. His friends sounded critical. She wanted to ask him about his co-workers but she suspected that was a forbidden topic.

"How old are you?" Isaac asked.

"Twenty-seven." She nodded at him. "You?"

"I have you by about ten years. Married?" He examined his plate like he'd just discovered the Holy Grail.

"No. I've never even been in a long-term relationship. My dad says it's because of my temper. Not many men are strong enough to stand up to me." Isaac glanced up at her and she smiled at the flick of his eyebrows, as if he considered taking on the challenge. What she wouldn't give for that to happen. "Are you married?" She held her breath.

"No. The job. It's not conducive to relationships." He shrugged and took a drink of water.

The giddy flush of pleasure at hearing he was single threatened to reveal her lack of indifference, but she managed to keep her voice level. Just two friends chatting. "But your friend has managed to have a family?" What did his friend do differently to allow him that happiness?

"Not many are able to...escape our profession." A sadness colored his voice when he spoke.

He seemed a lonely man. His friends were few, and he'd been shot. One of the first things he'd done when he regained consciousness was to clean his rifle, and he'd spent a few minutes every day, disassembling and cleaning it. "Are you a criminal, Isaac Cooper?"

His eyes snapped to her and his body tensed. He shook his head. "My organization works within strict confines. What I do is sanctioned. I am not a criminal." He was emphatic with his words, punctuating each one.

Lyric lifted her eyebrows at the intensity of his declarations. She stared at him, trying to read why he was so adamant, but she couldn't. Finally, she nodded her head. "I believe you."

Isaac held her stare for a moment before he nodded. For whatever reason, he needed her to believe him. She did.

~

Asp woke and rolled onto his side, barely flinching at the movement. Lyric wasn't sitting in her normal spot across from him. He rotated so he could look at the fire. She wasn't there either. He stretched carefully, feeling his muscles pull. It had been three days since he'd showered under the waterfall adjacent to the back entrance of the cave. His strength had started to return, no doubt because Lyric kept him fed, hydrated and corralled. She made an exacting mother hen. She kept a sharp eye on him. Hell, he told Lyric every day he was solid. She ignored him, every day. Why she was so damn stubborn was beyond him. She needed to get off this mountain and as far away from him as possible. He reminded her of that every chance he got. A small piece of him, however, was happy each time she rebuffed him and then fussed at him for not taking care of himself. Not since he'd left home had someone fussed over him. Was it wrong of him to covet it? Probably. Strike that. Try definitely.

He stank, and he wasn't the only thing that stank. He stood and risked bending down to remove the blankets from his pallet and toss them over a pile of rocks not far away. Those blankets needed as much attention as he did. He moved across the cave and rummaged around in his pack for his bar of soap, his toothbrush and powdered toothpaste and his straight razor. It was time to clean up and rejoin the land of the living. He also pulled one of his glow sticks out of the bottom of his pack. The chemical reaction lasted twelve hours so they could use it all day without draining her flashlight's batteries.

At the waterfall he stripped. A small flow of water still poured over the rock shelf. He stripped and grabbed his bar of soap and his straight razor before he washed quickly and sat down under the stream of water. God...he was finally clean. Asp caught a flash of movement. Dark pants and an arm. He pushed into the face of the rock. The waterfall area was concealed, still he moved further under the rock that hung overhead. It took no time to collect his belongings and move his ass back into the interior of the cave. Once inside, he threw on his jeans, stuffed everything in a blanket and grabbed his glow stick. He sprinted to the front of the cave, expecting to see Lyric. Only, she hadn't returned, and that was a huge fucking problem. Winded, he sucked air and tried to focus. Asp grabbed his boots and stuffed his feet into them before he snatched up his weapon. He grabbed a handful of rounds, shoved them into his front pocket and headed out of the cave.

His eyes bounced around the upper valley. *Holy fuck, where was Lyric?* There was someone out there, and chances were that particular someone was hunting for him. He moved to his left, looking for a way out of the bushes that would still keep him covered and at minimal risk. That was when he saw her. She was crouched down between a tree and one of the flowering marmalade bushes. She'd made herself as small as possible, and from above she may not be have been seen, but from the floor of the canyon, she was exposed. Her head shot up, and he knew she'd spotted him. She lifted her hand and made a small motion to point above him. Asp made the OK sign with his hand and then held it up in a stop sign fashion. Lyric folded into herself again, becoming as small as possible. That was one a smart woman.

Asp shifted back to the cave opening. It offered the most concealment if someone looked down from above. He worked on steadying his breath and listened for anything that was out of the ordinary. He heard the ghost whispers of gravel shifting. Too much to be from the breeze. The sound came from up above him and to his right. Carefully and quietly he drifted back out of view. The rattle of rocks became louder. There...the catch of a boot on rock and a muttered curse, in English. Whoever it was had no idea Asp was below him. Glancing to his right, and left, he weighed his options. Of course, he chose the most difficult, but quieter, of the two available avenues he could use to take the man out. He could shoot the bastard or kill him with his hands. Firing the rifle would have anyone in a five-mile area heading their direction. So, a close-in kill. Asp didn't have the strength for a long fight. He needed an efficient and quick kill.

He pressed against the rock and waited. A flurry of loose rock and dirt preceded the inelegant thump of the man's feet, not three feet from where Asp waited. He had a millisecond to determine if the man was friend or foe. The half-assed uniform and Russian made weapon strapped to his back told him everything he needed to know. Asp stepped out and sent a quick thrust of the butt of his weapon toward the man's head. The stock collided with the man's face. Blood and teeth sprayed across the rock surface. The man choked or gagged an inaudible plea or perhaps it was a curse. Asp didn't care. His target dropped to his knees. Asp planted his bad leg and swung violently with his good, kicking the man's chin back and up with all the force he could muster. He couldn't hear the telltale sound of the man's neck snapping because he was breathing too fucking hard, but the guy dropped like a bag of rocks, and the position of his head on his neck told the story. Asp dropped his hand to his knee and sucked air. He shook from the small amount of energy he'd expended and sweat sheened his body. The blank eyes that stared back at him told him nothing. Asp rifled through the man's pockets. No identification, nothing but a pack of cigarettes and a lighter. He stayed in his hidden position for twenty minutes, listening and waiting. There was no further movement. Taking the risk of revealing himself, he pushed away from the wall and the man he'd just killed. He'd deal with the dead body after he got Lyric back inside the cave.

Asp carefully slid along the wall of the cave and made it back to where he could see Lyric, but she was no longer there. Every nerve in his body tensed as he scanned the area. He moved from one bush to the next, carefully moving limbs to expose a wider expanse to his view. There was nothing. Fuck! Where was...

A scrape of a boot against a rock to his left plunged him into full attack mode. He spun and lifted his rifle ready to kill. Lyric skid to a stop, her eyes wide and her face pale. Asp lowered the weapon, reached out and pulled her into his chest. He cradled her there, relieved he didn't deliver the blow he'd intended and was fucking thankful she was alive.

"I'm sorry." She whispered the words over and over into his chest.

He held her to him and rocked her back and forth letting her seek comfort. She had to be terrified. He made shushing noises in her ear, before he spoke, "You have no reason to be sorry."

She pulled away and looked up at him, tears rolling down her face. "If I'd have stayed in the cave, he never would have found us. He was up by the fruit trees. I think he saw me and followed me. You had to kill him."

Asp nodded and pulled her against him again. He'd been honest with her. He'd told her he had enemies, and she'd just witnessed that in a front row seat fashion. "I'm sorry you had to see that."

"I'm sorry I made you do it." She leaned into him and fuck him if he didn't revel in the feel of her against him.

"You didn't make me do a thing. I killed him to keep both of us safe." Asp rubbed his hand up and down her back, still holding his M-21 in his right hand.

"We need to leave. By his uniform, he's FARC. If they are

this close, it's only a matter of time before they find us. Are you well enough to travel down with me?"

Asp leaned back and frowned. "I can't come with you. I can't bring this shit to your family's door. If anyone saw us together, it wouldn't go well for you, your father and grand-father." He backed away slightly and herded her toward the cave entrance. He would follow her and keep an eye on her, but he wouldn't go with her.

There was a sniper out there, somewhere. One of the basic tenants he'd always followed was to confirm your kill. He'd confirmed his kill. The sniper who shot at him, could not. The marksman hadn't been able to track him either. If the bastard was working for Halo, outside the law, he'd prob-ably take missing the kill personally. That meant Asp had to assume the man was out there, somewhere, and that he would still be hunted. Even if he made it off the mountain unseen, he still had over fifty vulnerable miles to travel to where he left his vehicle and his satellite phone. Asp wouldn't give up if the roles were reversed. He didn't expect the bastard who shot him would give up either. He'd deal with the dead body and get a game plan started.

He continued to shield her view as they entered the cave, and thankfully, she didn't try to go around him. Death was never something innocents needed to see. Death scarred. It ripped lives apart, and it was the one thing in which he excelled.

She spun on him once he managed to get them in the cave. "You, I..." She shivered and rubbed her hands over her arms before she looked past him to the entrance of the cave.

He moved to block her view. "What? What were you going to say?"

A small shake of her head preceded a deep breath. She straightened her back and tilted her chin up in a show of defiance. "Nothing. It is almost nightfall. I need to get my things together." She spun away from him and started gathering her belongings.

He watched her jerky movements as she picked up items that had migrated from the area around her pallet to the far corners of the cave. She didn't turn back to him. Instead, she ignored him. No surprise there. He'd killed someone in front of her. She was probably terrified of him. Asp set his rifle down near the mouth of the cave and returned to the corpse. He grabbed the man's leg, tugged him away from the entrance, and into the thickest stand of marmalade bushes. He used his boot to scrape out the soft bed of leaves under the bush. He rolled the man under the limbs and kicked the leaves and dirt over him. It wouldn't do anything to protect the body from wild animals, but it might hide him from anyone looking down from above, and right now, that was Asp's only concern. Exhausted, he made his way back to the cave. They'd sleep for a few hours and then leave during the dead of night.

CHAPTER 11

*S*he'd tried to lose the man on her trail this afternoon. She'd circled past the valley twice and thought she'd lost him before she came over the ridge and down the far side of the valley, but he must have seen her and moved to cut her off. He'd come down the face of rock that held her grandfather's shrine to her grandmother. She watched as he almost dropped on top of Isaac. She wanted to scream to him in warning, but fear kept her silent. She watched as Isaac reared up, struck the man with the stock of his weapon and then...the man's head snapped back from Isaac's kick. She knew at that moment Isaac had killed him.

The entire situation was her fault. If she'd just been more careful. Tears kept a steady flow down her cheeks. She swiped at them as she shoved her belongings into the pack.

Isaac wasn't coming with her. She would have to make her way alone down the mountain. Alone. Lyric's hands shook, and her mind raced. For the first time since she'd traveled up the mountain, she was really scared. She couldn't believe he was simply going to abandon her. He said he "wouldn't bring his enemies to her family's door."

Yeah. How noble of him. So what if that left her traveling alone down the mountain, dodging the FARC who were hunting him. If they found her? Oh, god. Lyric shivered and rubbed her arms with her hands. At the farm, her father and grandfather were armed and kept her safe. Here, with Isaac, she was safe, but a single woman traveling down the mountain alone, unarmed...she rubbed her arms harder trying to warm herself. She searched the area looking for anything she couldn't leave behind. There was nothing.

"You're probably in shock."

Lyric startled at his words, not realizing he'd come back into the cave. He draped a blanket around her. Lyric threw the blanket off her shoulders. "I'm not in shock, I'm..." She was in shock—but it wasn't for the reasons he thought. Her shock stemmed from pure disillusionment about the character of the man she'd saved. She shut her mouth and shook her head. So...she had to make her way alone down the mountain. Okay. She *could* do this. She was smart, resourceful and she'd be careful.

"Look, I know you're upset, but it's for the best."

The sound of his words hadn't faded before Lyric pounced. "Really? It's for the best? Sending me down the mountain alone when the FARC are out there, beating every bush looking for you? It's for the best?" She glared at him. "Don't worry, I hear the women they take don't last long." She spun on her heel to grab her pack and was jerked off her feet and pulled into his chest. His massive arms cradled her even when she kicked him. "Let me go!" Everything settled on her heart. The mistakes she made this afternoon, the man who lay dead because of her and the heartache from the realization Isaac wasn't the champion she'd built up in her mind—all of it crashed down on her. She crumpled, and he held her up. She cried, and he rocked her in his arms. This was the

Isaac she thought she knew. Why had he refused to help her down the mountain?

"You're safe with me. I won't let anyone hurt you." His words rumbled through his chest.

She shook her head. She really wasn't. She was terrified and she... "Wait, what?" She sniffed. "You said you wouldn't take me home."

"No, I said I couldn't bring this to your family's door. I would never leave you unprotected." He tipped her head up, and she blinked back her tears. "I can't be seen with you, but I'll be there."

"I don't understand."

"I'll be watching, but you won't see me. I will be there for you."

"Oh...you shaved." She had no idea why she said that. Perhaps relief had left her giddy.

He chuckled and nodded. "I did." He cupped her face with one massive hand. "Trust me?"

She stared at him. "I do."

"We'll sleep for a couple hours, pack up, only the necessities, and we'll head out. Staying here isn't safe any longer." His eyes flicked from hers to her lips.

Lyric ran her tongue over them because they were suddenly very dry. His eyes trailed the movement. Pressed against him as she was, there was little he could hide from her. His body wanted her, maybe as much as she wanted him. She lifted onto her toes and pressed her lips against his. He stood, stoic and still. Lyric threaded her arms around his neck and pulled away a fraction of an inch opening her eyes to see him. "Stop trying to protect me from you, Isaac. Kiss me."

She rubbed up against him. His body had reacted to her, and she was going to use that fact to her benefit. His hardening length against her stomach told her he wanted her, too.

Logically, this was a bad decision. Logically, she knew he was a man who wouldn't be tied down to a woman like her. He'd traveled the world and worked doing something mysterious and dangerous. Something that put them both in danger. Maybe it was stupid to push him, but she'd always wonder what could have been if she didn't. She'd learned from her mother's death, life was too short to live with regrets. He stared at her, the indecision in his eyes was easy to read. "Kiss me, now." She whispered her demand.

He lowered to her. The first sweep of his lips lingered for a few precious seconds. She opened for him, inviting him deeper. He clutched her tighter, kissed her softly once more and dropped his arms. "We need to pack up and get ready to go. When it is full dark, we move." He turned and walked out of the cave.

Lyric lifted her fingers to her lips. The kiss was everything and nothing. She wanted more. At the same time, she was terrified of more. More of Isaac Cooper meant certain heartbreak. He would leave her and she'd go back to her small existence in the foothills of the Andes.

She rubbed her arms again and looked around the cave. She had what she needed to travel light. Everything else could be left. Twilight was fading into early evening outside. To pass the time, she made some dinner. She ate and waited. Hours passed, and he still hadn't returned. It was full dark now. Lyric made her way to the entrance of the cave, careful to keep concealed along the darkest side of the entrance. She snuck a peek out and to the right and then left. She found him sitting against the outside wall of the entrance.

"Hey." She sat down beside him. "I have food for you." He nodded but continued to look forward, through the bushes. She tried to see what he was looking at, but the night was inky dark. Clouds shadowed the moon and the stars. "What are you looking at?"

He rolled his head and looked at her. A sadness had settled around him. It was easy to see and to feel. "I'm trying to estimate where a sniper would be, what he would be looking for and where. I believe he'll be looking for my entry point. That means we should have three, maybe four days of relatively safe travel."

"Sniper? The FARC has snipers?" Lyric shivered at that thought.

"No, the man who was organizing the remnants of the FARC had a sniper, and he was the man who shot me. Everything we do outside this cave will become a game of strategy. What would they do, versus what we will do? I completed my mission. I killed his boss. He missed me. He knows he failed. People like me don't like to fail. So, he'll try to guess what I will do, and he'll try to manipulate the terrain and environment to make me do what he wants me to do."

"You killed his boss?" Her throat tightened as she said the words.

"I did. He was my assignment. He...he was a monster."

"Your government sent you here to kill him?"

"No. Not the government."

"But it was...legal?"

"It was."

"How?"

"I can't tell you."

They sat in silence for a while before Lyric asked, "Is that what you do? You kill people?"

He nodded. "Yes."

She twirled the words through her mind. Gooseflesh rose on her arms. "This man who is waiting for you and trying to figure out where you will be, how would he even know where to start looking?"

Asp shrugged. "Simple. He had an idea of where I was when he took the shot. He would know he didn't fire a kill shot, so he'd start there. Track me if he could. Your grandfather said he saw men on the ridge, which lends credence to that supposition. If I took a shot, I'd know if I hit the target, even a glancing wound. I can almost guarantee he knows I'm injured. He knows I'll need help. Chances are the people he works for have people monitoring the hospitals and local doctors." He turned his head, his brow furrowed. "How did you obtain the medication you gave me?"

A small laugh escaped. "Jo-Jo."

"Excuse me?"

"We have a donkey; her name is Jo-Jo. She is small and stubborn and not too bright. She walks through barbed wire fences, usually once or twice a year. Dad told the vet that she'd done it again and the cuts were infected. He gave me the medication. I gave the medication to you."

Isaac turned his head back toward the field, but not before she saw his lips twitch. "It wouldn't be the first time I've been treated like an ass."

She chuckled even though the situation was dire. Lyric leaned her head against his strong shoulder. "What are we going to do?"

Isaac drew a deep breath. "That is up to you. We can make an attempt to reach your grandfather's farm. If we are being followed by the FARC, your family may be targeted. Or, we can try to make it to my vehicle. If we do, I can get us out. Safely."

Lyric's snapped her head around. "What? You mean to leave the country?" Leave Colombia? The old desire flicked inside her, like a small spark.

He nodded. "Only for a short while. Will your grandfather come back up here?"

"The banana harvest is in full swing. If he did come back to check on me, it wouldn't be until that finished. In just over a week, maybe a few days more." She'd lost track of time, but with the large crop this year, it would take a couple days longer to harvest the bananas. She shelved the dream of leaving Colombia and concentrated on his words.

"If we are where I think we are, and that could be seriously messed up because I was out of it during the last hours, we should make it to my exit point in four days. No, five. I don't have the stamina to make it in four days. When we get out, I can get word to them, so they know you are safe and that you'll be back."

"Unless this sniper finds us." She dropped her head into her hands. "So, my choices are to possibly lead the FARC to my family and jeopardize them or lead them away from my family and..."

"And possibly die because of me." His words were flat, hard and cold. But that was exactly what she needed to hear. The truth.

"You will be there to protect me, and I'll be there to help you. What are the odds we will make it out?"

He pinched his lips together, still staring out into the darkness. "Fifty-fifty."

Lyric swallowed hard. She'd hoped for much better odds. She nodded and croaked, "The odds of leading the FARC back to my family?"

He shrugged. "I don't know. I wish I did. We could crest the ridge and run into them, or we could make it down to your farm and not see a soul."

"You don't believe that, though do you? That we wouldn't see anyone or be seen by anyone?"

"No, I don't." He gestured down the path toward the cluster of marmalade bushes that concealed a dead body. "He wasn't out here alone. When he doesn't come back, someone will come looking for him. On top of that, when he cursed, it was in English. He's here with the people who were brought in by the man I killed."

Lyric rung her hands together for a moment as she thought. "Is he the caliber of man this monster recruited?"

That got a huff of air from Isaac. "Neither of us have any idea what that man was capable of doing. I got the drop on him. Luck on my part."

That was true, to a point. Lyric knew the man had no idea that Isaac was waiting for him when he dropped. But she knew what she'd seen. Isaac was a skilled fighter. She glanced up to the ridgeline of the small canyon. Even odds or walk into the unknown. She didn't like either situation, but she'd been the one to tell her grandfather she'd take care of Isaac. If her grandfather was here, there wouldn't be this discussion. He'd go with Isaac to lead them away from her and her father. She knew it. She couldn't do less.

CHAPTER 12

"I'm not going to chance leading the FARC to my family. Let's hope your luck holds out. I'm coming with you."

Her words were the ones he wanted to hear, but neither scenario was good. She leaned into him. He lifted his arm and let her tuck into his side.

"When we leave, you will need to listen and obey what I tell you when I tell you. Don't question or hesitate. It could mean the difference between life and death for us." She nodded and scooted closer to him. "The night is quiet. Our travels have to be silent. We will move slowly, very slowly until the sun starts to rise. We can't risk alerting someone to our presence during sunrise or sunset when the wildlife is most active. We will move when the night is darkest. No flashlights, no illumination of any kind."

"How will we see where we are going?"

"You'd be surprised how well your eyes will adapt given extended time in the darkness." Is there anything in the cave that could be used to identify your family?"

"In the cave? No. But remember I told you my grandfather built a shrine to my grandmother and his family just above here. Their names, the dates they lived and died. They are permanently etched in the stone."

Asp nodded. He remembered her telling him, but there was nothing he could do about the shrine. "Alright, if the cave was discovered and it was apparent someone had lived there, the next logical step would be to find the person who made the shrine above it and question them. We need to gather everything we aren't taking with us and bury it in one of the darkest corners of the inner cavern. I'll do that while you get leaves to obscure our footprints."

"Then what?" She looked up at him. Worry etched her expression.

He lifted a finger and traced the deep line between her eyebrows. The act seemed intimate, but he took the liberty after that kiss. He nodded away from the cave. "Then we get to the top of that ridge, and I get my bearings. We are heading northeast. We'll drop further in elevation but stay in the wooded area." He ran his finger over her cheek before he dropped it, removed his arm from her shoulder and stood up.

"Won't that make it easy to hear us?" She rose gracefully to her feet.

"If we were running or trying to escape, yes. We won't be. We are going to move slowly, and quietly." Not only because the darkness was their best defense, but because he knew he couldn't last if the effort was more taxing. Playing things safe wasn't his usual M.O. He had the scars to prove it, but this time he had someone else counting on him, a spitfire of a woman who was stronger mentally than most men he'd encountered. He ducked and headed into the cave. It was time.

$\sim$

Asp stopped just below the crest of the ridge and signaled. He waited for Lyric to catch up with him. They were moving in installments. He'd travel a distance, stop and hold up a hand when he noticed trouble with the trail, and let her mark the approximate location. The loud snap of a branch behind him echoed in the night. He studied the area around him looking for any sudden movement. Lyric was close, and he held a hand up, stilling her forward progress. He studied the terrain before he motioned her up to him.

"Sorry." She whispered, soft. Barely audible.

He put his mouth next to her ear. "When you step down, test the ground with your toe first. You can feel branches or loose rocks. Put your weight down only after your toe is on solid ground. Don't hurry. Just keep coming toward me." She nodded her understanding. "We are crawling over the ridge. I need you as low to the ground as you can get. If someone is looking for us, they could see us silhouetted by the moon if we stand." She nodded again and he low-crawled over the ridge and down the slope. When he motioned for her to follow she mimicked his movements. She was a fast study. When she reached him, he moved forward again, this time standing to move through brush and trees. He stopped about a hundred yards in front of her and adjusted the rifle he'd strapped across his back. The weight of it, plus the pack he carried, put additional strain on his stamina, but he couldn't stop. He needed to get Lyric out of his mess. She'd been his savior when he couldn't ask for help. He needed to be the same for her and her family.

Asp motioned her forward for the last time. There was a large thicket of vines and trees ahead. He found a place large enough for both of them to crawl into where they'd sleep and rest, hidden from sight, until nightfall. The last of his depleted energy reserves waned as the wildlife woke. She reached him and waited. He signaled, and they both dropped to their knees.

He whispered, "We are sleeping here. Go behind those trees to relieve yourself. We won't be able to come out until after dark."

She nodded and almost soundlessly made her way back behind a stand of trees. Asp moved away in the other direction and did the same. They came back together, and he pointed and motioned for her to follow him. He dropped to his knees, removed his gun and his pack and placed them beside her. He motioned for her to wait. She nodded. One well-placed hand in front of the other, he worked his way through the vines, opening a passage until they cleared against a stand of small trees. The area was tight. They'd have to sleep on their sides, but they could manage. He made his way back, folding back vines and branches that would impede her ability to follow him. When he emerged, she expelled a breath.

He took his rifle, shouldered his pack and motioned for her to go first. After she passed them, he grabbed the vines and slowly moved them back, blocking their entrance to anything but the most discerning tracker. When he reached her, she'd already pulled out a blanket and a water bottle. The blanket was on the ground protecting them from thorns and small branches. She sat on her heels and handed him the bottle after he placed his rifle on the ground with the muzzle pointed down the small tunnel in the vegetation.

He dropped his pack and pulled out two protein bars, giving one to her. They sat down on the blanket and consumed the bars and drank the water. They would have to find more to eat eventually, but in the tropical zone they were traversing, that wouldn't be a problem for someone with his skills. He dropped his pack to use as a pillow and lay down on his uninjured side. She dropped down beside him, used his arm as a pillow and fell asleep. This first night was successful. They were out of the cave and heading toward safety, but the obstacles before them were massive. Asp pulled her into a more comfortable position on his arm and closed his eyes. He'd take it one step at a time.

~

The mid-day heat woke him. Although they were protected from direct sun by the brush, vines, and trees, the foliage also blocked any breeze that might have alleviated the muggy intensity of the Colombian heat. Lyric had moved while they slept. She'd turned and was facing him with her cheek pillowed on her hand. The braid that held her long fall of dark brown hair back had loosened, and strands had been dislodged. Her long eyelashes rested on her cheeks. Asp noted the fine spray of freckles over the bridge of her nose. He cataloged each one rather than give in to the urge to reach out and touch her. She was a beautiful person, inside and out. He figured the beauty on the inside ran strong in her family. Her grandfather didn't have to help him, but he did. Lyric didn't need to stay with him once the fever broke, yet, she did.

Asp eased himself onto his back and stared up through the intertwined vines, branches, and leaves. It was rare he allowed himself to dream, to consider a 'what if' scenario. Hindsight was always twenty-twenty, and he rarely gave into the inclination to wonder what could have been, but...he glanced at the woman sleeping beside him. If he hadn't accepted the CIA's proposal, if he hadn't shielded his parents from the horrors of his life, if he had returned home and tried to live in nine-to-five suburbia, would he have had a family? Kadey's smile flashed brilliantly through his mind.

Before his life shattered into a million pieces, he'd wanted that. Children with a woman who could put up with his bullshit and love him anyway. He was wired to be a one-woman man. Before he officially died, he wasn't a serial dater. He liked being in relationships. Unfortunately, his career blocked every attempt he'd made, and he'd come to accept that, but...yeah, he would've loved to have had a family. A wife and children to love, protect, cherish.

"A penny for your thoughts?"

The whispered comment made him smile. He rolled back onto his side. Their eyes met, and she gave him a sleepy smile. "They aren't worth a penny." He reached out and pulled one of the stray wisps of hair from her cheek.

"How will I know unless you tell me?" She reached over and picked a dead leaf off his shoulder.

"I was wondering what my life would have been like if I had made different decisions. If I would have had a family." Sharing that information with her wasn't his plan, but for some reason, his mouth and brain had a disconnect concerning this woman. Talking to her was easy. He'd never tell her anything that would put her in any further danger, but he liked her, cared for her. Probably too much.

"Ah, reflections. We all have times in our lives when we question if we've done the right thing." She closed her eyes and settled her head against her hand again.

"You're too young to have those worries."

"You think so?" She opened her eyes and gazed at him. He nodded. She stared at him for several long seconds before she gave a slight shake of her head. "I don't. I think life doesn't discriminate. You make decisions when you are young and inexperienced, and you pay for the bravado and ignorance. Or someone you love pays. Regrets plague us all, don't you think?" She closed her eyes again and yawned, making a small sound at the end. Asp wanted to hear that contented hum again.

He stared at her long lashes laying against her skin for a moment before he answered, "I think you are an intelligent, beautiful woman, and I think you should have gone home after my fever broke. Staying with me wasn't the smart thing for you to do." Asp hated that she was forced to flee with him. If they were discovered together on the way back to his vehicle...

She opened her eyes and stared at him for a moment before she lifted up onto her elbow and gazed unseeing at something over his shoulder. Her lips thinned, and she shook her head before she met his eyes. "I have a lot of regrets. Staying with you is not one of them." Asp followed her movements as she lowered and scooted closer to him. The heat between them only intensified the temperature of the sun. She reached up and trailed a finger from his jaw to his shoulder. "I think any regret about you is yet to come. One day, you will walk away, and the colors that have painted my life since I saw you lying on that pallet will drain and fade. My world will return to what it has been, pale and uninteresting."

The words surrounded him like a soothing balm, one that he didn't deserve, but he'd cherish them nonetheless. "The excitement coloring your world at the moment will get you killed. I'm bad company. I can only put you in danger." He ran his hand down her arm. Her skin prickled from his touch, and she shivered. He lifted his eyes to hers. She pushed him onto his back and pinned him, lying half on his chest. She hovered over him. Her eyes strayed from his down to his lips and then slid back up to his eyes again. "Stop trying to protect me, Isaac. I'm a big girl. I do what I want to do. Right now, I want to kiss you."

"Protecting you is the least I should do." He swallowed hard. He didn't dare consider what he really wanted. He shook his head, still maintaining eye contact. "No, we can't." He knew if he allowed it, if she kissed him, it would lead to deeper feelings, further intimacies that would only lead to disaster. At least for him. It would be too hard to let her go.

"I don't want your least. I want your everything."

Her words caressed his skin as she pressed her lips against his, and then seduced his mouth with her tongue. He let her control the kiss and allowed himself to respond. Allowed? Hell, he couldn't stop. He wasn't sure when the protectiveness and care he felt for her gave way to something more intense—but it was there. That intensity of emotion had a name, and a fist of fear gripped his chest. He had nothing to give her. No future, no life...only death.

She deepened the kiss. Her hands threaded through his hair, and she tightened her grip to stop him from pulling away. Her insistence destroyed his lingering hesitation and he relaxed into the sweet taste of her. Their tongues danced, and he slowly took command of the kiss. Her small whimper of need when he rolled her over and deepened the kiss reverberated through his body and settled like an electric charge in his balls. The attraction between them destroyed his defenses.

Since Isaac Cooper had died and become Asp, sex had been a physical release for him. He didn't kiss the women he fucked. It kept emotions out of the act. Knowing the danger she posed to him, Asp would never have initiated any intimate contact, and he successfully pulled away when she demanded a kiss at the cave. But now? There was no place left for the long suppressed inner man, the one who dreamed of "what ifs" to flee. Lyric's small gasps and hums as they kissed tended a desolate, dry place in his soul. Her laugh when he jumped as her fingers trailed over his ribs watered the parched expanses of his need. She was beautiful music to his soul, even when the only sound was her skin caressing his.

She pushed on his chest, and he lifted off her, his body rigid with desire, and his mind clouded with lust. Fuck him, from just a few kisses and touches, he was worked up to the point of coming in his pants. Hell, she hadn't even touched his cock. But he had to be responsible. "We don't have protection." His words fell on a heavy exhale.

"Then we'll have to improvise." Her smile stretched slowly as she reached down and palmed his cock.

His eyes crossed, and he groaned as she slid her hand up and down the length of his shaft. She pushed his chest again, and he allowed her to move him to his side. She inched down his body, kissing her way down his chest, past his ribs, to his stomach. Her tongue circled and then delved into his belly button. He gripped his cock through his jeans. If he didn't, he'd fucking bust his nut before she ever put her lips on him, and God help him, if that was what she was promising, he'd make damn sure he didn't finish until he felt the warmth of her sweet mouth.

She unbuttoned and unzipped his jeans. Her tongue played hell with the skin on his groin that she slowly exposed. Fuck, his legs already shook, and his breathing sounded like he'd run a damn marathon. She pulled his cock out from the folds of denim and... *ohmygodyessofuckinggood.* He snapped his mouth shut against the shout of absolute fucking delight her hot, warm mouth pulled from the deepest parts of his soul. He bucked against her mouth. He couldn't help it. Her fingers clawed at his hip, pulling him toward her again, and *sweet mother of everything right with the world*, he thrust. He thrust again. The sounds of her taking him intensified the sharpness of the edge he'd been walking. He thrust again, and as Lyric pulled him deeper, he felt his cockhead push past the back of her mouth into her throat. Her moan vibrated up his cock, through his spine and blew out the top of his fucking head. He lost it, lost everything in that moment. He had just enough discipline to choke his bellow of gratification into some faint, wounded animal, sound. She pulled away enough to suck his shaft, taking everything as he spent down her throat. He pulled her off his cock and crashed his mouth against hers. He needed to...

He slid onto his back and pulled her on top of him. His arms slid down her sides, under her legs and he lifted, bringing her up to straddle his chest. Her eyes popped open, and she looked down at him. "Drop your jeans. Ride my mouth."

Her mouth opened in an "O" as his words registered. She moved off him, unbuttoned and unzipped. It took some maneuvering, but she was able to shed the jeans and her panties quickly. She straddled him once again. He lifted her shirt and bra baring her full, round breasts. His eyes traveled from her sex, up her stomach, over her ribs, and to her breasts. If he thought the woman was beautiful with clothes on, the sight of her disheveled and partially clothed was erotic as fucking hell. When his hands followed the path charted by his eyes, his spent cock made an admirable attempt at getting hard again. He pulled her down and circled one nipple with his lips while his hand tended to the other. Lyric's hips bucked forward, and she ground her sex against his stomach. He lowered his free hand to her and teased the folds of skin hiding her clit. She growled at him, and his eyes snapped up to find hers.

She narrowed her eyes at him and warned, "I didn't tease you. You damn sure better not tease me."

Asp smiled, and in one smooth movement pulled his hands away from her body, slid them under her legs, and lifted her over his mouth, centered where he could taste her.

He wrapped his arms over her legs and used his fingers to separate her folds. She was already wet for him. He zeroed in on his prize and pressed her pelvis down, not that she needed encouragement. He felt her hands plant above his head. Her hips moved in small jerks as she chased the perfect sensation of his lips, teeth, and tongue against her lips and clit. Her gasp, "Yes, there, like that," floated through to him. He locked his arms, keeping her in position and feasted. Her thighs shook and clenched and her body tried to move away or move closer, he wasn't sure which. The only thing he did know was she was close to orgasm. So fucking close, and he was using every technique his vast repertoire to shove her over the edge. He wanted to taste her when she came. So. Damn. Bad.

Lyric's legs tightened, clenching around him. She bucked against his grip. Her body froze for a moment, and then he felt the rhythmic spasms of her orgasm. He worked her through it, even when she tried to pull away, keeping after that hard pearl until...she gasped with a low cry and came again. Asp released her to slide down his body until she lay on top of him, her head tucked into his neck, her breathing labored and interlaced with delicate whispers of, "Oh, my God." The heat of the Colombian sun and the strenuous efforts of their love making covered them in perspiration. He'd give anything to be able to take care of her, to wash her body with cool water. But that would assume they had a relationship. They didn't. He had some kind of fucked up desire that would only end in him hurting her. She had...hell, he didn't know why she wanted him, but there was no way this wasn't ending with one or both of them getting hurt.

The heat was too much to keep the skin to skin contact. He drew a deep breath and let her roll off him onto the blanket and her side. She flopped to her back and started laughing. A low, melodic sound. Asp lifted up on his elbow and looked down at her. "Do I need to tell you that laughing after sex can make your partner wonder if A, you are laughing at them, or B, your orgasms broke something inside you."

She rolled her head toward him. The smile on her face was a thing of beauty. "I'm not laughing at you. I'm laughing at all those bumbling bastards I let try that before. No, actually that's not true. What started me laughing was the thought you should give lessons, and *that* started me thinking about the lack of satisfaction I'd received in the past, compared to the mind-blowing sex we just had. In the middle of the forest. On the run. I'd love to see what you could do in a proper bed."

Asp leaned over her and tipped her chin up, so she'd look directly at him. "You know that probably won't happen, right?"

"What? You giving lessons or the proper bed?"

"I'm definitely not giving lessons." He rubbed his thumb over her bottom lip. "What I meant is, you know this thing between us isn't going to last. It can't." He watched the smile fade off her face, and a furrow built between her eyebrows.

"We just had *really* good sex. I'm not going to start dreaming of bridal dresses and writing Lyric Cooper in my notebook a million times. I have no expectations beyond maybe an orgasm or two. Stop worrying. I'm not deluding myself this is permanent. " She jerked her chin out of his hold and worked to get her jeans pulled up and her shirt back around her body. While he tucked himself back into his jeans, she rolled on her side away from him and grabbed a book out of her backpack before tucking her backpack under her head and opening the cover.

He rolled onto his back and closed his eyes. How the fuck did she do that? She'd handed him his ass on a silver platter when all he'd wanted was to make sure she wouldn't get hurt.

Fuck him standing. He worked at relaxing his breath into an even pattern. He needed to sleep, to recharge for tonight's trek, but he couldn't because, damn it, even though she had no illusions about what was going on between them, he suddenly found he did. That thought scared the fuck out of him.

He rolled away from her and focused on the vines that protected them from the rest of the world. He turned the problem over and over, examined it from every conceivable angle. There was no way he could walk away from the world he lived in to be with her in hers. His past would find them, and she would pay the price. No, she could never be pulled into the reality in which he existed. *Face it, asshole. If you care about her, the only thing you can do is walk away.* The caustic voice inside his brain melted his hopes and dreams and seared his reality into focus.

He'd allowed himself a small reprieve, a chance to hope, and it had fucked with his mind. He was done. Done with hoping. Done with looking at the woman he was with and pretending they could have a life. They would travel. They would escape, and he would leave. He had no other option but to leave because, while she may have no expectations, he did.

CHAPTER 13

*L*yric put her toe down carefully, feeling for a branch or stick. She slid her boot until she felt solid ground and stepped forward again, glancing up at where Isaac stood in the distance. He'd said about three words since they'd woken up tonight and picked up the pace of their travel. Whatever, he could be a douche. Let him. Lyric had been surprised at his impromptu, 'this can go nowhere speech' this afternoon. *Seriously, who did that?* She was complimenting him on two fantastic orgasms and boom...he goes all serious and shit. Like they both didn't know whatever it was between them wasn't permanent. What was she going to say to him, *"No, you made me orgasm. Now I want a wedding band and kids?"* Or maybe, *"you fucked me, you keep me?" What did he think she was going to do? Tell her daddy that her virginity had been compromised?* Hell, that had happened in Jacksonville when she was fifteen in the back room at a college frat party she'd snuck off to without her parents' knowledge.

Lyric stepped carefully and glanced up again at where Isaac was waiting and froze. He wasn't there. She dropped to the ground instantly. He was supposed to be...she saw him further on up the trail. The asshole hadn't even waited for her to reach him this time. She ground her teeth together and stood up. Well, fine. It seemed as if he couldn't wait to get rid of her. She picked up her speed, trying to be as soundless in the forest as he was, and succeeding for the most part. She'd snap an occasional branch or slip on a rock she didn't feel under a layer of leaves, but she kept up. She glanced up at him and noticed she'd gained on him. He stood about twenty feet away. She stopped where she was, not intending on going further until he led the way. He nodded to her right. She looked the direction he indicated and blinked to try to figure out what she was seeing. There was a dark void in the pale shards of trees up the ridgeline. She studied it for several moments before the form made sense. A shack. She glanced around the area and noticed flat acreage below the building. Coca fields. *Cocaine.*

Lyric moved forward until they were squatting down next to each other, hidden by the underbrush. "It may not be vacant," she whispered.

"It is. I passed it on my way here." His eyes studied the place as he whispered his reply.

She noticed a distinct furrow in his brow. "What is it?"

"This is a perfect spot for us to wait out the day, to rest and to get ready for tomorrow night."

Lyric couldn't agree more. She started to lift so they could make their way to the shelter, but he gripped her arm and kept her from moving. His grip didn't loosen. She could see his eyes darting around the area. He was completely immobile. Something was wrong. She didn't know what he sensed, but she'd learned his mannerisms. This hesitation wasn't because he was trying to be a dick like earlier tonight when he'd set a grueling pace. No, something had made him wary.

He still gripped her arm, and Lyric wasn't going to disregard his silent warning.

She relaxed against his hold and watched him as he systematically scanned the landscape in short bursts. He was working closer to where they were crouched. She couldn't see as well as he could at night, but she could see his face, and she watched as he worked. He jumped ever so slightly. His grip intensified for a fraction of a second, and his eyes bounced back and forth. He lifted the hand not holding her and put his fingers to his lips. *Yeah, like she'd say a word.* He turned his head and looked at her before he pointed at her and then at the ground. He lifted his hand in a stop sign fashion. She nodded and sank to her knees, taking the strain off her legs. He nodded and carefully, soundlessly, took the strap of his rifle off his shoulder. He set the weapon down and slipped out of his pack. He pointed to himself and then indicated the area he'd been scanning. He pointed to his watch and lifted all ten fingers, closed both fists and lifted them again. Twenty minutes? Okay, he'd be gone for about twenty minutes. She nodded and leaned against a small tree. He made a move to rise but stopped, dropped his hand toward hers and squeezed it once before he stood up and ghosted off into the trees. Lyric had no idea what the final touch was for, but she'd hoped it was an attempt to put things right between them. Not that he needed to do that. *Okay, yes, he did, because she wasn't going to make the first move.* She wasn't the one who made it weird. She would have. Eventually. But he beat her to the punch. She *did* have hearts and flowers and dreams of a happily ever after with him floating around inside her head, but she was an adult. She knew they weren't right for each other. Having him beat her over the head with it, though? *Ouch.*

His form melded with the shadows, and she lost track of him, but she had a vague fix on the area where his attention had focused before he left her. She leaned against a small tree and shifted her weight to relax her muscles as quietly and as slowly as she could manage. The night sounds enfolded her as insects sang a quiet song around her. A bird launched from the bushes. She snapped her head toward where the sleeping bird had been frightened from its perch. There were no other movements or sounds. Perhaps something hunting at night. A feral cat...or a jaguarundi, what her grandfather called a gato moro. She dismissed that idea immediately. Her grandfather told her the gato moro hunted during the day and slept in the forest trees at night. Lyric closed her eyes and then slowly opened them, glancing up into the trees overhead. She examined the branches and gave a silent shudder of relief when she couldn't see signs of a big cat. She glanced back at the area where the bird had startled. Whatever it was that caused the bird to take flight also caused the entire forest to fall into an unnatural silence.

She listened for any sound that might tell her where Isaac had traveled. She had no watch to tell her how long he'd been gone, only her sense of time elapsed, and that seemed to have disappeared the second she'd lost sight of him in the forest. What happened if he didn't come back? She glanced at his rifle and then to his pack. He'd come back. He had to come back. She studied the area around her, her eyes jerking from image to image. She gripped her hands together to keep them from shaking. He'd come back. The thrush of the insect song started up again. Isaac *would* come back. The bug song slowly built. She pulled in a deep breath and held it, counting to twenty before she released it. She'd count until he came back. Count the seconds. Yes, it was a plan. She could keep track of the minutes by counting. Her mind popped off with one Mississippi, two Mississippi, so she went with it. Her thumb touching a finger with each sixty-second count that passed.

A slide of sound to her right brought her head up and around. She leaned into the tree to try to blend into the surroundings. The insect song continued around her. She blinked and scanned the area where she'd heard the sound and picked out a form moving slowly toward her. Lyric shrank as small as she could make herself and watched the shadow moving closer. She almost cried in relief when she was able to make out his identity. Isaac didn't speak but knelt and gathered his pack. He put it on before he strapped his rifle to his back. He motioned for her to follow. She didn't hesitate and stayed within five feet of his retreating form. He didn't go toward the shelter. Instead, he moved rapidly away from it, almost back the way they had come.

They moved fast and silent through the forest. He turned in sharp right and left angles. Any hope of knowing which direction they were traveling in ended with the third radical turn he made. Her thighs burned from moving forward in a perpetual crouch while staying light on her toes. Her thighs shook from exhaustion, and her lungs burned, but she kept up as well as she could. Finally, Isaac slowed. He signaled for her to drop and she did. Immediately and thankfully. He disappeared from her sight, but she was too exhausted to do more than crouch as low to the ground as she could get. She saw him come back toward her and signal for her to follow. Her legs screamed in complaint, but she pushed up and moved forward.

He stopped and motioned for her to come closer. They both sank to the forest floor. He put his lips next to her ear and whispered, "There. Through the trees. Do you see it?"

Lyric followed his finger and squinted. A vehicle? There was no road that she could see, and it appeared one of the tires was off the chassis. Her head snapped toward him. "Is it safe?"

He actually smiled at the question but shrugged. "It was

probably deserted by drug traffickers." He nodded in the other direction. "The stream we've been following is over that small rise."

"We've been following a stream?" She swung her head toward the hill. She heard his response in the form of a low rumble of laughter. She nudged him with her shoulder and grumbled, "Shut up."

He looked up at the night sky and then nodded toward the truck. They moved forward carefully. Isaac managed to open the back hatch. He pushed inside and explored the interior before he took off his pack and laid his rifle in the empty back cargo space. The SUV had been gutted, probably to carry more bales of coca leaves. He dug into his pack and handed her a bar of soap, a tin of toothpaste powder and a toothbrush. He grabbed his rifle and motioned for her to follow. She blinked at the items in her hand and at his disappearing back before her feet started to move of their own accord. He stopped beside a low bank and sat down, taking off his boots. Lyric stood motionless as she watched him disrobe. He glanced back at her and smiled. He whispered, "Take your clothes off. We'll wash us and then our clothes. I'll put them on top of the vehicle to dry during the day."

He peeled his clothes off and carried them into the stream with him. His light skin and naked form were illuminated by the moon. The word impressive didn't do him justice because it didn't begin to describe the masculine beauty that held her mesmerized. Lyric jolted from her observation when he turned toward her and extended his free hand. She slid her backpack off and made quick work of stripping. She wasn't ashamed of her body, and they'd already been intimate, but she felt her face heat at his blatant examination. She carefully moved forward but slipped when she entered the stream. Isaac's hand was there immediately, steadying her. He led her into the deepest part of the stream where he sat down into waist-deep water. The water was cool, but not cold. She held out his bar of soap, and he wasted no time scrubbing himself clean. Lyric carefully sat down and submerged her clothes, and then his, in the water. She put a rock over the stack of clothes so they wouldn't move. They washed without sharing words. He ducked under the water and then washed his hair. They shared the soap back and forth. He scrubbed soap into their clothes while she washed the suds from her hair. They left the stream not more than five minutes after they entered it with few words exchanged. Naked except for the boots they shoved their feet into, they made their way back to the hollowed-out SUV. Isaac spread their clothes on top of the vehicle to dry. They were invisible from the side or from the sky because of the canopy of trees that drooped over the roof.

Isaac got in and covered the floorboards with the blanket they'd slept on last night. She climbed in as he pulled two more protein bars from his pack and placed one beside her. She pulled a shirt and a comb out of her pack. She used a t-shirt to wipe herself off and then handed it to him while she worked a million snarls from her hair. It was all she could do to keep her eyes open while she braided her hair and ate the bar. Isaac moved around the vehicle and was able to roll down the windows to allow a slight breeze to waft through the interior. He lay down, still naked, using his pack as a pillow. He extended his arm and patted the blanket beside him. Lyric's mind had stopped functioning. She was so tired she felt as if she were vibrating. She was naked. Shouldn't she have clothes on?

"Lyric. Come on. Lie down. We need to sleep." He extended his hand, and she took it. Sleep. She was going to sleep naked with him?

"Yes, sweetheart, naked. I'm too tired to do anything but sleep. I promise."

She blinked at him. She didn't know she'd spoken aloud. Her movements slow and jerky, as if her brain weren't communicating with the muscles of her body, she lowered herself next to him. He curled around her back, and his arm wrapped her waist and pulled her into his chest. The hard metal bed of the vehicle felt like heaven.

CHAPTER 14

A snap of a branch woke him from a dead sleep. He was instantly alert. Another snap, immediately next to the truck, brought him to a crouch, with his rifle lifted and ready for a target. A large hog rooted near the truck followed by a host of piglets. He watched them for several minutes. They were unalarmed and foraging, which was a good sign, particularly after last night. Lowering his weapon, he glanced at the sun. It wasn't noon yet. A breeze circulated through the vehicle. Asp lowered back down onto the thin blanket next to Lyric. She sought him out in her sleep, moving into him.

He let her snuggle into his side while he gazed at the roof of the old SUV. His gut had told him the shack was being watched. Hell, every nerve in his body screamed the building was a deathtrap. He noticed a guard posted on the perimeter of the cabin and easily overpowered him. A search of the body produced American money which meant he was probably a local, hired to kill whoever came to the shack. A silenced bullet sank into the tree next to Asp and startled a bird into the air. The impact was so high it never had a chance of hitting him but did alert him to the position of a second gunman. Asp moved quickly, but instead of retreating, he advanced at a full run. When the shooter stood to fire, he threw himself forward and drove the man into the ground. The rifle dropped to the forest floor. Asp broke the man's neck with practiced ease and turned to the rifle the unfortunate guard had carried. The suppressor on the rifle was homemade. If another round had gone through it, the report would have been heard and more than likely, brought whoever else was in the area on the run. Small graces. Whoever hired these two would be checking in. Asp didn't see any radios on either body, but didn't he stay long enough to search further. What he needed now was to get him and Lyric as distant from this location as possible.

He'd set a grueling pace, but Lyric kept on his six. They worked long, hard hours to travel not only away from the shack, but in the opposite direction he'd normally go. Whoever pursued him was damn good. His hunter had identified where he'd normally stop, so it was time for Asp to stop behaving normally. He worked them back up the hills, toward the higher elevations, away from his phone and help. The dead bodies he left last night would alert his tracker that he'd been there, and the hunt would begin in earnest. There was no way he and Lyric would be able to reach his vehicle. If it were just him, he would step up and take the fight to the bastard who was playing fucking chess with his life. But it wasn't just him. The woman sleeping next to him depended upon him for protection.

Asp narrowed his eyes as his brain churned through the possibility he'd considered last night. What could he do that was so counterintuitive the bastard would miscalculate? How could he turn the tables and become the hunter? A simplistic answer formed. His only concern? He needed someplace where he could safely hide Lyric. Where would the people hunting for him never look? He smiled at the roof of the vehicle. The plan he'd formed last night was sound.

Asp let himself drift in a semi-sleep state. Resting and comfortable, he heard the hog and her family outside the truck and felt the breeze cool his skin. The birdsong and sounds of the day filtered around him. Peaceful and natural. Lyric's rhythmic breathing fanned across the skin at his neck. He tightened his arm around her. She moved closer to him and settled again. His fingers found her braid and played with the weave, mindlessly following the bumps and hollows. She rolled onto her back, and his eyes followed her. She was spectacularly beautiful.

Asp closed his eyes to stop the visual torture. His body reacted to hers. He ached to have her. He wanted to feel her under him, wanted to stroke the beautiful tan skin he'd memorized when she stood nude before him last night. His cock kicked up at the thought. There was no way he could let that happen, though. Even if he discounted the physical danger it posed to her, he couldn't afford the emotional cost. Not only to her, but damn it, to him. As strange as it sounded, the intensity of his desire became his strongest deterrent. He wanted her with a soul-deep longing that he couldn't ease with anything but total denial. Tonight, he'd guide her to safety, or at least to a place that should be safe, and then he'd go on the hunt. If he didn't succeed, she'd at least have a fighting chance.

"You're thinking too hard." Lyric's voice carried to him.

"Always. It's because of my big brain." He smiled at her inelegant snort.

"What happened last night?" She moved closer to him, and he tightened his arm around her.

"We took a bath." He got an elbow in his ribs for that one. "There were people waiting for us at the shack. They'd been paid to kill me. I don't think they know about you."

"How long until they know we've been there?"

Asp glanced at the sun. It was descending. Maybe four o'clock in the afternoon. "They know by now."

"What are we going to do? Will they track us?"

He could hear the tremor in her voice. Her bravado was convincing, but he'd heard it. She was scared. As well she should be. "I doubled back several times. If I'm not mistaken, the stream we bathed in last night is the stream that feeds the shower at the cave."

Lyric lifted up on her elbow and blinked the sleep from her eyes. "You mean we've gone in a circle?"

"Intentionally. After dark, we are going to slip back into the cave, coming in from the back. We have the advantage. We know the area." Asp's plan firmed in his mind. He liked it. It gave them both a chance.

"Won't they be looking for us?" Her voice rose to an incredulous squeak.

"Yes, but they'll have found the valley by now, found their man and retrieved him. If they made the connection to your grandfather, they have already been to the farm to question him. There is no reason for them to remain in the valley. They are out here, searching for me."

A furrow formed between her brows. "What's your plan?"

"I'm taking you back to the cave, make sure you're safe, and then I'm taking the hunt to the hunter."

"What does that mean?" She stared intently at him.

"It means I'm done running." Taking her back was the only thing that made sense. To his knowledge, nobody knew he'd been assisted. The cave had been sanitized, tracks had been obliterated. They weren't seen the first night. The second night his position would have been pinpointed. When he ran with Lyric, it went against every instinct he had. He'd tried to confuse those who'd tried to trap him, and in doing so, he'd given himself one chance to take out the bastard hunting him.

"You're leaving me in the cave." She dropped onto her back and rolled away from him. He rolled onto his side and ran his hand down her arm, keeping the touch reassuring, not sexual.

"I want you to stay there for three days. That will give me time to get where I'm going, get set up, and take out the bastard hunting me." He leaned over and kissed her shoulder softly. "I'll either succeed and eliminate any threat against you, or they will have been successful and stopped searching. Either way, you won't need to worry about the FARC roaming the hills looking for me. Go home and live your life."

"If you get the man hunting you, you won't come back." Her whispered statement burned like acid, but it was the truth.

He dropped his forehead against her shoulder. "I can't." He felt her tighten at his admission. He'd tried to be indifferent to her—to stay away. God knew he'd tried to warn her not to feel anything for him. But fuck him, she was his idea of perfection, and he'd taken a small sip of heaven. He'd realized too late a sip would never be enough to satisfy his thirst. Lyric lightened the darkness that surrounded him. She was the music he longed to listen to every day of his life, to cherish and embrace, but because of his choices, she was the melody he'd never hear again.

She rolled over, facing him. Her eyes held tears, and she swiped one away as it fell. "I've always known that. But we have now, don't we?"

He interrupted her ramblings with a finger to her lips. The temptation was too great. "We have now." God help him, they had now. He rolled on top of her, his cock hardening at the contact of her chest against his. She was soft and fit against him perfectly. They both groaned when she lifted her legs around his hips, and he pushed his cock against her sex, rubbing the length against her pubic bone. He didn't want to dry hump her. Fuck, he wanted to be inside her heat, but without protection...

She cupped his head and pulled him up from her neck where he'd been working his way toward her breast. "Make love to me." She shook her head when he started to close his eyes, in preparation to deny her. "No, I want you inside me. I need this. Pull out when you get close."

"That isn't foolproof." Hell, it wasn't even safe. He wouldn't leave her with a baby to raise by herself. He'd heard what Sky had to go through to raise Kadey alone. There was a real chance he wasn't walking away from this mission.

"I'm a big girl, Isaac. I know how to take care of myself, how to take care of my body. I want you inside me. I want you to make love to me. Pull out when you are close. Let's pretend we can be together. Let's pretend we have forever."

His mind screamed no, don't take the chance of ruining this woman's life. His heart, however, took her offer and ran with it, leaving the objections of his rational mind in the dust. He lowered for a kiss and got lost in her unique taste. He pulled away only to breathe. Her hands traveled his body, and he felt every nerve ending fire and respond to the feel of her small hands. He worked his way down her neck and paid homage to her breasts before he moved back up and centered between her legs. He fingered her and devoured her mouth, capturing the delightful gasps, whimpers, and moans. He lifted his leg, forcing her leg up and over his thigh, opening her for his cock. He ran his arms under her shoulders and captured her head with his hands, holding her steady, so he could watch her as he entered.

She locked eyes with him and nodded. He slid forward, retreated and slid forward again, deeper into her tight, wet heat. The next thrust seated him against her and both of them closed their eyes. He'd had good sex before, but nothing compared to what he was feeling right now. It wasn't just the physical. The emotional connection they shared put this experience into a category all its own. Was he a fucking idiot? Hell yes, but if it meant five minutes with Lyric, like this, he'd make the same mistakes again. All of them. He wouldn't change a thing, because she was goodness, and happiness and love—the essence of light that momentarily illuminated his dark-as-fuck world.

He held her tenderly as he thrust forward, taking them both to a shattering point, one that acknowledged their desires for each other and at the same time signaled the beginning of the end for a passion he couldn't permit. She clenched around him. Her hips lifted under him as she worked her body, meeting and seizing her need. Her orgasm swallowed him, and he pulled out, reared up, and stroked himself once before he exploded over her, painting her slight frame with stripes of his cum. He held himself up with one hand as they struggled to catch their breath.

She reached up and put her hand over his lips. "If you say one word about this not being a permanent thing, I'll rack you." She lifted her knee settling it against the underside of his ball sack.

He couldn't help his smile. "Fair enough, I deserve that."

"You most certainly do. Now find me that t-shirt we toweled off with last night and a bottle of water." Lyric waved a dismissive hand at him.

He leaned down and kissed her smiling face before doing as she bid. But only because it was the gentlemanly thing to do.

CHAPTER 15

The moon provided the only light as Asp sat down on the slab of rock that formed the overhang of the waterfall and lowered himself down into the blackness of the sheltered area of the cave. It seemed like a lifetime ago he'd sat in front of Anubis' desk and been handed the folder detailing Halo One-One's demise. In reality, it had been just over two months. Taking out Halo had settled some kind of cosmic sense of justice—justice that he'd needed more than he'd realized. That bastard was gone, but his people still moved. The machine that Cavanaugh had started may have stalled, but with men still out there like the hunter currently after Asp, people like Lyric and her family would never be safe. Drug trafficking was too profitable for those in control.

He turned around and waited as Lyric handed down his rifle, stock first. He took it and set it to the side along with the two backpacks she dropped one at a time. She sat down, and he reached up, grabbing her waist as she dropped, controlling her descent against his body. She leaned into him, and he wrapped his arms around her for a moment.

"I'll go first. You stay here and wait." If there was a sentry in the area, Asp would need to skirt him so as not to reveal their return. She nodded against his chest. He kissed the top of her head and stepped away. He'd have to go blind through the larger cavern that held the pool of water, but he had a good recollection of the walls, shelves, and pathways of the cave. His eyes were adjusted to the moonlight, but the pitch black of the cave forced him to close his eyes and react to his memories of the cavern and the feel of the walls under his fingers. He took small steps, quietly placing each foot as he traveled toward the other entrance.

The front cave received a small amount of light. Asp sat on his heels inside the larger cavern and listened. The emptiness of the area echoed around him. There were no sounds to make him cautious, yet something felt off. He waited ten more minutes before he entered the main cavern. The neat area he'd left with Lyric two days ago had been trashed. Garbage littered the floor, and as he approached the cave entrance, the stench of human feces assaulted his senses. At the mouth of the cave he examined the small area of the valley that he could see. He ghosted out of the entrance and made his way to where he'd concealed the dead body. The corpse was gone. He continued down the face of the rock and pushed through the marmalade bushes as far from the entrance as he could go. He lay down and started a strip and grid search of the entire area, looking for anything that would register as different or foreign since the last time he'd looked across to the ridge. He paused about halfway through the search. A large mound at the base of the shrine Lyric's grandfather had built caught his attention. He carefully pulled back from under the bush and moved silently to a better observation point. There. He carefully pushed through the bush. A grave. Large rocks were placed on top of the mound of dirt. It was intended to be a permanent resting place. Whoever buried him wouldn't return.

Asp pushed back and made his way to the mouth of the cave. He curled his nose in disgust at the piles of shit. When he entered the back cavern, he reached into his pocket and withdrew a chemical stick. The rod snapped under the pressure of his fingers, and he shook the vial, creating a pale glow. The only footprints were his and Lyrics. The interior of the cavern hadn't been disturbed. Before he went to get her, he retrieved the buried equipment they'd left. He found a container that would work and headed back to the front of the cave. He couldn't bring her back to that mess.

It took fifteen minutes to make the cave livable. He moved the rocks that made up the fire ring back toward the larger chamber and built them pallets to lie on. He covered hers with the blanket he'd buried their equipment in after he shook out the dirt. He wasn't going to take any chances that she'd be seen, but he wanted her to be comfortable for the next three days. The fire took a few minutes to build and light. He waited until it caught before he went back for Lyric.

She hadn't moved from where he'd left her. She appeared exhausted—and worried. Her usual vibrancy and, hell, he didn't know...inner light, maybe, had diminished. He hated the part he'd had in that loss. "Come on." He extended his hand to her. She stood and grabbed her pack and his. "Leave that. I have a fire going. Come inside, you need to rest."

Lyric shook her head and walked past him, carrying both packs. "I'm not an irresponsible child. Get your gun. I've got these."

Asp drew a deep breath and rolled his shoulders after she slipped down the fissure that led to the front of the cave. The woman made him crazy. He slung his rifle over his shoulder and followed her. His priorities shifted as he crossed a safe shelter for Lyric off the list. Next came food, sleep and then at dark, he'd once again become the man who delivered death. Lyric would be free. Hopefully, her family had survived any inquisition by the idiots who found the body—if they'd even put two and two together. He wasn't so sure, but it wouldn't do to underestimate them. Underestimating them would put Lyric at greater risk, and that he wasn't willing to do.

Lyric dropped his pack and hers and sat down next to the fire. "Why did you move the fire back?"

"Added security." He sat down with her and fished in his backpack producing another of those damn bars. He held it out to her.

"I'm not hungry." Not for that anyway. They tasted like crap. Yeah, she knew she was being a bitch, and she knew why. She didn't want him to leave. She didn't want him to risk his life. She didn't want to wait three days in this cavern and then go home like nothing had happened. How could she when Isaac was in danger? How could she when she'd fallen in love with the man? Her life had changed. Isaac was the reason her heart beat. She knew everything she'd ever wanted was encapsulated in the man. How could she go through life comparing all the men who crossed her path to him? No one could measure up. No one matched his integrity, his kindness, his...no, she didn't want to wait three days. What she wanted to do was to fall on her knees and beg him to stay.

So...what was she going to do about it? If she did nothing, he was gone.

He leaned back from the fire and unwrapped his food, eating half of it in one bite.

She studied him as he studied the fire. "Why do you have to go back?"

His gaze swung to her. "What do you mean?"

"Why do you have to go back to the States when you stop this guy?" She was grasping at straws. "You could stay here, in Colombia. You could live and work on my grandfather's farm with me." Lyric blinked at the utter stupidity of that thought. Isaac wasn't a farmer. She sighed and dropped her head into her hands, pulling on her hair. "Ugh...never mind. That was stupid." She shook her head and then dropped her hands. When she lifted her head, he was staring at her. What she saw in his eyes looked like pity. She once again shook her head, but this time it was because she was pissed. "Do not give me that look, Isaac Cooper. I don't want your pity." That wasn't going to happen. "Forget I said anything. Go back to the States. Do your dangerous job. Get your friend's daughter a pony and live your life."

"You don't understand."

"No, I don't. Why don't you make me? Why can't you come back or take me with you? Why?"

He stood and ran his hands through his hair as he paced back and forth. "Right. Fine, let me spell it out. I am an assassin. I kill people. Monsters, horrible people who are beyond the reach of normal law enforcement. I take them out to make the world a better place. Fuck, Isaac Cooper isn't even my real name! I am a killer, Lyric, a murderer, and I am not someone you need to be involved with!"

Lyric stood and wrapped her arms around herself. "Murderers kill for greed or lust. You kill because it is your job." The thoughts were out of her mouth before she could censor them.

"I kill. Period." He still hadn't met her gaze.

Lyric stepped closer to him, and he moved away keeping the fire between them. "Take me with you, Isaac. I know you are a good man. I know you have a difficult job. I see the way you worry, the way you protect me. The way you don't want to make love to me because it will be harder for you to leave. You want me as much as I want you. Take. Me. With. You."

He turned and looked at her. His eyes held his answer,

one she didn't want to hear. "I can't. How could I? Didn't you hear a thing I just said?"

Lyric walked around the fire and stood in front of him. "I heard. I don't care. I have fallen in love with you, whoever you are." She reached out with a shaking hand and placed it over his chest. "I don't need a name to know the man who owns this heart is a good man, and I can't help but love him."

He closed his eyes and lifted his hand to cover hers. "I may die tomorrow."

She stepped into him and wrapped her arms around his waist. "Tomorrow is never guaranteed. We only have now." She leaned away from him to look into his eyes. She saw it then, the love he held for her. "I want all my now to be with you. Only you."

"I..."

She lifted her hand and put it to his lips, stilling whatever objection he was going to raise. "Answer one question. Do you feel what is between us?" She stared into his eyes.

The firelight danced around them, sending shadows across his face. He couldn't deny his feelings for her, not when his eyes confessed them. He nodded his head. Once.

Lyric collapsed into him. "Then nothing else matters. I will wait three days, and I will go down this mountain. I will wait for you, and Isaac?" She leaned up and narrowed her eyes at him. "You will come back for me. Finish your job here, but don't you dare think you can walk away from me."

"You are the most demanding, frustrating, loving, and beautiful woman I've ever met." He lowered and kissed her.

Lyric shivered at the first brush of his lips. He hadn't said he loved her. He didn't need to say it. His lips, the way he held her, and the emotion in his eyes told her. She slid her arms around his neck and let him lead the dance of their tongues.

He pulled away only to move her to the pallet he'd built.

He held her as he lowered her to the ground and hovered over her. "I can't make you any promises. I will try to come back for you, however long it takes."

Tears threatened, but she fought them back, instead running her hands up his shoulders. The joy of hearing the promise she'd only dreamed of won over her valent attempts not to cry. Fat tears pushed over her lashes. Her voice emerged thick with emotion. "I don't care. I'll wait for you. Whatever it takes to make that happen, Isaac. Whatever it takes."

He lifted a few inches and a dazzling smile spread across his face.

"What?"

"Nothing. It's just...nothing. I think you may be perfect."

She slapped his shoulder and laughed. "See? That is what I've been telling you!" Their laughter rolled around the cavern.

He stilled and stared down at her. "I'm in love with you, Lyric Gadson."

Lyric closed her eyes as their lips met. She lost herself in the sensation of the man above her. Clothes disappeared, and skin met skin. She touched and memorized his strong back, the scars on his arms, the breadth of his chest as he made love to her. Tears again formed in her eyes as he centered over her. The newfound love between them and the uncertainty of their future became a maelstrom of emotion. He carried her to a mountaintop of sensation, a crest that left her shattered into a thousand pieces. She held him as he chased his own release. Her name pushed past his lips as he withdrew and crashed through his climax. His shoulder hit the pallet beside her, and she was rolled into his arms. He held her close to his chest where she heard the rapid beat of his heart. Lips against her hair whispered the confirmation of his love. Exhaustion, both mental and physical, swamped her in a heavy, warm embrace. Her last thought as she let sleep take her was that Isaac *would* come back.

Isaac watched Lyric as she finished her shower under the waterfall. They'd slept until late afternoon and had made love again. Twice. He could say he couldn't get enough of her body, and that would be true, but it wasn't the whole truth. What he felt for her was more than the lust for sex. Her strength, temper, sass, and willfulness were intertwined with a loving, giving, and beautiful soul. She was everything he wanted and did not deserve. If he was successful...no. *When* he was successful and had shut down the threat to her and to him, he'd go back to the complex and talk to Anubis and Bengal. Fuck, he'd even try to talk to Fury—if the man didn't gut him first. Since he'd mistakenly commented on the... assets...of Fury's wife, things were kinda...tense...between them. Like he knew the knockout redhead was Fury's wife. He'd thought the assassin dead. Actually, "Fury" *was* dead, but the man beneath the code name wasn't. Asp lifted a mental eyebrow at that. He'd sure as fuck like to go back to who he was before he "died", but that person was long gone.

The thoughts ran through his mind as he watched the water sluice over his woman. *Mine.* Lyric's hair fell like a sleek pelt down her back to the curve of her ass. This beautiful woman wanted him even though she knew his truth. He handed her a dry t-shirt as she stepped out of the water and watched her as she dried off. Fuck, that was another thing he'd need to address. She knew he was an assassin and she knew his employer. Anubis and Bengal were going to have his ass. He'd never breached protocol regarding his cover but, leave it to him...when he broke a rule, he did it right. Hell, it was the biggest breach in the history of breaches. Not that he'd change a thing. She knew, and she still wanted him.

"Like what you see?" Lyric's words pulled him out of his thoughts and back to the present.

He smiled. "You know I do." He pushed away from the rocks he was leaning on and made his way over to her. "You're beautiful."

"I'm not, but I am yours." Lyric lifted up and kissed him.

He slid his arms around her and deepened the connection between them. She moaned into his mouth, and he inhaled her desire, consumed it, as if his existence depended on it. She linked her arms around his neck and dropped her head back when he released her lips. She stared up at him, and he used the time to memorize her. Dark, arched eyebrows, high cheekbones, a small, straight nose and lips that begged to be kissed.

"You *are* mine." He dropped another kiss on her lips. He glanced skyward before he spoke again. "I have to go soon." She gazed up at the twilight evening sky and closed her eyes. He grabbed her hand, and they made their way back into the cavern. He made short work of gathering his few items and his rifle. She waited for him by the smaller cave entrance. Asp set his equipment down and pulled her into his arms. "I love you. Be safe. Don't take any chances. Wait at least three days before you go down the mountain."

He kissed her as she started to speak. He needed a minute, a chance to stomp on emotions he wasn't used to dealing with before he'd let her talk. When he left this cave, he'd be forced to leave everything behind. He couldn't take any emotional baggage with him. He couldn't worry about her, or about a future, because the second he did, he'd open an opportunity for a mistake—a mistake that could cost him his life. He lifted away. "Three days. I have to know you won't leave this cave, for any reason, for three days. If I'm worried about you, I won't be able to concentrate and not concentrating will get me killed." Was it wrong of him to lay that on her? He didn't think so. She needed to understand.

"Three days. I promise."

She lifted up on her toes again, and he took her invitation one last time. He broke away, strapped his backpack on and shouldered his rifle.

She moved closer to him and took his hand in hers. "You promised to take me with you, Isaac. I look forward to seeing America again. Don't make me wait too long." She squeezed his hand and stepped away.

There was so fucking much he wanted to say, but nothing else could be said—no more promises made that might never be kept, no more futures planned that might never come to pass. He nodded at her and turned on his heel.

CHAPTER 16

*A*fter hours of travel Asp hunkered down in the same depression he'd dug a little over a month ago. A month. Fuck, if someone had told him when he first dug out his shallow hasty scrape and started to camouflage it that he'd be back here after being shot and falling in love, he'd have laughed in their faces. He grabbed an empty bottle made of clear glass out of his backpack. Sliding forward on his belly, he positioned the glass to catch the afternoon sun. The camp below slept, and the cloud cover obscured his movements in the brush as he cast no shadow. He backed away, taking the time to brush away his tracks, drift leaves over the bare spots and fade into the underbrush. He dropped back to his secondary position and covered his observation post with branches, vines, and leaves before he settled in and pulled one of the last two power bars out of his knapsack. His view of the camp was unobstructed as was his view of his trap. Now he'd wait for the minion that would lead him to the rat.

Asp stirred from a fitful rest. He blinked away any traces of sleep and scanned the area. The sky had cleared and the position of the sun told him he had an hour, maybe two, before it reached the glass. He rolled his shoulders and systematically clenched and released the major muscle groups in his body. Staying inactive for such a long period of time forced a person to learn how to keep alert. This was his tried and true method. He continued his exercise as his mind drifted and his eyes scanned the camp below him. There were more people and more cars than a month ago, but then again if Halo was intent on resurrecting the FARC malcontents, the addition of personnel made sense, although without Halo on scene, who ran the show? Who funded the effort and what was the primary goal? Granted the FARC made money off the coca trade, but only because they taxed the farmers who grew it. To the best of his knowledge, the FARC did not produce or sell the drugs. Maybe Halo had something different in mind? Asp flashed back to the shack on the other side of the mountain. It had a hidden coca field below it. The FARC wouldn't go to the trouble of hiding a field of coca. Of course, he worked on the assumption that Halo or his people knew about the field. It was one hell of an assumption. Asp ran the scenarios around in his brain a few more times before he noticed movement below.

Three men stood at the edge of the camp. He lifted his rifle, making sure not to catch the light and shine a reflection. Three men, in battle dress uniforms. No insignia of rank and all three wore their black berets like a chef's hat. Asp didn't stop the sneer that crossed his face. Posers. He watched one motion toward where he'd set up his mousetrap. The fattest of the three shook his head adamantly. Whatever they were discussing, two of the three were against what the scrawny one wanted to accomplish. Finally, the one that was gesturing up the mountain threw up his hands and stalked away from the group. He lifted the barbed wire, slipped through the interior fence line, and motioned for something. He waited until one of the men he'd left sent a whistle his way and then he opened a panel in the fence line and left the compound heading straight up the mountain.

Occasionally, Asp could see the brush moving below him. Whoever the man was, he wasn't a skilled climber. He bounced his view from the camp to the man's progress. A convoy of three, open-cabbed Jeeps pulled into camp. Asp raised his scope and unlike the glass bottle that glinted and twinkled in the afternoon sun, again made note of the position of the sun to avoid any reflection. The men in the vehicles congregated at the middle Jeep. Asp leaned into his scope to get a look at the faces just as *Dora the Explorer* broke through the bushes in front of him. Asp froze and waited.

The man lowered his hands to his knees and bent over, panting like a dog. "Fucking hell, it was around here somewhere."

He had an American accent. Asp's rifle pointed right at the asshole. He remained still and shifted his eyes to the right of the man, keeping him in his peripheral vision.

"Where the fuck?" The man spun around as if to get his bearings.

The radio that hung from his belt squawked. "Durbin, the boss wants to know what the fuck you're doing up there?"

The man grabbed the radio and directed all his attention down the hill, standing not more than seven feet from where Asp held a weapon, trained on his chest. "I'm checking something out." Durbin lifted his finger off the button that activated the microphone. "Stupid fuck, do you think I'd climb this fucking rock for fun?" The man swung his attention away from the camp and headed toward Asp's mousetrap. Little did Durbin know, he was most definitely the mouse. And the mouse would lead Asp to the rat's nest.

"Boss says to get your ass back down here. You're not supposed to leave camp without permission."

"Fuck you. What am I, five?" Durbin damn near shouted the words down the mountain. He found the bottle Asp had left and picked it up. "A fucking bottle." Durbin lifted his radio again. "Tell Jose his fucking eyes are shit. There wasn't anyone up here. It was glass reflecting off a bottle." There was silence for a moment, and Durbin chucked the bottle down the hill. It crashed into the rocks below and shattered.

"Dude, boss is pissed. You didn't tell anyone Jose thought he saw something. It could have been the sniper."

"Well no fucking shit, bird brain! Why the fuck do you think I came up here? For my health? If I could have gotten that motherfucker, Mr. Flowers would be fucking impressed, wouldn't he?" The man ranted as he walked back to the bushes in front of Asp. He lifted his radio to his mouth and spoke, "It was nothing. I knew it was nothing. No sense wasting resources. I'm on my way back down. Tell the fucking wannabes not to shoot my ass."

Asp waited until the man had dropped forty feet before he worked his way soundlessly out of his observation post and shadowed the man down the hill. Durbin fell, cussed, bellowed and made one hell of a lot of noise, drawing all attention toward him as he crashed down the mountain. Asp couldn't have asked for a better diversion.

The double fence line was new. Money had been poured in to reinforce the encampment. As long as the fence line wasn't electrified, Asp could navigate the physical barriers. The interesting thing about fortifying your camp was it gave you a false sense of safety. First and foremost, a sniper could wreak havoc, raining down death from above. A fence couldn't stop a bullet. Asp didn't doubt whoever was on the ridge a month ago was still around. He hoped the bastard made the mistake of showing himself. He'd love to teach the son of a bitch a lesson. Never miss your target and if you miss, shoot the fucker again. He chuckled at the old saying. Asp moved to the bushes immediately outside the fence line. There was no clear zone. The brush should have been pushed back to give the people inside the compound a clear, three-sixty view of the area. Piss poor planning.

He hunkered down and watched. There wasn't much structure under the activity in the camp. No dogs–always a plus. The lighting was minimal, and he could slip through the fence in several areas. What he needed, however, was to find 'the boss.' He studied the men who walked from building to building. He could identify a handful of prior military types. Most were over six-feet-tall, still wore high and tights and they took notice of their surroundings. They searched the tree line every time they exited a building. They wore side arms and didn't fuck around like the rest of the men who went about their daily activities. The low growl of several vehicles made him shift to watch the inbound personnel. Two Hummers appeared and were immediately passed through the gates. Asp contorted around a young sapling to see who had entered the compound. He smiled as an older gentleman exited the lead vehicle. The deference shown to him by everyone told him what he needed to know. This bastard was the reason the camp hadn't splintered after Halo One-One's brain matter painted the shack behind him. Asp twisted to see who...

No.

Impossible.

Asp wiped the sweat out of his eyes. He lifted his scope

and brought the man into focus. Fuck! *Billy!* Billy was fucking alive, and he...he had to be the sniper who'd shot him. Asp watched his old spotter take his M-21 out of the truck and follow the bankroll into the largest building. His back hit the tree. Billy had died. *Those motherfuckers! They'd told him Billy had died!* He'd visited the man's grave. Rage boiled through his veins. Rage and hate. Not at his spotter, fuck that. He raged at the fuckers who'd manipulated his life. *Had they lied to Billy? Manipulated him the same way?* Asp's gut clenched. Lyric and her family were in danger, and not just because of the dirtbag in charge. No, he knew Billy. The man he trained and served with wouldn't stop hunting until he knew for sure the man he'd shot was dead. Sooner or later Billy would piece together the relationship between the shrine to Lyric's grandmother and the dead body, and that connection would take him straight to Lyric's family. He knew his spotter. Billy was intelligent—and lethal. It was only a matter of time before the information about the dead man made its way back to this camp. The rag-tag group obviously didn't have a central communications system. That meant each new person entering the camp was a threat. A threat Asp needed to deal with—tonight.

He monitored the movements within the camp. As twilight cast longer shadows he watched Billy exit the largest building with his equipment. He watched him as he strolled down the main road of the camp, perhaps too intently. Billy's head came up, and he appeared to sweep the area where Asp watched. The man stood motionless, but Asp knew he was raking through a search of the area. He flattened to the ground, knowing if Billy saw a difference in the landscape, he'd respond. The longer shadow played in his favor. Billy rolled his shoulders and gave one more glance toward the brush before he entered a smaller structure, the same building the rest of the men Asp had pegged as prior military had entered. A barracks. Considering his options, Asp laid out a plan. It was stupid risky, but it was the only scenario he could fashion that didn't include dying. A memory of Lyric flashed through his mind. No, today wasn't a good day to die. He'd opt for Plan B, as in Plan Billy. Fuck, he hoped his spotter would remember.

CHAPTER 17

*a*sp shimmied under the outside fence line after an hour of cautiously digging out space to worm through. He was exposed, but there was no routine patrol. Which was good and bad. The lackadaisical guards had just meandered by, but there was no telling if they would double back. Asp unfolded his knife and popped the staples that held the chicken wire to the wood posts of the second fence. Asp targeted the area because it wasn't constructed as well as the first fence. He figured they were about a week from having the camp buttoned up.

Asp bent the wire and shimmied through. Being stealthy and shit wasn't necessarily his gig. Not close in like this at least. That was Lycos' gig. The guy was like a fucking ghost. Sweat poured off him and soaked his shirt as he worked his way through the camp to the barracks building. He darted into the shadows created by a vehicle when the door opened. A man stumbled through the door and headed to what Asp assumed was the communal toilet. His heart beat against his chest like a ten-pound sledgehammer while he waited for the man to pass. He inched closer to the door of the barracks. He would leave his calling card on the wood planks that made up the porch. He'd place it to the right of the door so it wouldn't be disturbed by nocturnal wanderings caused by full bladders. He reached into his pocket and retrieved the three flat stones, placing one on top of the other. Two smaller stones pointed ninety degrees from the position where Asp would wait for Billy. Two stones meant two clicks, and they'd always used ninety degrees to the right when identifying a meeting place. It was their twist on markers, something they'd come up with and something nobody else would know. *If* Billy saw the signal and *if* he wasn't too caught up in whatever Halo One-One had concocted, he'd come to Asp. *If,* a small word and a huge fucking chance. If not, then Asp had given Billy a way to pinpoint his location. Everything hinged on Billy being the same man he'd served with. Everything.

Asp retreated from the camp the same way he'd entered it. His entire body shook as he slithered through the hole he'd dug. As he entered the brush and collected his equipment, he took a moment to breathe and center himself. He glanced back at the sleeping camp and the reality of his situation fell heavy on his shoulders. He'd gambled his life on a man he hadn't seen in years. One that worked for criminals. He had one more power bar in his backpack and half a bottle of water. He'd left the chlorination tablets with Lyric. Could he survive off the land? Yes. Could he survive off the land while on the run from an elite sniper? Asp drew a deep breath and nodded to himself. If it meant getting back to Lyric, yes. He shouldered his backpack and carefully picked up his weapon. It was time to move.

～

Asp trained his scope on the front of the small barracks. Nothing else in the camp mattered as the compound started to come to life. He'd made sure his position was on the shade side of the sunrise so no reflection from his scope would be seen. The door opened, and two men exited. Both walked right by the marker. He watched as Billy exited in animated conversation with another man. They walked past the marker. Billy laughed. Asp couldn't hear the sound but his memory reproduced the deep rumble of the man's laugh. Asp tracked him until they entered the latrines and then swung his scope back to the markers and watched three other men leave the structure. The markers remained untouched. Asp clocked Billy and the other man as they left the latrines and crossed to the largest building. He lowered his scope and waited.

When the men emerged, the mood wasn't as jovial. Billy was still with the other man, and they were headed back toward the barracks. Asp watched and held his breath. Both men's heads were down as they neared the boards. Billy stopped. The man beside him took several strides before he swung his attention back to Billy. Billy nodded and continued walking. As he passed the marker, Billy kicked the stones to the dirt. The other man entered the barracks, and Billy turned, looked directly at the location Asp had indicated and nodded, once, before he entered the building.

Asp held his position. He wasn't where he told Billy to go. He couldn't take the risk that the man he once knew might double-cross him. He trained his scope on the building and watched as Billy left, with a full pack and his weapon. The man went back to the largest building and remained in the facility for over an hour. When he exited, he walked toward the gate and waited for the guards to let him out. He slipped into the bush. Asp lost track of the man, found him, lost track and found him again. Billy was heading straight for the marker's location. Asp watched as Billy entered the clearing. His crosshairs painted Billy's chest. The man stopped, took off his backpack and lowered his weapon to the ground. Billy raised his hands and turned around. He then took five large steps away from his weapon. "For fuck's sake, please don't tell me I imagined that marker. Mac, dude, please, don't fuck with me."

Asp lifted from where he had camouflaged himself, his gun still pointed at Billy. The man's face split into a tremendous smile. He dropped his hands and walked towards Asp. "Mac, you son of a bitch! You're alive. Holy fuck, they told me you were dead!"

"Stop there, Billy." Asp barked out the command. "They lied to me, too. They told me you'd died. I went to your grave, saw the headstone."

The man froze, and his smile dropped. "Mac, what's going on, man?"

"You tell me, Bill. Why are you working for those criminals?" Asp tipped his head toward the camp.

Billy's brow furrowed. "Criminals? Fuck, man, I work for the CIA. We've been sent to restructure the remnants of the FARC into a paramilitary organization to assist the National Police." Billy crossed his arms over his chest. "Son of a bitch. It was you. You killed..."

"Cavanaugh. Or as I knew him, Halo One-One. He'd been coded by the international community. He was rogue."

Billy scoffed, "Bullshit! We are here on a U.S. Government-sanctioned mission."

"Really? Who is your diplomatic contact? Tell me your chain of command." Asp kept his voice level.

Billy stiffened and blinked before his head jerked. "I don't know."

"Why don't you? Think back, Billy. When was the last

time you knew that information? Five years ago? Six? I bet you stopped getting that intel when Cavanaugh went rogue. Did you have six months or a year when you didn't have missions?" He watched a myriad of expressions cross Billy's face. "I 'died' and went to work for the CIA, also. I was the one that outed Cavanaugh. He was my handler. He was using me to kill people for his own agenda. I figured it out, and I went to the top. I exposed the bastard for what he was, and I left. I've been working for Guardian since. They sent me here. *Guardian*, Billy. You know their rep. You know they don't play the bullshit political power game."

His friend's face went pale under his tan. His eyes displayed disbelief. His head shook slowly from side to side. "That can't be right." Billy sat down in the middle of the clearing. He glared up at Asp. "Fucking put the gun away, man."

Asp shook his head. "Not yet, Bill. Did the CIA recruit you after the bombing?"

Billy shook his head. "Yeah. Told me that Amanda had already buried me. Showed me pictures. Told me she miscarried." His grief-stricken face looked up at Asp. "We were supposed to get married when I got back. I told you that right?"

"Yeah, man. You told me when we met up back in country."

"Right. Things that happened right before the bombing are hazy. She was pregnant. When the service told her, she miscarried. She was admitted to a mental health ward. They asked me if I really wanted to put her through more anguish by reappearing and then dying in combat. They told me I wasn't injured enough to be sent home. The service was sending me back—without you. Fuck man, how could I work with someone else?"

Asp cleared his throat before he spoke, "They showed me

pictures of my parents. They told me almost the same thing. The CIA stole our lives, Billy. Cavanaugh has been rogue for years. Your pay isn't going to the same account the CIA used originally, is it?"

Billy shook his head. "They changed it…five years ago, security precautions."

"This camp, it isn't a liaison effort. You're reorganizing the malcontents left over from the disbandment of the FARC."

"You've killed two of the men I deployed."

"No, I killed three."

"Three?"

"There was a man who found the cave where I was recovering." Asp lowered his weapon but kept the business end of the rifle trained on his friend, just in case.

"Sanders? We got word he'd been killed yesterday. A courier brought photographs. Benedict sent a team to question the old man who had a shrine up there. He made some calls. If there isn't an actual liaison or training going on, then there are dirty National Police personnel. The team they sent out is meeting up with a local from the NP. Did that man help you?"

"He and his granddaughter saved my life after someone from your camp shot me in the thigh. Wasn't you by any chance?" His mind raced, how the fuck was he going to get to Lyric's grandfather? Her father was there, too.

Billy nodded.

"You're slipping, Bill. The man I knew would have killed me."

His friend gave him a look through narrowed eyes. "Yeah? Well the man I knew wouldn't have presented a target." Billy reached into his pocket, and Asp snapped the rifle to his shoulder. "Chill, Mac. I have a Sat Phone." Billy tossed the phone, and it dropped at his feet. "I want to hear the call. I want proof that my people are on the take. Set it up. I have nowhere to be." He tipped his head down the slope. "They think I'm gone for the next three days."

Asp lowered his weapon and reached for the phone, careful to keep his friend in sight. Billy growled and flopped onto his back. "I can't get any fucking less intimidating, Mac. Make the call."

Asp lifted the phone and entered the numbers he'd memorized. He put the phone on speaker wanting complete transparency for Billy. The phone rang twice before one of the disembodied mind readers who ran the switchboard answered. "Operator Three-Seven-Four."

"This is Six-Six-Eight. Send me home."

"One moment, Six-Six-Eight."

Billy put his hands behind his back. His eyes were focused on the sky, and the furrow between his brows deepened with each passing minute.

"Authenticate Roast Beef," Bengal's raspy voice growled over the connection.

"Swiss Cheese," Asp responded as Billy laughed. The man knew him, and his appetite.

"Where the fuck have you been and who is with you?" That was Anubis.

Asp sat down across from Billy. "I'll tell you in just a minute. Is Thanatos still in country?"

"Yes," Bengal growled.

"I need him to get to a farm owned by an old man. Fuck, I don't know his name." Asp let out a string of curse words. How could he be so fucking stupid?

Billy lifted his head. "The guy we are going to question is Mateo Garcia."

Asp drew a deep breath. "Thanks. The old man is Mateo Garcia. His son-in-law, last name Gadson, lives on the farm with him. There are a team of FARC and National Police going to question the man. The only thing he's guilty of is saving my life. He needs protection."

"Omega team is close. I'll deploy them." Alpha's voice cut through the connection, and Asp's eyes widened as he glanced over at Billy. Billy raised an eyebrow and cocked his chin toward the phone.

"Alpha, mission complete, but there are complications," Asp spoke as he acknowledged Billy's silent request.

"Standby," Alpha barked, and Asp snapped his mouth shut.

"Archangel online."

Shit, the boss of all bosses. Asp wiped his hand over his forehead. "Sir, mission complete with complications."

"Bring us up to speed." Archangel's distinct voice grated over the line.

Asp laid out the mission from start to taking out Halo One-One.

"Why didn't you call in before now?" Anubis asked when Asp paused in his narrative.

"I was shot."

"By who?" Archangel and Alpha asked at the same time.

"By me." Billy chimed in.

There was silence on the phone. Complete silence. Asp assumed he'd been muted and the others were having a conversation that he couldn't hear. "Couldn't keep your mouth shut could you, Bill?"

"What's the fun in that? Do you think I broke them?" Billy got that stupid half smile on his face that Asp remembered so well.

"Authenticate, Noodle." Anubis came across the connection demanding Asp reconfirm his safety.

"Lasagna." Asp sighed as Billy burst out laughing.

"If you're done with the chitchat, I need a full debrief. Leave nothing out." Archangel demanded.

"Yes, sir." Asp told them about Lyric and her grandfather, their attempt at leaving and what brought Asp back to the camp. He told them about Billy and about their connection and what the CIA had done to both of them. He finished with his observations on the camp and his signal to Billy.

"Mr. Pearson?" Alpha asked, and Billy's head popped up.

"I haven't been called that in a long time, sir." Billy looked at Asp and mouthed, *'How do they know that?'*

He shrugged his shoulders. His assumption was Bengal's wife was listening and mining data as they spoke, but that was just an educated guess.

"If you were here, I'd have you in a conference room, and I'd debrief you for days. I don't have that kind of time. I need to know what you know, and I need to know it now." Archangel's voice whipped the command across the connection, snapping the air with authority.

Billy clamped his lips shut and shook his head before he responded, "With all due respect, sir..."

"That means he has no respect for you, by the way." Alpha dropped that chip shot in as Billy gathered his thoughts.

"With all due respect," Billy repeated before he continued, "I don't know who is telling the truth in this matter. I know Mac. He's never lied to me, but it's been years, and he was supposed to be dead. I want to talk to Deputy Director Munson. He was section chief when I was first recruited. When I talk to him, and he tells me the shit we are doing down here is illegal, I'll tell you what I know."

"Done." Archangel agreed immediately. "Give me five minutes to track him down and wake his ass up."

The line went quiet again. Asp leaned against the nearest tree.

"If this story you're spinning is true..."

"It isn't a story." Asp interrupted.

Billy sat up and stared back at Asp. *"If* Munson provides

validation, and right now I have a lot of reasons to doubt he will, but *if* he does, the other American advisers down there in that camp? I'd bet my left nut they've been played just like I was."

"Like Durbin?" Asp lifted an eyebrow as he asked.

Billy laughed and shook his head. "No, he's a hired merc and not a very good one at that. No, there are five others down there, company men. I've worked with most of them for years."

"Can you get word to them?" Bengal's voice floated from the phone.

Billy shrugged. "I could go back in. Talk to them one at a time."

"That would put you at risk. What if they aren't being duped? No, I won't jeopardize one of our assets."

"Again, with all due respect," Billy started, and Alpha busted a not so humorous laugh across the connection.

"Right, your lack of respect is noted Mr. Pearson, but when we get Deputy Director Munson on the line, and he authenticates our claims, you will be working for us, either as a loan from the CIA, or if you are no longer employed by them, you'll be under Guardian's authority. Both ways, you are my asset, and I don't gamble with my men. Ever."

"Archangel, Deputy Director Munson is on the line, and I have routed the satellite call through our systems. The line is secure." The crisp female voice snapped both men's attention to the phone that lay beside Asp's leg.

"What the fuck is going on, King? I was getting ready to head to the hill this morning to testify before Congress. Those asshats are already pissed and I need some quiet time to prepare for that stupidity. This had better be good."

"Like I'd pull you away from your ramp up time without good reason, Daryl. We need to discuss the assets Halo One-One formerly handled. How many of them did he have?"

"That's classified." Munson whipped out the automatic response.

"Fuck you, Daryl. How many of Halo's assets went missing when he did?"

There was a long silence. "You're sure this call is secure?"

"Yes, if Jewell says it's secure, nobody but us is hearing this." Archangel's growl carried menace, a warning not to stall any longer.

"He had a total of six assets. Five disappeared when he did. The asset that figured out what he was doing and turned him in left our employment. We have no record of his whereabouts. He fell off the face of the map. The other five were scrubbed from our systems by Halo's minions here at the Agency. He threatened one of our best security systems operators. Had pictures of her daughter at school. She deleted all the information. Permanently. We only know there were five records."

"Do you have backups of those systems?" The woman's voice interrupted.

"We do, but our best and brightest tried and failed to recreate the information."

"Yes sir, but that was five years ago. Our tech is capable of putting information together based on what is missing. If you have a courier send over that hard drive, I can get you the information."

"I could do it, but my question is why I would want to?" Munson asked.

"Because we believe some of Halo's assets are still working in Colombia trying to continue his quest to reestablish the FARC," Archangel explained.

"Halo was the brains behind that debacle, and we took him out for his crimes. Why would his flunkies still be in the area?"

"Because he was second in command, sir," Billy responded.

"Who is that?" Munson whipped the question out like a knife, ready to attack.

"Billy Pearson, sir. I was one of those five. We believed Halo still worked for the CIA."

"You've been with Halo the entire time?"

"Yes, sir."

"Enough of the reunion, who the fuck is leading the spin up down there?" Archangel demanded.

"Robert Flowers."

There was silence for a scant second before the woman's voice cut in. "Sir, someone in Colombia is trying to triangulate the position of Pearson's Sat phone. I'm bouncing them, but we need to cut the transmission. Power down the phone and get the fuck out of there."

Asp and Billy were on their feet before the woman finished speaking. Asp tossed Billy the phone and grabbed his weapon and pack. Billy had the phone open and the battery out in a matter of seconds. He threw the phone at Asp and pocketed the battery before he grabbed his pack and weapon. "Where the fuck do we go?"

"Follow me. I know a place." Asp set off at a jog.

Billy laughed at him. "No shit, Mac. You've gotten really good at hiding."

CHAPTER 18

$\mathcal{L}$yric jumped for the millionth time since Isaac left. She sat by the cave entrance, just outside of the setting sun's rays. Tonight she'd be leaving, going down the mountain. Only birds and butterflies traversed the small meadow. She'd spent the majority of the last two days watching their movements through the spaces in the marmalade bushes. Her fingers traveled over the book she held. Isaac had pulled it out of the hole where he'd buried it. Mentally, she couldn't concentrate on the words. Every time she tried, the print blurred, and her thoughts returned to Isaac.

She'd gathered her things and packed up her backpack. There was nothing to do but wait and worry. Worry about Isaac, about her family, about the trip down. She hadn't slept more than a few hours. Her head hurt from running the worst-case scenarios through her mind. She hated that she always defaulted to the worst possible thing that could happen.

A soft scurry of sound popped her off her ass and sent her scrambling back into the darkness of the inner cavern.

She'd put out the fire this morning because she'd be leaving tonight. The darkness consumed her, but she could see the front of the exterior cave. Her body shook as fear, no, terror, dropped adrenaline through her system. Lyric gasped. Her book! She could see it by the wall. *No, no, no!* She moved forward. If she could get to it before…she heard footsteps of more than one person and quickly darted forward to grab the book. She sprinted back into the darkness but forgot to duck. Her head slammed into the lip of rock that hung down. The pain and her momentum dropped her like a ten-ton stone. She blinked up, her vision wavered. She turned her head as a pair of boots came into view.

A stranger's voice echoed, too loud in her mind, "Well, well, well, what do we have here?"

~

Asp held back, watching their six. He hadn't seen anyone following them but bringing danger back to Lyric wasn't an option. Once they made it into the cave, they could reassemble the phone and get an update. He held his position and let his eyes find any movement that shouldn't be there.

Billy emerged from the cave, "Dude, there's a woman in here, and she's hurt."

Asp sprinted past his friend and slid to a stop beside Lyric. "Oh fuck, baby." Asp's hands shook as he cupped her face. There was a huge goose egg on her head. He looked up to the lip and grimaced. The wound was fresh and still swelling.

"You know her?" Billy knelt down beside him. "She was just lying there when I came in. I thought she was asleep until I saw the abrasion. Oh hell, that is going to leave a nasty bruise." He reached out to touch Lyric's forehead, and Asp couldn't help himself. He snarled, literally snarled.

"Wow, dude, not touching the pretty woman." He raised his hands and sat back on his heels. "See? No touchy."

Asp shot Billy a quick glare before he lifted Lyric and took her into the smaller cave, into the sun so he could assess her wound. Asp gently laid her down and moved the hair away from the blood that seeped out of the abrasion. She moaned and shifted her head. "That's right, wake up, sweetheart." Asp cupped her cheek and rubbed his thumb gently over her cheekbone.

A low moan parted her lips. Her eyelids fluttered for a moment before she opened them. A smile curled her lips, and she lifted her hand to touch his face. Her fingers tickled over the thick beard that had grown since he last shaved. Hell, that seemed like forever ago, but it was just over a week. The things they'd been through in such a short period of time. Lyric closed her eyes for a moment before they popped open. She gasped and bolted upright, nearly braining Asp with her forehead in the process. She grabbed her head and her stomach at the same time and moaned.

"You're safe." Asp ran his hand up her arm. She swung toward him and then lunged forward, wrapping her arms around his neck, and damn near strangling him in the process. She knocked him off his knees, and they both tumbled back onto the cave floor. Asp ran his hands over her back, trying to quiet the sobs that wracked her body.

He opened his eyes to see Billy standing over them, hands on his hips. That shit-eating half grin slid across his voice. "So, are you seeing anyone, Mac?"

Lyric jumped at Billy's voice. Asp released her when she twisted in his arms and sat up. "Lyric Gadson, Billy Pearson. Billy Pearson, Lyric Gadson." Asp made the formal introduction.

Lyric wiped her tears and blinked up at Billy before she reached out for Asp's hand without turning around. He placed his hand in hers and gave it a squeeze as he sat up beside her. Lyric looked over at him, her pupils a little too dilated for his liking. "You got help?" "After a fashion. How did you hit your head?"

"I forgot my book," Lyric responded as if the answer made perfect sense. Asp could assure her it didn't.

"This one?" Billy leaned over and picked up the small book. He brushed it off and handed it to her.

She took it and murmured her thanks a second before she leaned into him, "I'm so happy you're back. Is it over?"

"Yes, and no. I'll explain in a minute. First I need you to look at me." He checked her eyes. Both pupils were the same size, and the dilation could be due to the darkness in the tunnel. "Now explain it to me again. How did you knock yourself out?"

Lyric cast her eyes down. "I heard someone coming and ran into the back cavern. I needed to see who was coming but I didn't want them to see me."

Asp smiled and nodded. "Of course, you did." His woman was a spitfire.

"I looked back, and I must have dropped my book when I was startled. I couldn't leave it there because if whoever was coming saw it, they might come back farther and find me, so I ran out, grabbed it and ran back."

Billy chuckled. "I think you forgot to duck."

Lyric frowned at him. "Exactly who are you?"

Asp stood up and offered Lyric a hand to help her up. He nodded his head at Billy. "That's the guy who shot me."

Of all the actions or responses Lyric could have come back with, he would never forget the sight of Lyric doubling up her fist and clocking Billy's smiling face. She dropped him on his ass and reared back with her boot ready to kick the man right between the legs. He shot an arm around her waist and lifted her off the ground. He spun her, putting down behind him. She shoved at him and lunged at Billy again, screaming at his friend. It was a recital of every Spanish curse word he'd ever learned and a couple that he hadn't.

"Stop! Lyric, stop!" Asp put his arms around her pinning her arms to her sides. She still kicked at him with both feet. Billy slid on his ass as far away from her flying appendages as he could get.

"Holy Shit, man. Control that hellcat!"

"Hellcat? I'll show you a hellcat, you…" Lyric launched into a string of Spanish that singed Asp's ears.

Once Billy was out of the reach of her boots he reached up and moved his jaw as if he was afraid she'd broken it.

"Lyric, he's helping us. He has a phone, and I called my company. They are sending a team to take care of your family." That got her attention.

She stopped struggling and turned to look back at him. "What about the FARC? Did you stop them?"

"Not yet, but we will." He loosened his grip on her, but only a little bit.

"He was the one who shot you?" She pointed at Billy without looking at him. Billy's brow furrowed behind her as he continued to move his jaw.

"He was." Asp tried to suppress the smile that Lyric decking Billy brought to mind.

"And you *know* him?" She glared at Asp.

"I do. We worked together and were friends." Asp glanced over her shoulder. "Close friends."

Lyric's eyes got wide, and she nodded. "Oh, so your close friends shoot you and leave you for dead?"

"I didn't leave him for dead." Billy made the mistake of talking, again.

Lyric snapped, "No, according to what he said, you were hunting him to kill him, you bast…"

Asp spun her and dropped a kiss on her lips. She tried to speak for about three seconds, then melted into him. He kissed her until he had to come up for air. He tucked her head under his chin and held her. "Billy didn't know it was me when he fired that round. He's been a pawn in a seriously fucked up situation. He could have set a trap for me today, but he didn't. He's had my life in his hands all day and not once would I question anything he's done."

"So, you trust him?" She picked at his shirt when she asked.

Asp glanced over at his old friend. The man stared at him. Asp met his eyes. "I trust that he is trying to do the best thing for himself right now. He's in a fucked-up situation. I've been there. I know what it's like when your trust is violated, and you're used as a weapon against innocent lives. He won't betray us, because we are his one shot at redemption."

Billy tipped his head slightly and lifted a brow. They held each other's gaze. Billy nodded. Once. Asp had an up close and personal relationship with what he believed was going on in Billy's mind right now—the idea that his handler had fucked him, for years. Asp returned the nod before he rubbed circles on Lyric's back. "Besides, if he makes a wrong move, I'll let you loose on him."

Lyric snorted and squeezed him tighter. "Are we going to the farm?"

"No." Billy shook his head. "There are patrols in this area. We increased them when we got information that Sanders was killed.

Lyric turned in his arms to face Billy, but Asp made sure to keep them secure around her. He wasn't sure how the man would respond to getting clocked again.

"Then what do you suggest? We can't stay in the cave

forever. We don't have food." She tilted her head back and winced. "I could slip out and get some fruit."

"I brought food. Just MREs but there is enough."

"MREs?" Lyric parroted the acronym. Billy grabbed his backpack and opened it, pouring out nine brown plastic packages.

"Meals Ready to Eat. They're okay. If you're starving," Asp interjected. Speaking as someone who enjoyed food, MREs were his last choice. Hell, he'd take a protein bar over an MRE, but he was curious. "Why so many? Wouldn't filling your ruck with food raise questions?"

"No. Not anymore. I'm supposed to be gone three days, but hunting you, I'd stay out longer."

"So we have food, but how do we get out of this cave?" Lyric leaned her head on Asp's shoulder and closed her eyes. "I need something for my headache. I have some pain relievers in my pack."

"Do you always travel with meds?" Billy asked as Asp helped Lyric sit down.

She narrowed her eyes at him. "I do when I'm trying to save a man's life."

Billy lifted his hands in surrender before he stood. "Fire pit?"

Asp motioned with his head towards the back cavern. He grabbed his last chem stick and popped it, lighting their way. Billy busied himself stacking a fire while Asp searched through the pockets of Lyric's pack.

"Does she know what you do?" Billy struck metal against flint sending sparks into a bit of dried bark he'd stripped from a few logs.

"Yes." Asp found a bottle of pain relievers and shook two out.

"And she's sticking with you?"

Asp zipped the pouch and gazed across the fire pit at his friend. "She is. Why?"

Billy shrugged. "Not sure Amanda would have." He gently blew on the smoldering spark igniting a small flame. Billy looked up at him for a second. "Not that I'll ever be able to find out."

"Do you keep track of her?" Asp stood and glanced out toward Lyric.

"Yeah. She hasn't had an easy life." Billy's expression hardened, and his jaw clenched. He drew a deep breath before he shrugged and nodded his head toward the front of the cavern. "Go take care of your lady. We can call the cavalry when she's settled."

As soon as the fire was burning, and Lyric was relaxing beside it, Asp led Billy through the back entrance. They assembled the Sat phone and called in. This time the operator acknowledged him by number and patched him through immediately.

"Authenticate Cookie." Anubis' voice snapped across the connection.

"Monster," Asp responded and looked at Billy. Of course, he was laughing. "I don't choose these damn authentication codes."

"Yeah, but the person who does knows you well." Billy grinned at him.

"Yes, yes I do," Anubis confirmed.

"All parties online, and I'm bouncing the hell out of their signal." The female voice had to be Bengal's wife. At least Asp assumed it was, he'd never met the woman.

"Let us know if the tracker comes back online," Archangel commanded. "Let me get straight to the point, gentlemen. Robert Flowers is a cover identification. We've traced it through shell corporations and offshore accounts to one Gerald Layman. Does that name ring any bells?"

"Multimillionaire investor? Building mogul from the Midwest? The guy that golfs with the President of the United States, that Gerald Layman?" Asp asked.

"The one and only. The thread connecting the two identities is as clear as crayons on a white wall, and that is the problem. Someone wants us to react to the breadcrumbs, but any criminal worth his salt would have made it harder to find his real identity. The entire situation stinks worse than a three-day old dead fish," the woman replied. "Additionally, Gerald Layman hasn't left the country in six months. He is currently the keynote speaker and lead partner at a business development expo in Kansas City. So the question is, who is the man in the compound and what connection does he have with the President's friend."

"Just thinking out loud here, but it sounds like someone wants to discredit Layman." Billy threw that thought out.

Asp nodded. "If they taint Layman, it could throw shadows on the President. They could say he has knowledge of what is happening down here."

"That would be disastrous," Alpha spoke for the first time. "A close friend of the President trying to undermine governments by funding terrorists. I can see the headlines now."

Asp tapped his thumb against his thigh. The shit down here just got thicker and thicker. The mission he'd originally been assigned should have scattered the masses. Billy's involvement stirred the pot and convoluted everything. Add the latest information about an arrow pointing to Layman and the entire thing resembled a powder keg with a ticking timer on top. "What are my orders?"

"We are still working that. Are you in a secure location?"

"Yes, sir. For now, but there is a female, American civilian with us, the granddaughter of the man who found me."

"Fuck me," Anubis mumbled the comment, but Asp caught it.

"Omega team made it to the farm. Someone beat them to the house. It was a recovery operation, not a rescue." Archangel's words sent a frigid chill through Asp's soul. Some bastard had killed Lyric's father and grandfather. He closed his eyes and torqued his jaw shut, screaming silently.

Alpha broke in, "Hold where you are. Do we have their coordinates?"

"Within a meter of where they are standing," Bengal confirmed.

"Alpha, order Omega team to proceed to Asp's location. They will take charge of the civilian. Pearson, you are a free agent. You can go with Omega."

"With all due respect sir, fuck that and fuck you if you think I'm leaving this shit half done." Billy sneered at the phone.

Alpha replied instead of Archangel. "Then you fall under Guardian's umbrella. Fuck this up, and you'll be on your own when the CIA comes asking questions because you and I both know they are all about covering their assess."

"Affirmative. Don't fuck up. Got it."

If he hadn't just been told Lyric's family had been murdered, he might have found Billy's attitude funny. The man was walking a thin line. Nobody screwed around with Alpha or Archangel. If Billy didn't watch his step, he'd find out firsthand what happened to people who fucked with the Kings of Guardian.

"Asp, we have a plan. Thanatos and Lycos are holding near the encampment. Tango and Foxtrot teams are landing in country as we speak. We can't set off alarms by using helicopters to retrieve the civilian, so Omega team will be traveling on foot to your location. The bastard posing as Layman can't be afforded the opportunity to escape. We need information."

"Roger that sir, what's your plan?" Asp leaned over the

phone and listened. As Archangel outlined the plan, he lifted his eyes to Billy. The man nodded. After Archangel finished, Billy spoke. "It can be done, sir. The security is getting better as Flowers brings in more mercs, but they know me. They trust me."

"Alright. Call back in when Omega Team departs your location. We will work the details from there. Archangel out."

Asp heard a series of clicks and was about to disconnect when Anubis' voice came across the connection. "This civilian, do you want me to bring her to the ranch?"

Asp closed his eyes. "Yeah. Yeah, I do. And if I don't make it back..."

"You're making it back. Kadey thinks you have a birthday present for her. You can't disappoint my baby girl."

Asp nodded, not that Anubis could see him. He picked up the phone, took it off speaker and held it to the side of his face. Billy lifted a chin and headed back into the cavern. Asp walked past the waterfall and looked out through some marmalade bushes. "Her name is Lyric. She's mine, Ani."

"Then she's coming home. She'll be here waiting for you when you get back. Take care of this shit, Asp, and we'll take care of her."

"Her father and grandfather?"

"I'll handle the arrangements."

"Thank you."

"You never have to say those words to me. Whatever it takes."

"As long as it takes." Asp disconnected and automatically popped the battery out of the phone. He had to tell the woman he loved that her family was dead. He lifted his eyes to the sky. His life had cost them theirs.

CHAPTER 19

$\mathcal{L}$yric clung to Isaac. She'd cried until she had no more tears. Her father and grandfather had been murdered. *Murdered.*

Isaac held her and let her cry. His hand brushed small circles on her back. Soothing and grounding her.

"I've lost everyone." The words fell from her lips, the agony imprinted on them dripped with despair. Somehow, they'd ended up on the ground. He leaned against the cave wall and held her in his lap. Her body trembled from her anguish. Her eyes were swollen from hours of crying, and it was painful to open them. The ache in her head matched the ache in her heart—dull and throbbing with moments of intense pain. She clutched at his shirt and pulled it. He glanced down at her. "Do you know who did it?"

"We have some assumptions. Omega Team will know more. I'll find out everything I can." He kissed her forehead. "I'm so fucking sorry. If it hadn't been for me, your family would be safe."

Billy's voice floated to them from across the cave. "That's not true." He shifted along the wall where he was resting against his backpack. "I was the one who shot you. If you want to push the blame further up the hill, Halo committed the atrocities that brought you here. Back it up further and the CIA fucked us all and before that it was the insurgents in Iraq that lobbed bombs at us. There is no one action or person who is directly responsible for her family's deaths. You didn't order the men who killed them to do it. Taking the blame for the evil other people did is useless, and it will only drive a wedge between you." He stood up and lifted his weapon onto his shoulder. "Lyric, I'm so sorry for your loss, but Mac, you didn't cause this. This tragedy is a result of events that started years ago. Don't torture yourself over things you can't change." He walked toward the front of the cavern. "I'm spending the night under the stars. I get claustrophobic."

She drew a shaky breath. "As much as I hate to admit Billy is right, he is. It wasn't your fault. We would make ourselves crazy with what-ifs, and I cannot lose you, too." She snuggled tighter into his chest. "What's going to happen now?"

"People from my organization are in country now. Five men are on their way here. They will take you to safety in the US. My friend is taking care of arrangements for you grandfather and dad. His name is Kaeden Lang. He's going to take care of you until I join you."

"You're going to stay here in Colombia?" Fear slid over her skin like oil being poured out of a cask. The cloying feeling was impossible to wipe away.

"I have to stay. There is something Billy and I need to do." He kissed her forehead again.

"What? This thing you have to do, will you be in danger?" She pushed away from him so she could see his face, to see the truth in his eyes.

He gave her a sad smile and pushed the hair that had fallen out of her braid behind her ear. "Yes, but you know what I do, what I am. I regret I didn't keep that knowledge from you." He trapped her chin lightly between his thumb and forefinger lifting her eyes to meet his. "But I've trusted you like I've never trusted another soul. Nobody else outside a handful of people in my organization know about me. I won't start lying to you now. Every operation has risks. I mitigate those risks as much as possible."

She let him press a soft kiss against her lips before she slid both arms around his neck. She'd lost everything. She couldn't help clinging to the man she loved. He was her life-line in a raging storm that threatened to overwhelm her. Isaac kept the storm at bay. He provided her shelter. "You better be careful." She pulled on his shirt as she spoke.

He twisted her, so she was straddling his lap. "I promise I will always be careful. I find it is necessary now that I'm in love with you."

"I love you, too." Lyric closed her eyes and leaned her forehead against his. "My dad and grandfather would have loved you." Tears formed in her eyes again. She swiped them aside and snuffled. He cupped the back of her head and kissed her. She trembled under his lips. As he pulled away, she tightened her arms around his neck.

"Isaac?"

"Yeah, babe?"

"Will we ever be able to be happy? Are we dreaming of things that don't exist?"

"I'm not going to sugar coat it. Life is going to suck for a while. But when I'm done here, we'll find a normal. We'll find a way and make it through this, and we'll come out stronger on the other side."

Lyric tucked herself under his chin and closed her eyes. Her world had spiraled out of control. She'd lost her family, and her only anchor in life was the man who held her in his arms. Grief overwhelmed her. In a few short hours, it had become an anguish laced backdrop to the uncertainty of her future. She was so damn cold and longed for any solace to mend her shattered heart. She let her tears fall as they came, the possibility of holding them back long abandoned. Her sanity and cornerstone was the man holding her. She sobbed again when her father's smiling face flashed through her mind. She was unable contain the pain. Lyric held on to him as gut-wrenching grief ravaged her once again. Somehow, she managed to send out a plea to her lover, "Hold me. Please don't let go until they come?"

"I'll hold you as long as it takes, babe. I promise."

~

The sound of footsteps and muffled whispers woke her. She managed to open her swollen eyes, lifting the heavy lids to no more than mere slits. She was still wrapped in Isaac's arms. He rubbed her back. "It's time, babe."

She shifted in his lap and turned toward the front of the cave. Five men stood at the entrance to the larger cavern. Lyric took in the weapons and uniforms. They weren't like the FARC forces. These men wore matching uniforms. Their weapons were numerous and modern. Each man carried himself with a purposeful ease that reminded her of Isaac. "Your people?"

He nodded before he cocked his head to the back of the cave. "Why don't you go wash your face and take a minute. I need to talk with them."

Lyric lifted from Isaac's lap and grabbed the glow stick lying beside him. He held her hand until her steps pulled them apart. The men didn't talk while she was present. Either out of respect or caution, she didn't know and couldn't find it in herself to care.

It took a tremendous effort to leave Isaac and to walk

outside to the waterfall. She splashed her face several times before she scrubbed it, trying to erase the effects of a night spent mourning the death of her family. Her eyes began to tear up again, but she fought them. No, no more tears, she had to pull herself together, but how was she supposed to do that? She tipped her head back and looked heavenward. The sun peeked through the foliage meaning she'd made it through the night. A butterfly flitted across her vision, fragile and beautiful. Lyric watched it float to a leaf, where it landed and fanned its wings in time with a slow beat that only it could discern.

She admired its beauty and immediately felt guilty for taking a small pleasure. She closed her eyes and fought back another wave of grief and tears. That was the way of things, wasn't it? Life continued even when bad things happened. She drew her legs up and hugged them as she opened her eyes and stared at the swirling water. The world should have stopped when her family died, but it didn't. The universe should have screamed at the unfairness of the acts of violence, but the only screams had been hers. She pulled a leaf off the bush near her. Perhaps what Isaac did, the monsters that he removed, perhaps his missions were good things, some small redress by the universe in the face of all the injustice.

In reality, his impassioned admission of his profession had been an abstract thing. Something she heard but her brain and heart had yet to rationalize. Now she understood the reason for people like Isaac. He made the world safer. Not completely safe. The world would never be safe because there were monsters who prayed on people like her grandfather and her father, but the monsters wouldn't be able to touch her. Not any longer. Isaac would make sure she was safe. Lyric drew a deep breath and glanced up at the sky again. She sent up a silent prayer that the universe would keep Isaac safe while he hunted his monsters.

~

Asp waited until Lyric was gone. He'd spent the night holding her while she grieved. Now it was his time to take matters into his own hands.

"Who killed them?"

As one, five heads swiveled to look at one man who responded, "We don't think it was the FARC. Whoever took them out was invited inside the house. There were no signs of forced entry. The father put up a fight. His knuckles were scraped and bloody. The old man was tied and gagged. They made him kneel, and they put a bullet through his brain. From what we could deduce it was done prior to killing the father, so probably as an incentive for him to talk. There were three, forty-five caliber casings—one next to the old man and two on the floor in the kitchen where her father was killed."

"Any idea who it was?" He needed any information he could get because before he left this country, the bastard or bastards who'd murdered Lyric's family would be dead.

"Guardian is working that. They have contacts down here, and there is another team collecting intelligence. Alpha told me to tell you he'd try to have answers for you when you were done with your mission." The man smiled and rubbed the back of his neck before he shook his head.

"What else did Alpha say?"

"He said you better not get your ass killed."

"Not my plan." Asp threw a look back toward where Lyric had exited. "I need some time with her. Give your men some time to rest."

"No hurry. We'll get her off this rock. We've been directed

to take her straight to the airfield and get her out of the country. Archangel is worried that if someone was crazy enough to commit double homicide they may have a reason to take her out, too."

"I appreciate that. Is someone going to stay with her?"

"We all are. She has a five-man body guard, assigned by Archangel himself. We are to take her to the Complex in South Dakota."

Asp finally was able to take a full breath of air. Anubis and Sky would watch out for her. He'd be able to concentrate on his mission and not worry about her. They could come back and bury her family. There would be time to mourn after the danger threatening the country was put to rest.

"Alright. Thank you." Asp took two steps towards the rear of the cave. "Make sure we have some time alone?"

"Nobody will bother you. I have orders to debrief Mr. Pearson. Take your time."

"Thank you..." Asp grasped the man's hand and looked at him expectantly.

"Leif. Leif Nilsson." The man gave his hand a squeeze. "Whatever it takes, brother."

"As long as it takes." Asp dropped the man's hand and headed out to see his woman, perhaps for the last time.

CHAPTER 20

*a*sp stepped into the sunlight and listened to the
sound of the water falling from the stream overhead
into the enclosed area behind the cave. He pushed past the
bushes and found Lyric sitting beside the water, her legs
tucked close to her chest and her eyes staring sightlessly at
the small pool at the base of the waterfall.

"It is hard to believe they are gone." She spoke without
moving.

"It is." When he lost his parents, he went through the same
thing. Even if he wasn't able to see them, he'd checked up on
them and made sure they were comfortable and safe. He
would have found a way to help them out if they needed it,
no matter what the CIA had directed.

"I'm all there is left of my family."

Asp sat down beside her. She leaned into him and
dropped her head on his arm. "No, someday we'll have children. Your family will live on through us."

She sat silent for several minutes. "So, you want a family?"

He put his arm around her and ran his hand up and down
her arm. "With you? Yes." He didn't know how that was going

to be possible, but he'd figure it out. Even if he had to leave Guardian and go sell insurance, or do clerical work in a cubical, he'd make it happen.

"Boys or girls?"

"Five of each," Asp grunted when her elbow connected to his ribs. He chuckled and leaned down to kiss the top of her head. "Okay, four of each."

"How about we start with one and go from there?" She gave him an illusion of a smile. Her eyes were puffy and red. Dark circles cut half-moon trenches above her high cheekbones and accentuated her pale, drawn face, but she'd never looked more beautiful to him.

He gave her a sad smile and winked. "Deal."

A smile ghosted across her face before sorrow swamped her expression again. "You'll need to head out with the team soon."

There was so much he wanted to say. He regretted the fact that he wouldn't be taking her down the mountain, that he wouldn't be the one to take her to safety. Entrusting her to strangers, even his brothers in arms, left an acidic taste in his mouth, and it burned all the way to the pit of his gut.

"You said Isaac Cooper wasn't your real name."

Asp shrugged. "It is as real as any other I've used."

She glanced up at him. "I like it. I think you make a wonderful Isaac."

"Then I'll be Isaac. For you and for our family."

"Billy calls you Mac."

"Caught that, did you?" He pulled her closer to him. "It was another name, from another time. I've used dozens. I like Isaac because that was who I was when I met you."

She turned and lifted onto her knees and then straddled his lap, looking at him. "I'm afraid you won't come back for me." She looked down and played with the button on his shirt.

He nudged her chin up with his index finger. "You're going with Omega Team, and they are staying with you all the way to my friend's place, Kadey's dad. They live in the middle of nowhere, but it is safe. When I finish here, I'll come for you."

"The people you are going after, the monsters. Are they the ones who killed my family?" She blinked back the tears that banked in her eyes.

He'd be lying if he didn't admit the expression on her face damn near gutted him. It was a cross between hopeful and terrified. He lay back and took her with him. Her forearms rested on his chest as she looked down at him. "I don't know. We are working on finding out what happened." He ran his hands up her arms and cupped her face gently between them. "I will make sure that whoever did this pays."

She stared at him, not blinking. Finally, she closed her eyes and nodded. She lay down on his chest, and he wrapped his arms around her.

"How long until I have to go?" Her soft question barely reached his ears.

"You have as long as you need."

She lifted her head to kiss his jaw. "I'm scared you won't be able to come for me. Will you make love to me, one last time?"

He rolled her, so she was on her side and made her look at him. "I have every intention of coming for you."

"I know you do, but..." She swiped at a tear that pooled in the corner of her eye and then dropped over the bridge of her nose. "What happens if you don't? Please, Isaac. I need to feel something good. I need..." She closed her eyes and took a shuddering breath. "I need you."

Asp moved slowly. How the hell did he show her how much she meant to him? How did he express the absolute fury that swirled through the deepest recesses of his soul and raged wildly against the shackles of his obligations? He'd been lost without a reason to exist until Lyric, and he hadn't even known it. She was the beacon of light in a life that was consumed by shadows. He needed her. He loved her, and he would move any mountain to make sure she knew how much he loved her. But he didn't want to hurt her, and he'd never take advantage. Asp lifted up on an elbow and traced her cheek with his fingers. "I'm here for you. I'll always be here for you, but I have to know you're alright with this. I can just hold you." He would. Whatever it took to make her happy. His needs and desires be damned. She was all that mattered.

Lyric pushed against his hand and turned to kiss his palm. "I'm sure. Make love to me, Isaac. Give me something beautiful to hold onto when the grief is unbearable."

He cupped the back of her neck and brought her to him. He didn't deserve this woman. He didn't deserve the possibility of a life with her, or the possibility of a family, but he was damn sure going to try to seize that golden ring and hang on. He'd put a stranglehold on the chance, and he'd do everything he could to ensure it never slipped out of his grasp.

Asp rolled her onto her back and slowly undressed her, removing clothing and committing her body to memory. The swell of her breast, the curve of her hip, the small, brown mole on her upper right thigh, all were permanently etched in his mind's eye.

Their lovemaking was slow and profoundly moving. He fought against the physical needs of his body to meet the emotional needs Lyric deserved to have met. She wrapped her arms around him trying to get closer. Closer wasn't possible. Her fingers dug into his back as she shattered. He pulled out and grabbed his slick shaft, pumping his cock through his fist twice before he followed her over the edge.

He lay down beside her and for the first time noticed the dirt that clung to his legs, forearms, and hands. Dirt and cum streaked Lyric. He swirled his finger through the mixture and held up his fingers. "I think we need a shower."

"Agreed. I have dirt in places dirt shouldn't ever be." The sound of laughter in Lyric's voice warmed the cold places in his soul.

"Then we should rinse off." He leaned down and kissed her. He nipped softly on her full bottom lip until she opened for him. The kiss was his promise. His promise that he'd find a way back to her. It was his promise that he'd find who was responsible for hurting her. It was his promise that he could be trusted with her heart.

She stared at him when they finally pulled apart. "I love you. No matter your name, no matter your profession. I love the man you are."

The words branded his heart. He dropped a soft light kiss on her nose before he answered. "I'm not going to list the reasons you shouldn't love me because there are so many." A smile played on her lips at that comment. He loved that, even in her misery, he could pull a smile from her. "I will tell you I'm going to try every day to be the man you think I am. I love you." He lifted to his knees and extended a hand to her helping her off the ground. She leaned into him, and he wrapped her in his arms. "We need to clean up, and you need to go with Omega Team."

"I know." She didn't move for several minutes.

Asp was okay with that. He knew what was waiting for her and he knew he couldn't be there to help her through it. Finally, she drew a shaky breath and pulled away, then stood up. Asp got to his feet and followed her into the pool. He ran his hands over her body, washing the dirt from her back. He rinsed off quickly, and they dressed without a word.

When they were ready, he extended his hand, and she

took it but pulled him to a stop before they entered the cavern. "Promise me you'll be safe?"

"You have my promise." He pulled her in for one last embrace and held her against him, breathing in her scent. "It's time."

She nodded her head under his chin. "I know."

CHAPTER 21

*A*sp watched as the team surrounded Lyric and they moved out. He followed them until she crested the ridge and he could no longer see her. Even then, his eyes held to the skyline.

"When do we rendezvous with the other teams?"

Billy's question returned him to the task at hand. He rolled his shoulders before he spoke. "The teams will be in place tonight at dark. If we push it, we can be back at the camp at the same time."

"Still going with the original plan?" Billy gazed at Asp steadily. "There are other options."

"None that will allow you to find your brothers and alert them to what is going on." Asp leaned over and packed up what was needed from the camp. Very little was left. Omega Team had taken all of Lyric's possessions, incorporating her meager belongings into their kits. Asp had his rifle and his backpack, freshly stocked with food and ammunition and a couple surprises, thanks once again to Omega Team.

"You have a reason to live. This plan your bosses put

together puts you in front of those bastard's crosshairs. What if shit goes sideways?"

Asp finished strapping his pack on before he looked up at his old friend. "There are two teams of highly trained warfighters on our side."

"They won't be able to help from the outside."

"I won't be alone."

"We don't know that my guys aren't on the take. If I say too much to the wrong person, I won't be any help."

Asp grabbed his weapon but thought better of it and rested it against the outside wall of the cave. He wasn't counting Billy as his primary means of help inside the camp. He had two aces up his sleeve. Thanatos and Lycos. He didn't need Billy, not when he had his fellow Shadows. Billy had no idea what Asp had become and that, well, that fact was alright with him. He smiled and winked at Billy. "I'm not worried. You do what you need to do, and I'll do the same."

"Dammit, you are either the stupidest person I know, or you've developed mad skills above and beyond being able to shoot a pimple off a gnat's ass."

"Skill sets can be acquired." Asp squared himself off in front of Billy. His friend shot him a 'what the fuck' look. "You need to put some damage on me, or they won't believe the goods we're trying to sell."

"Fuck me." Billy scrubbed his hand over his stubble. "We can say I snuck up on you when you had a bead on the camp." Asp lifted an eyebrow and stared at Billy. He watched as Billy acknowledged the truth of their situation, "Yeah, that isn't going to work, is it?"

"I'd like to keep my teeth, but you need to do some damage. Two good punches. Don't make me suffer through a..." The word *third* was forgotten in a nanosecond. Lightning bolts of pain lit him up with a million kilowatts of fist to face. Asp spun and bounced into the rock wall outside the cave.

Out of natural reflex, he doubled his fist and started to turn only to hesitate. Billy didn't. The following uppercut to the jaw sat him on his ass. Hard.

"Motherfucking son of a bitch!" Billy danced around holding his hand. "I think I fucking broke my hand on your damn hard head!"

Asp spit out a mouthful of blood. He'd bitten through his lip on that uppercut. "Stop being such a fucking princess." He used the cave wall to help himself up and worked his jaw as he leaned against it. "I owe you two, motherfucker."

"Bullshit." Billy held his arm like he'd broken it. His injured hand protected in the "L" of his elbow and bicep. "If you'd been expecting it, you would have tensed, and I probably would have broken your jaw. Fuck man, did you have a fucking steel plate implanted in your jaw after we got blown up in Iraq?"

Asp cracked his neck, first to the left and then to the right. "Stop whining. Were you always this much of a crybaby?"

"Hell, yes. Damn, did you forget everything you used to know about me?" He lifted his pack with his good hand and shrugged it on. "How am I going to explain having you in custody with a broken hand?"

"Easy, we fought, you knocked me out and tied me up before you wrapped your hand, which you probably should do, because daaamn, that bitch is swelling."

Billy scowled at him. "Not any more than your eye or lip, asshole."

Asp reached up and touched the knot forming on his cheekbone. Fuck, that was going to be a technicolor exhibit. He shrugged and reached for his weapon and strapped it on. "Yeah, but I got hit. I didn't break my hand do the hitting."

"Fuck you and your hard head."

Asp threw back his head and laughed. "Either wrap that

bitch up or quit whining, we have some serious distance to cover."

"Give me a couple minutes." Billy grabbed a wrap from his med kit and managed to compress the swelling. If it was broken, he'd have to get it set after shit hit the fan.

Asp stopped his friend before they started out. "That's your shooting hand. When this goes down, you hunker down and stay low."

"Why the fuck would I do that?"

"Have you ever seen a Guardian operation?"

"No."

"Hunker down. Do not pick up a weapon or you'll be dead. You can fuss and cuss about it after the event, but trust me, if they don't know you and you have a weapon in your hand, you are dead. Tell your men, Billy, make them believe you." Asp leveled an 'I fuck you not' stare at Billy.

"I'll do my best." Billy shouldered his weapon and nodded to Asp. "After you."

Asp pushed through the marmalade bushes and headed across the small field, making his way to the other wall and the climb out to the ridgeline. He gave himself one last opportunity to think of Lyric and the team taking her down to the misery that awaited her. He sent a silent plea to the universe to watch over her and protect her. They crested the ridge and set off toward the encampment at a jog. They had a shit-ton of mileage to cover before darkness fell.

~

Asp plopped his ass down and sucked air. His eyes pinpointed on the horizon and started searching the hills for potential threats.

"Fuck, man, you're out of shape." Billy sat down beside

him, his eyes scanning the surrounding area the same way Asp's were.

"You fucking shot me, asshole. Remember?"

"Oh, yeah. Well, there is that. Kinda easy to forget with you being such a big, fast motherfucker."

Asp glanced at the man. At least he had the decency to have developed a sweat. He, on the other hand, could be wrung out to refill the Dead Sea with the salt water pouring off him. "Whatever. We need to tie me up. The camp is..."

"Yeah, I know where the fuck we are." Billy took off his pack. "Do you think your people are here?"

"They're here." Asp had a vague idea of where the teams would be positioned, but Thanatos and Lycos were either in the camp or ready to make their move the second they saw Asp. He hadn't worked much with Lycos, but he and Thanatos went way back. He knew what the man would do, or at least he hoped he did. Asp held out his wrists.

"No, behind your back. I'm not stupid. If I bring you in with your hands tied in front of you, they'll know something's up."

A sliver of apprehension fingered his spine. The plan was simple, and he'd have backup. Backup that Billy didn't know about, but Billy had been working for the enemy for a long time. Keeping small details like two deadly-as-fuck assassins from him...meh...he'd get over it. Eventually. Probably. Maybe. He pushed his wrists back behind his waist and waited. The nylon rope slipped over his wrist and wound around the other. Billy tightened the cinch knot digging the rope into his skin. Asp let out a hiss of air. "Motherfucker."

"Yeah, I am, but you know if I take you in there with loose ropes, we're toast. What was it you said to me? Stop being a crybaby, princess?"

"I never said that." Asp watched as Billy hid his weapon under some brush and tucked his kit after it.

"Well, those words in different order, seriously, who the fuck cares." Billy stood beside him and drew a deep breath. "Whatever happens, I'm glad to have known you, Mac."

"We'll make it through this. Remember the timetable and don't fucking pick up a weapon when the show starts."

Billy nodded. His eyes darted past Asp's shoulder before his face became a concentration of anger. "Let's go."

CHAPTER 22

*B*illy tugged on Asp's arm, putting pressure on his shoulder socket and nearly sending him to his knees. He snapped his head sideways. Billy pushed him again, causing him to stumble over some brush. Billy let him fall on his face. "You are one sorry son of a bitch, you know that asswipe?"

Asp snapped his head to glare at the man he thought was his friend.

"Halt, who goes there?"

A voice from his right explained Billy's sudden shift in attitude. Asp jerked his arm from Billy's grasp only to have the man cuff him across the ear.

"Bastard," Asp growled.

"Princess," Billy whispered.

He pushed Asp harder and sent him to his knees, slamming his size twelve boot onto his back and pushing him into the dirt. The motherfucker seemed to be enjoying this shit way too much. The business end of Billy's rifle was lodged against Asp's ear. There was no way in hell he was moving, no matter how good of a friend Billy used to be.

Billy shouted, "Who the fuck says that? Seriously, Durbin, you are one lame son of a bitch?"

"Pearson? What the fuck are you doing up here?"

"I could ask the same question, asshole. You're supposed to be supervising Sanchez and Diaz while the civilians fortify the fucking chicken wire on the inner fence line."

The man's voice was closer when he spoke. "Yeah, Sanchez and Diaz have it covered. I figured if I could find that fucking sniper...oh..."

"Yeah, oh, you stupid fuck." Billy's heel ground into Asp's kidney. The growl that came out of him was instinctual. The stomp on the kidney from Pearson's boot shut his ass up. "Yeah, that's right motherfucker. Shut up and keep your mouth shut until Mr. Flowers asks you a question."

"Flowers?" Asp heard the confusion in Durbin's voice.

"Yes, Flowers. What the fuck is the problem?"

"Flowers is leaving, hell he may be gone already. There was a big dust-up earlier today, now he's busting his ass getting everything in line so he can leave. You'll have to hurry if you want the boss man to have a shot at this stupid fucker." Asp ground his teeth together stopping the biting comment he wanted to spit at that fucking walking, talking, cartoon-sized bag of clichés.

"Right. Come on, motherfucker, we have to make sure you meet the boss." Billy turned to Durbin. "You've got our six. I'm pushing us down the hill, and I don't want to have to step over your dead body when you fall and break your neck."

"I fell once. Once!" Durbin lamented but waited for Billy and Asp to pass before he took up the rear position. Billy's grasp on his arm loosened and while he still shoved Asp, he didn't push him enough to hinder their progress down the hill. Asp did attempt to pull away on occasion, making sure Durbin knew he wasn't going willingly. They made it to the bottom of the hill in record time. Asp was sweating bullets, as was Pearson. He could hear Durbin gasping behind them as he slid and scrambled to keep upright as they descended.

They approached the compound, and Pearson once again shoved Asp to the ground. This time the gravel tore the skin of his face, and several pieces of rock felt like they embedded in his cheek. Asp thanked his lucky stars it wasn't worse. He damn near hit his head on a rock. The sharp point would have killed him if Billy hadn't shoved him at the last moment sending him to the left and into the gravel. He'd have to thank his friend for that little piece of humanity. Asp groaned as he was jerked back up. Oh, hell yeah, he was going to thank Billy, up close and personal. He was beginning to wish he hadn't stopped Lyric.

There was a barrage of voices in both Spanish and English. Asp tried to keep up, but honestly, the people talking over each other sounded like a gaggle of geese. Billy put his fingers to his mouth and rent the air with a loud, sharp whistle. "Shut the fuck up!" Billy growled in the sudden silence. "You, go get Flowers, and tell him to come to the main building. I have a present for him. You, yeah, you, get these assholes back to work."

The drone of voices lessened. Asp risked a glance up and saw two sets of government issued combat boots heading his way.

"I see you caught the motherfucker who took out Cavanaugh."

"I caught him. Gleason, Harper, do me a favor. Round up the company men and have them meet me in the barracks in fifteen."

"What's up?"

Asp felt Pearson's hand tighten on his bicep. "Intel briefing for company ears only. Barracks in ten. Get them all there. I don't care what you need to do." Billy pushed Asp forward toward the main building in the camp.

There was a slight hesitation before Asp heard one of the men speak. "Everything okay?"

Billy stopped and turned, still holding Asp's arm in his grip. "No. Not even close to being okay." He pushed Asp forward again, but not with the force he'd used earlier. Billy shoved him up a set of steps, which Asp pretended to stumble up. He landed on his knees and used the time it took for Billy to lift him to his feet to get a lay of the exterior of the buildings surrounding the one where he was being taken. He noted the shadows, knew the distance between the structures and where the lights were. Asp glanced behind him to the fence line. Still chicken wire. That is where his help would come from, and if they didn't, that is where he would escape this camp should Guardian's teams somehow fail.

Pearson rewarded his drop to his knees with a kick to the back, not hitting the kidney this time. Asp rolled away from the kick, and it may have looked vicious, but the boot barely made contact with his ribs. Thank you, sweet Jesus.

Billy hauled him up and pushed him through the door past a radio room that looked like a set from a 1950's sci-fi movie. Asp fell on purpose and from floor level noted the radios were not on battery backup, nor were they on an uninterrupted power supply. When the teams cut the power, the camp would be isolated.

"Get up, you motherfucker!" Billy grabbed the back of his shirt and yanked him up. Asp lifted to his feet. He was shoved into a windowless room. Once again, he went down from the force of Billy's propulsion, but managed to spin and land on his shoulder. Three pairs of boots surrounded him. Hands grabbed him, and he was unceremoniously dumped into a chair. Within seconds his legs were zip tied to the chair. His hands, still tied behind him, were shoved through the opening in the back of the wooden chair. A rope cinched his chest and tightened until he couldn't breathe normally. Shallow pants kept him from passing out.

Billy circled behind him and cuffed his head. He yelled, "What is your name, motherfucker?" Asp felt the ropes at his chest loosen. He groaned when Billy slapped him with an open hand. His lip started bleeding again. The two men who helped Billy tie him into the chair laughed. The bastards. He felt something pressed into his hand. He cupped the instrument, shielding it from view. Billy cuffed his head again. Asp ground his teeth. He was so going to enjoy thanking Billy for all his wonderful hospitality. *Motherfucker*! Another backhand, this time across the swollen bruise from the first punch this morning. "Talk, asshole, and this will be easy. We can put you out of your misery and be done with it."

Asp kept his gaze pointed toward the floor. He'd been through enough training and a fuck-ton of real-life experiences. He knew no matter what he did, the people beating him wouldn't suddenly turn into sugar plum fairies and cut his ropes. No, first they'd try to break him and then after they got the answers they wanted, they'd either dehumanize and humiliate him or execute him. Hell, probably all three. He knew from experience. The scars on his arms were a testament to how insane people worked. At least this time he knew a rescue party would be coming and coming soon.

Pearson left, but that didn't stop the men who remained from taking shots at him. He lost a molar with one particularly vicious punch. Blood dripped from his nose and mouth and pooled on his lap. He watched the thread of blood and drool stretch. He had no idea how long Billy had been gone. Boots dudes had tired of using him as a punching bag, at least for now. Asp made sure he could see both men before he slid the razor blade between his fingers and started sawing on the ropes that bound his wrists.

Boots dudes must have thought he'd passed out because they ignored him. They sat at a small table by the door covered with paperwork of some sort. Their conversation about what the locals thought of the camp leadership droned on, but at least he had a vector on both of them. The blade sliced the nylon with ease, and his wrists tingled as a thousand needles stabbed him when blood flowed to his appendages again. The rope was still wrapped around his wrists. He didn't have to fake keeping his arms suspended behind him, yet he could move when the time arrived for action.

The door opened, and the dynamic duo complaining about the stupid Americans who had no fucking clue that the workers were stealing from them, ceased talking. Asp lifted his head and looked through lids so swollen they restricted his vision to slits. Flowers. The man nodded toward the door, and the two locals fled like their assess were on fire and Flowers had gasoline.

"Well, well, well...who do we have here?" The man's voice was so far from what Asp thought it would be it was shocking. High pitched, breathless and almost musical. Flowers stopped by the door and continued, "From what Pearson tells me, you were the shooter that took out one of our best men." Asp's head dropped again. His chest caught on the rope that bound him to the chair. He could remove them with a shrug. Billy hadn't actually tied the knot, and if he leaned forward anymore, the ropes would fall down. The sticking point of getting out of the chair would be the zip ties around his ankles. Breaking the rickety ass folding chair would alleviate that problem but having the time to manage that feat was questionable. He could lunge and attack with his arms free. The chair was only a limitation.

Shoes came into his view. Asp blinked, surprised at the sight of the light tan handmade leather loafers. Expensive shoes. He'd been around the elite, and he knew a tailor or two on Savile Row. Obviously, this man did too.

"So the questions I have for you are, why did you kill him and who sent you?" The man's quiet voice sent gooseflesh down Asp's spine. He tried to calculate how much time had elapsed since he'd been shoved into this room. The team was supposed to hit exactly ninety minutes after they saw Pearson and Asp enter. Ninety minutes. How long had he been here? A quick calculation put him at an hour, maybe a few minutes more or less. He needed Flowers to talk to him. He needed anything Guardian could use to unravel the riddle that Halo's death had spun. Personally, he didn't give a fuck if Flowers lived or died during the raid on the camp, but there were considerations. The man was a small part of a bigger problem. It wasn't Asp's job to figure out the larger picture, but if he could find an edge piece, he'd bet the puzzle masters at Guardian would figure it out.

He lifted his head and tried to smile. His smashed lips hindered the process. "I killed him because he fucked me over."

Flowers lifted an eyebrow and then cocked his head. "How did he do that?"

Asp sneered at the bastard. No, it wasn't going to be that easy. "Why would you want a fucker like that in charge of your business down here?"

"Ah, well, sorry, I don't believe I will be answering any of your questions. You see, this is an inquisition. That means I ask the questions and you answer them." Flowers moved a smaller chair from the side of the room. He sat down, stared at Asp and then moved it to the right, so he was not sitting directly in front of him. "Yes, this is perfect."

"Manuel?" Flowers sang, calling to someone outside the room.

"You have a very interesting voice." Asp imagined the man

rather liked that idea. He seemed to preen at the Asp's observation as if it were a compliment.

"Thank you. You know it really is too bad we didn't meet under better circumstances. Unfortunately, I can't spare much time today, so I'm going to ask you one more time. Who sent you and why did you shoot our employee?"

"I told you why I killed him." Asp lifted his head to speak. He hadn't realized he'd lowered it. Over the course of his life, he'd had worse beatings, but between Billy and the clowns that had worked him over, he was hurting.

"When did my employee, as you say, fuck you?"

"When we both worked for the CIA."

"So, you killed him because he made waves for you at the CIA? I'm sorry, that is thin. Too thin." Flowers turned toward the door and yelled, "Manuel!"

There was no movement. Asp had a damn good idea why. He spoke to Flowers, "It's the truth. He sent me out to kill an innocent man. A professor. He told me the man was a traitor to the country. He wasn't."

Flowers crossed his leg and regarded Asp for a moment. "Ahh...that makes sense. Well, first the professor wasn't a traitor, but he did have useful attributes that would have furthered our goals. Economics is such an interesting field of study. The saying money is power is true, you know." Flowers waved his hand dismissively, "We approached him, and he refused to help us. He threatened to expose us unless we stopped our...work, I guess is a good word for what we are doing. He gave us two weeks to prove we'd complied. Instead, Cavanaugh sent in one of his assassins to kill the man. Then all hell broke loose." Flowers uncrossed his leg and leaned forward with his forearms resting on his thighs. "Was that you?" He smiled and then laughed. "It was, wasn't it! You cost us. Time, money, effort, but we were able to right the ship. We've learned and grown in the past few short years." Flowers stood and went to the door and looked out. "Manuel!" The man huffed and crossed his arms in frustration. "Where is he? I don't have time for this."

"Where did you get your shoes? Was it the little shop on Savile Row? The one at the end next to the haberdashery?" The man's head whipped around. "Yes! Farrows! How do you know it?"

"They make most of my dress shoes." Asp had to keep the man talking. He was a self-important ass. The best way to keep him talking was to let him talk about himself.

"Oh, Farrows does fine work. Fine work! Now, see, killing you is going to be such a pity. I think I would like you. Who did you say sent you to kill Halo?"

Asp chuckled. "I didn't."

"Ah, but you see, I need to know. I need to know what entity sent you because that would let us know if we need to worry. I've been recalled. I'm assuming it is a knee-jerk reaction, but he's always paranoid."

"Who's paranoid?" Information from this man was hard to come by, but Asp already had a few nuggets, and he could dig deeper, maybe reveal the mother lode. Hard to do being zip-tied to a chair and on the wrong side of the inquisition table, but what the fuck, he'd do the best he could.

"Who?" Flowers blinked at him as if he'd just seen Asp. The fucker was a bubble off center. He brain wasn't level with the rest of the world.

"Who is paranoid about someone finding out?" Asp tried to judge the time. He unwound the rope from his wrists, gathering the excess in this cupped palm. The one that didn't have the razor blade.

"Oh, well I guess we all are. You can imagine what happens when six men as smart as us get together. Conspiracy theories will abound." Flowers giggled and then laughed. He laughed so hard he had to sit down. He wiped a tear from his eye. "Oh, that was golden. Conspiracy theories. Oh, that is rich. Don't you think?"

"Why? Because there actually is a conspiracy?" Asp shifted his weight, and the dime store folding chair groaned. He glanced over at Flowers who'd gone silent.

"You are very perceptive for a paid hitman."

"I'm not a hitman." Asp considered the time it would take to cut the zip ties with the razor blade. Everything depended on the moves his prey would make, and Flowers had become his prey the moment he walked into the room.

"You can call it what you want. You are a drone that kills on command." Flowers once again gave a dismissive wave of his hand.

"You've made a mistake. Perhaps I was that when your employee knew me, but I'm not that man any longer."

"Really? And tell me, tiger, how do you become a leopard?"

Asp cocked his head to the side. "Second mistake. I'm not a tiger. I'm a viper."

"Wouldn't that be a shade of the same mistake?" Flowers quipped before he asked, "A viper? Oh, like a rattlesnake?" The man laughed again. "Should I consider this your tail rattling?"

"No, not a rattlesnake." Asp stood, shrugging the ropes off as he rose. Flowers jumped to his feet and sprinted toward the open doorway. Asp lunged forward and tackled the man around his knees. They both hit the floor. Flowers brought his knee up, catching Asp under the chin sending his head backward. Asp grabbed a fistful of shirt and pulled the motherfucker down to him. Flowers kicked, his hands punched Asp around the head and shoulders, but Asp barely felt the abuse. He was face to face with the man, and the terror in his prey's eyes was almost euphoric. Asp lifted the hand with the razor blade. Flowers saw it and arched his back bringing his arm up to stop Asp from what Flowers must have assumed was his goal. Asp pushed his chest over Flowers as he struggled. He snarled at his soon to be prisoner. "I'd kill you, but you have too many answers."

Asp heard a sharp metallic sound. Somehow Flowers had palmed a knife. Asp rolled his shoulder a split second before he felt the blade slice at his back with a downward strike. Asp pushed harder against the smaller man. Flowers' arm moved again, and again. The knife ripped at his back and shoulder, the last slice went deep.

Asp roared in pain and anger. He was physically spent, but his rage crested his exhaustion. He managed to grab the arm with the knife and pin it to the ground. Flowers other arm came up. A flash of metal caught Asp's eye.

Asp blocked the other arm by turning and that released the pressure on Flowers' knife. He realized the time had come to end the situation. Asp reached up and drew the razor blade across Flowers' throat. Flowers' eyes widened, and he grunted as he thrust the knife against Asp's shoulder again. Asp let a sinister smile spread across his face. The man's struggles turned into convulsive jerks. Asp pushed off the smaller man, arched his back and used the blood-soaked razor blade to slice the zip ties that held his legs to the metal chair. He stood with blood trickling down his arm and shoulder and looked down at the dying man. He'd sliced the artery. Flowers would bleed out as evidenced by the blood spurting out around Flowers' hand. "Do something good with your life. Tell me who the others are." Asp heard the sound of gunfire. His people were storming the camp.

Flowers gasped and jerked. Asp watched as the man's last breath hissed out of him. Flowers' scared gaze froze into a death stare. Asp needed the fucker's DNA and fingerprints. He solved both issues with one action. He grabbed a piece of paper off the table where boots dudes had lazed. Then he grasped Flower's wrist. Asp pressed and swiped the lifeless hand against the floor removing most of the blood. He then set Flower's entire hand to the paper and lifted it away carefully. The handprint was damn near perfect, and the blood on the paper could be used for DNA. Asp held the paper by the edge, so he wouldn't smudge the damn thing.

The battle outside the room where he stood suddenly quieted. A few random shots were fired. A floorboard creaked outside the room. The siege was damn quick. Obviously, the trained warfighters in the camp had listened to Billy and not taken up arms. Asp glanced at his back. He'd need stitches, a couple of the wounds were pretty damn deep, but he'd survived worse. He grabbed a wad of paper towels and shoved them under his shirt, then pressed back against the wall and waited. Thanatos walked into the room. "Well, it took you long enough. You missed all the fun." Asp drawled even though he was relieved to see the man.

"You have a really disturbed definition of fun," Lycos said as he walked in behind Thanatos. He glanced at Flowers before he turned his attention to Asp. "You are one ugly bastard on a good day. Today isn't a good day for you."

Asp chuffed out a laugh. "Fuck you. Blood red, black and blue are my colors."

"Nah, dude, they really aren't." Thanatos righted one of the chairs and sat down. "Who was this?"

"Flowers, or the man who was pretending to be Flowers. I'm not up on the circle jerk that is going on with the name game." He leaned against the wall. "The CIA men?"

"They're safe. I made sure of it." Lycos stepped over Flowers and glanced at the paperwork that covered the desk. He did a double take and started shuffling through the stacks. "Did you look at this?" Lycos glanced over his shoulder when he spoke.

"No, I was kind of tied up. I used a piece of paper to identify this fucker."

"If that doesn't work, we can find out from his tailor." Thanatos snapped a picture of the man's face. "His clothes are bespoke."

"Yeah, we established that during our little meet and greet. If all else fails, his shoes come from Farrows in London." Asp would have chuckled, but he didn't have the damn energy and his face hurt too badly.

"Guardian is going to want to see this. Invoices, companies, rosters. There are a couple of emails here...shit." Lycos picked up a sheet of paper. "WTF over?" The tone of his question sent a specter of apprehension up Asp's spine.

"What is it?" Asp pushed himself up and away from the wall. His knees still felt like jelly, but his curiosity got the better of him. Lycos handed Asp the document. Asp scanned the top and stopped. He glanced at Lycos and re-read the words. His gut dropped. That meant... "You've got to be fucking kidding me?"

"Okay, I'll bite." Thanatos stood and grabbed the paper. His smirk dropped from his face. Asp shook as he pushed his hair back from his eyes. The shaking wasn't only because he'd been through hell, but if the information was correct...

"But they're a myth?" Thanatos jerked his head up. "Right? Stratus is a myth?"

Asp shook his head. "I don't know, and that's above my pay grade. Lycos, you take that and get it back to Guardian. Thanatos, help me get Pearson and his people situated. I need to find out if they have any information on the bastard that took out Lyric's family.

Lycos stopped what he was doing. "Who is Lyric?"

"Nobody, you damn horn-dog." Thanatos cuffed Lycos on the shoulder. "You go through women like fire goes through flash paper."

Lycos shrugged. "I have urges."

"Yeah, well keep your urges to yourself. Lyric is mine and fucking off-limits." Even amongst friends, there was no way Asp could keep the feral growl out of his voice.

Lycos chuckled and resumed stacking the information he'd take back to Guardian. "Another one bites the dust."

"I'd say so." Thanatos clapped Asp on the shoulder, sending him forward two steps.

"Dammit. Can't you see I'm injured?"

"Stop whining, princess." Billy's voice turned all three of them toward the door. He stopped short and winced, pulling a whistle through his teeth. "Fuuuck, man."

"Yeah, your friends liked beating up a defenseless man." Thanatos nodded toward Flowers. "I made sure they ended up like this one."

Asp glanced at Thanatos and gave him a slight inclination of his head, acknowledging the professional courtesy, for lack of better words. His friend dipped his in return.

Billy lifted his hands to his hips and stared down at Flowers. "Did you find out who he was working with?"

"Nope," Asp spoke quickly. He knew Thanatos and Lycos would never discuss Guardian business in front of others, but it never hurt to make sure they knew Billy wasn't to be trusted. Yet. "He asked his questions and then died when the shooting started.

"Strange. He liked to boast. I was sure you'd get something out of him." Billy rubbed the back of his neck, still staring at the corpse on the floor,

"He came in, said he didn't have time to chat and asked me who sent me and why I killed one of his best employees. The teams entered on the heels of that question. He bolted, and I couldn't let him escape." Asp let go of the bloody paper he was holding when Lycos tugged on it. "Your men okay?"

"All but one. He wasn't with us when we first started out.

I spoke with him last after the rest of my crew had signed on. He went out in a blaze of glory." Billy motioned toward the door. "Your mercs told me I had two minutes. They have to keep us segregated. I get that. I'll see you on the other side, brother."

"Take care of yourself, Billy." Asp shook the man's hand and watched him walk back through the door. He knew chances were he'd never see the man again.

Several Guardian team members walked into the room, moving to the side to let Billy pass. Asp recognized one from a previous operation. "Duke, how's it hanging?"

"Low and heavy." Duke stuck out a hand and Asp took it. "That your kill?"

Duke's team member stepped over the body and took out a digital camera. Asp, Thanatos, and Lycos all grabbed for the device at the same time. "Whoa! Dude, what the fuck?"

Duke chuckled. "Shadows don't like cameras, dumbass." He nodded his head toward the man who'd pulled the camera. "F.N.G."

Asp took the camera and scanned the disk. He handed it back to Duke. The fucking new guy, as Duke labeled him, paled and swallowed hard. "Have you gotten any intel from Billy's crew?"

"Haven't even started questioning them. Something specific you're looking for? I've got one of the best interrogators in the business with me." He glanced at the man beside him. "Go get Giovanni."

"Roger that, skipper."

Asp waited until the kid left and nodded toward the paperwork Lycos had stacked. "Keep your eye out for anything, either electronic or paper. We found some interesting information. Not sure if it is useful, but…"

"Oh hell, believe me, we learned how to process a scene from Jared King himself. When we were taking down that human trafficking ring, he and his people ran a scope up our evidence collection process." Duke laughed and shook his head. "It was a pain in the ass, but those bastards are off the streets now."

"You called for me, skipper?" The soft, sensual female voice drew every eye in the room.

Duke nodded and held up a finger towards her. "What do you need to know?"

"There were two executions, roughly four days ago. An old man, Mateo Garcia, and his son-in-law. His last name was Gadson. The younger was tortured. Omega team gathered intelligence that the FARC weren't involved. I need intelligence on who killed them."

"Do you want to know why?" The woman asked.

"I want the motherfucker who killed them. *He'll* tell me the reason why." Asp had a few tricks up his sleeve. He'd skin the bastard alive to get the answers he needed. This time it was personal.

Her eyes widened, and she popped the gum she'd been silently chewing. "Roger that." She swung her head to her skipper, totally dismissing the three assassins in the room. "You want me to start with the Company guys or the survivors?"

Duke narrowed his eyes at her. "Who do you suggest?"

"Survivors. They are terrified right now. If I wait, the shock will wear off. Company guys know what's coming and they've been trained to avoid and evade. I'll get more intel from the ones crapping themselves."

"Do what you have to do. If you get any information regarding the situation he mentioned, let me know ASAP. Other than that, you run your investigation."

"Roger, Skipper." She ducked out of the room.

"Where did you find her and more important does she have sisters—ones who don't carry automatic weapons? I prefer my women less lethal." Lycos picked up the papers as he asked.

"She's one of a kind, and she's off-limits. I don't let anyone fuck with my team. Literally or figuratively." Duke hid the threat with a shit-eating grin.

"Your people must hate you. You're cockblocking everything and everybody with that rule." With his arms full he nodded toward Asp. "Get him to sit down before he falls down."

Asp would have made a smart-ass comment but sitting down sounded damn good. Better yet, being horizontal and sleeping would be heaven. God, that thought was almost orgasmic. But he had shit he had to get done.

"Got him. The barracks are in order. They should be clear by now. I'll send Doc in to check you out." Duke motioned toward the door. "Come on, big guy, I'll escort you to a cot and make sure you get a hot in about twelve hours."

"I need to debrief first. The bosses need to know what he said." Asp motioned towards the corpse.

"Hold tight, I'll get a Sat phone in here." Duke headed out of the room.

Thanatos brought the rickety ass folding chair over and pointed at it. "Sit."

Asp shook his head and moved to the wall to lean against it. "If I sit down, I won't get up. I was running on fumes. I don't know what the hell's keeping me upright now."

"Sit, I'll get your big ass up or enlist one of those teams to carry you to a bed." Thanatos pointed at the chair again.

"You know I'm not going to be able to sleep here, right? I gotta find a hole and..." They were shadows. The sooner they got lost, the better for everyone.

"Bullshit. I've got you, and so does Lycos. Just get some sleep. We've got your back, my brother."

Duke came back in and handed a brick to him. "Alpha's online."

"Sir." Asp acknowledged his boss.

"The connection is secure. What do you have?" Alpha's strong, loud voice was jarring in his ear.

"There is a group of six, well, now five, people. The leader is paranoid, Flowers' words, not mine. I don't know what they are planning, but it is a conspiracy of some sort. Somehow the economics professor Halo had me kill was involved in the situation. That was the case that caused me to open the black door and expose Halo to his superiors. The professor's name was Regis Thornton. Flowers, or the man acting as Flowers, indicated Thornton could have helped further their plan but refused. He threatened to expose what was going on, so Halo used me to shut the man up. And we found documents. They mention Stratus."

"Repeat your last?"

"What did you say?"

"Say again?"

Through the phone, three voices jumbled over the top of each other. He recognized Alpha, Archangel, and Bengal. "Sir, I repeat we found documents that mention Stratus. Lycos has the papers. He'll get them to you."

There was a distinct pause at the other end of the line. Asp waited, assuming he was muted and another conversation was going on because of the information he'd conveyed.

"Roger that. Good work. Get some rest and food, or in your case, food and then rest. Is Duke nearby?" Alpha was the one to speak.

Asp chuckled, because, fuck yeah, he was hungry. "Yes, sir. Sir...may I inquire..."

"Omega Team got her down the mountain. She spent yesterday taking care of her family's funeral arrangements, wouldn't leave until she took care of it herself. We've intervened with the government on her behalf. The burial can happen anytime, but she wanted to wait until you could be there. She boarded a plane and is probably in our airspace as we speak." Alpha knew what he needed to hear. She was safe. Thank God.

Asp let out a long sigh and shook his head. The events of the last seventy-two hours rested heavily on his shoulders, weighing him down. He was crashing, and he knew it. The hand holding the phone started shaking. He glanced up at Thanatos who stared at him intently. "Roger that, sir. Here's Duke." Asp fell against the back of the chair and tried to lift the phone. He blinked at his hand and then rolled his head, so he could see Thanatos. The man was on his knees in front of Asp. His lips were moving, but his voice sounded like it was making its way through sludge. He was so fucking tired.

CHAPTER 23

*L*yric stood on a small hill and turned in a three-hundred-sixty-degree circle. The rolling hills to the east turned into mountains in the west. The Black Hills were nothing like the Andes, but the country was beautiful. Cattle dotted the horizon, and every now and then she could hear a momma cow calling for her calf. The little buggers were so cute the way they frolicked in the deep grass. She glanced up at the vast blue sky and sighed. It had been three weeks since she'd flown out of Colombia. Three long weeks without Isaac.

Kaeden, the friend Isaac spoke of was, in fact, a very nice man. His wife Sky, and daughter Kadey, had taken her into their newly constructed home. She played with Kadey and her friend Elizabeth, so Sky was free to paint and decorate the beautiful house.

Lyric could imagine a life here. The women who lived here were close. One night a week they got together, drank wine and watched Supernatural. That made Lyric laugh. She'd watched the show before she left for Colombia, and Sam and Dean were still going strong. She'd met many women whose spouses worked for Guardian. There were still others that had nothing to do with the company, but their men worked the ranch. Ranch, heck it was a village. It was bigger than the villages she traveled to in Colombia. Strange how she now compared everything to Colombia instead of Jacksonville. Jacksonville seemed like someone else's life.

"You okay?" Kaeden's voice pulled her back to earth, or rather, South Dakota. She turned to watch him walk up the small knoll where she stood.

"I am." She could acknowledge that. She was lonely, but she was okay.

"I know it isn't easy. The waiting." He sat down and stretched out his long legs and leaned back on his arms.

Lyric sat down beside him and picked a stem of grass to play with. "When he called last week, he said he would come to me when he was finished." Lyric hadn't asked him how long it would take. She didn't want him to worry that she wouldn't wait for him, because she would wait. Forever if need be.

"Thank you, by the way. We don't expect you to babysit Kadey."

"I don't mind. She's adorable." Lyric smiled at the surprise the little girl and momma would get if Isaac ever did get her a pony.

"So, you and Isaac, huh?"

Lyric turned to give Kaeden her complete attention. "Yes. Why?"

The man shook his head and then gave a small shrug of his shoulders. "He's my friend."

The statement said more than anything else could. Lyric called up images of her lover. First, when she'd nursed him back to health, and then the first time they'd kissed, the first time they'd made love. She felt herself smile and closed her eyes. "You are lucky to be his friend. I don't think Isaac lets many people close. He's an amazing man."

"Who has a tough job."

Ah, there was the purpose of this visit. Lyric opened her eyes and turned her head toward Kaeden. "I know what Isaac does. What do you want from me, Kaeden?"

He stared at her for several long seconds. "Do you? Do you truly understand what he does?"

Lyric repositioned herself, so she was facing him. "I do. What is your concern?"

"Frankly, I'm concerned you'll leave him. That you'll hurt him. He's a friend. I have, like, five people that can claim that title."

"Then you have four more people than I do. Isaac Cooper, or whatever his real name is, is my only true friend. There are no guarantees in life, but I know I would rather die than hurt that man." She cocked her head and asked, "Does your wife know what you do for Guardian?"

"In abstract terms, yes." He glanced over to where the new house sat nestled against the tree line,

"Abstract terms." Lyric mused over the words. She knew what her man did. Isaac fought monsters and won. There was nothing abstract about it. "I don't have that luxury. I've seen the ugly reality." She picked a stem of blue-eyed grass and twirled it between her fingers. "He makes the world safer without people knowing."

"He does." Kaeden sat up and brushed his hand free from the dark, fertile earth. "Are you okay with that?"

She was. "The world needs a hero who will battle the monsters that live among us." She'd made peace with what he did.

"You know what?" Kaeden stood and offered her a hand up.

"What?" She took it an allowed him to help her stand.

"You'll do, Lyric Gadson. You'll do."

"I'm not sure what that means, but I feel like I should say thank you." She brushed off her hands and jeans.

"No, I need to thank you. Take care of my friend, Lyric."

"Do you know when he will return?"

Kaeden shrugged. "Any day now. He had a loose end to tie up, but I have a feeling he'll be back within the week."

Lyric squeaked in surprise. "A week? Isaac will be back within a week?"

"I believe so. Sky and I took the liberty of cleaning out the Drover's Cottage." He nodded and pointed to a small house settled behind the massive barn and next to the main house, an enormous log home with a wraparound porch. "We figured you'd want your privacy. Kadey has terrible timing, and she has no idea what a closed door means." The man's cheeks turned a dark red.

"I take it there is a story there?" Lyric laughed as they made their way toward the cottage.

"Oh God, several." He groaned and rubbed his face with both hands before he laughed.

"You are lucky to have them." Lyric's heart lurched. She missed her family. Grief often hit her the hardest when she witnessed others with the ones they loved.

"I am. I almost didn't have them." He stuck his fingers in the front pocket of his jeans as they walked. It took almost ten minutes to get to the cottage. They walked in comfortable silence for the most part.

"We can go back up to our house and get your things. We wanted to make sure you were okay with staying here. It isn't much."

She stepped inside. There was a kitchenette at the front with a window looking out toward the big house with the porch. To the left of the door as you entered was a small table and two chairs. A loveseat, radio, and bookshelf sat mere feet from the queen-sized bed. She wondered if Isaac's feet would hang off the end. The thought made her smile. He could spoon her when he slept. That would keep him on the bed.

"It's perfect. Thank you." She ran her hand across the little table before a thought struck her. "Do you know what Isaac's favorite meal is? I would like to have it ready for him when he comes home."

Kaeden's eyes got large, like silver dollars. "What did you eat in Colombia?

"I made him stew once. But for the most part, we existed off fruit and the protein bars he had in his pack. I never asked him what he liked to eat." Not that she could really cook that well, but surely the ladies here on the ranch would help her? Right?

Kaeden covered his mouth, and his shoulders moved up and down. A low rumble of laughter filled the small cottage, and the man doubled over, slapping his leg. Lyric had no idea what Kaeden found so funny.

"What do you know how to cook?" When he was able, he gasped and started to compose himself.

"Chicken and rice, slow roasted pork…"

"That, cook that and make oh, about three times the amount you would normally make. Isaac eats anything and all the time."

Lyric lifted an eyebrow. She doubted that, but Kaeden seemed to think he was right. She couldn't imagine the man whose entire subsistence for a day was one protein bar would eat to excess the way Kaeden suggested. Isaac had said his friends had harassed him. Maybe that was why he didn't eat much in front of her.

"I want to be a fly on the wall the first time you feed the man. Oh, better yet, invite us down." He opened the door and shook his head. "Yeah, no. We probably won't see you two for a week or so, but seriously, I'll remind Sky to help you stock up on groceries down here."

Lyric followed him out and closed the door behind her. "Ahh...thank you?"

"What are you thanking him for?" Lyric twirled toward the voice. She recognized the man as Drake. They'd been introduced by several different people.

"She's never seen Isaac eat." Kaeden started laughing again.

"Isaac? Who is...oh...*oh*...no way, seriously? How is that possible?" The man joined Kaeden in the joke.

"Field conditions, dude." Kaeden managed between laughs.

"Well, sh...shoot, that would explain it," the man conceded. He tipped his cowboy hat towards Lyric. "Nice to have you as neighbor for a while, ma'am." He nodded at Kaeden. "Make sure she stocks up."

"I know, right?"

Lyric put her hands on her hips at Kaeden's agreement. One thing was obvious. According to his friends, Isaac liked food. God, she needed help. She'd ask Sky and maybe Miss Amanda. She was the wife of the ranch owner, and she always brought good food to the Wine & Winchester Wednesdays. Hopefully, she wouldn't burn down the cottage in the process. No, her mishaps in the kitchen were something from her past she'd like to keep firmly buried. Lyric's smile faded. She still had to bury her family. Kaeden had assured her they could do it when Isaac got back. She'd bury her father next to her mother and send her grandfather's ashes to the wind from the mountain shrine where her mother, grandmother and uncles were memorialized. That was his wish and one she intended to honor. She'd like to find someone to engrave her father and grandfather's names into the granite face beside that of her grandmother and mother.

Kaeden seemed to pick up on her change of mood. He nodded toward the 'Guardian' side of the settlement. "Shall we?"

They started down the path together. She watched Drake reach down and scoop up a cat as he headed toward the large house just across the clearing. "I wouldn't take him for a cat person." She pointed at the odd couple.

"Yeah, from what I heard, that thing adopted him not too long ago." Kaeden shrugged. "Cats are self-sufficient, and with the amount of time that man spends at work, a poor dog would pine away."

They made it back to Kaeden's house after stopping to visit with others who were out on the warm spring afternoon. Kadey launched herself off the porch at her daddy and immediately started to chatter about her day and adventures. Lyric followed them into the house. This is what she longed for with Isaac—simple times wrapped in love and spent with family. She'd have the possibility for that type of love home, in her arms, within the week. Her heart soared at the prospect.

CHAPTER 24

*A*sp waited in the front room of Lyric's family; the home where her grandfather was murdered; the place where her father was tortured—and watched the evening shadows lengthen. There was no intelligence regarding the deaths of Lyric's family from Halo's camp. In fact, most of the intelligence they gathered had fortified the information in the paperwork Lycos had found. It was a stroke of luck that led Asp back to the small farm today. He'd wandered down to the closest village because he was fucking tired of the crap he was eating in the field. It was late and dark as Asp sat outside the local cantina in the outdoor dining area. Though food was still served, the interior was full of locals, and they were drinking. Asp didn't give a flying fuck about the locals. From the interviews Guardian's people had conducted, they didn't know who had killed Lyric's family. But it wasn't locals he overheard that night. He'd finished his beans and rice and some sort of mystery meat and had drifted into the shadows. The music and laughter coming from inside lessened the stress of the past two weeks. It was comforting to hear humanity laugh and live. Two men in National Police uniforms exited the cantina, and after casting glances around, they sat at a table near the entrance, obviously intent on talking in private.

"The man is fucking insane."

"No shit. When he put a gun to that defenseless old man's head, I left. I wanted nothing to do with that."

"They were found dead."

"Man, I can't wrap my head around it. Why would Ricardo do such a thing?"

"She threatened him. Then she was gone. He thought she'd gone to the district commander to file a complaint. The old man, he ranted crazy shit about her finding a real man. Ricardo lost it. He shoved him down and put a gun to his head after he pistol-whipped the other, knocking him out. I told him to leave with me, but...I should have done something, you know? But how could I even conceive that he'd kill both of them?"

"If you report him now?"

"He'd kill me. He has people who take care of him. How could he progress so quickly if he didn't?"

"Have you seen her?"

"No, and I pray I never do. I hope she left like they said. You know he still goes out there to look for her. Even after processing his own crime scene. How can they catch the killer when he is in charge of the investigation?"

"Insane. What happens if he gets away with this? Where will it stop?"

"I don't know, Miguel. I don't know. Our life, it is never easy is it?"

The door opened, and a large crowd of laughing men fell out into the small courtyard. Asp took that moment to ease his way over the low wall and walk away. He had a name, and he had a profession.

He waited in the darkness. It had been two days since he took up his vigil. He'd wait two more before he'd have to track down Ricardo Castro de la Mata. Asp preferred to make the kill here, where the bastard had committed his own acts. Only he wouldn't sully the interior of the small ranch house. He had plans for Ricardo.

Asp had never wanted to kill someone before. The missions he'd accomplished were done out of duty, to help thousands by taking a life. Rationalization? Perhaps, but it worked for him. Until the night he overheard that conversation. Now? Well, now he knew what Anubis went through when he tracked down and killed the bastard who'd gone after his woman and child. Now he understood the white-hot fury that embedded inside a man's heart and prevented him from seeing the correct way to do things. Now he understood, and he'd apologize to his friend because the desire to kill Ricardo Castro de la Mata ate him from the inside like acid. It was a slow, painful burn and with each passing hour that Lyric's family wasn't avenged, it killed a little more of his soul. Asp's muscles tightened at the sound of a motor. He stood and moved to the window. A set of headlights bounced down the pothole infested road. He pushed back into the shadows. He'd turned on the small lamp in the bedroom. It would be noticeable from the driveway, but the bastard wouldn't be able to see who was in the house.

He heard the car stop and idle for a long span of time. The bastard was either amping himself up to come inside, or he was running through his options of confronting Lyric. Whatever he was doing it ended with a twist of the ignition key. Asp listened to the computerized ding when the car door opened and noted the absence when the door shut, although there was no slam. The bastard was going to try to break into the house, then.

The door handle jiggled and then turned. Asp hadn't locked it. A slight crack between the door and the jam let in a sliver of moonlight. The door inched open, carefully and quietly. What was the motherfucker's intent? The man entered. Asp saw the gun pointed toward the floor, and in the hand that controlled the door, he saw a rope. Another cascade of fury slithered just underneath his skin. He planned on abducting Lyric. Planned. Past-fucking-tense.

Asp took one step from the shadow and lowered the butt of his newly acquired forty-five caliber automatic in a sharp motion. The crack against the back of the man's skull preceded the whap of his unconscious body hitting the terra-cotta tiles of the living room floor. Asp grabbed the bastard's leg and dragged him back out the door. He'd gone over this plan countless times. He'd debated with himself. His inner devil's advocate warred with the voice of reason. He'd run the pros and cons against the outrage and hatred that coursed through his veins with every pump of his heart.

Asp made his way behind a small shack where an over-hang covered a stone wheel used to sharpen tools. Asp had put it to good use when he'd arrived. He dropped the man's leg and moved to the wood stack. The bastard was short. He needed something. *Perfect.* Asp set two large logs on the inside of the overhang's frame, directly beside the two support beams on either side of the door. He reached into the shed and grabbed a rope. He took the machete he'd sharpened this afternoon and cut the rope into lengths. A quick flick of his wrist and he had the rope attached to the man's wrists and ankles. It took a bit of effort, but he managed to get the unconscious man into position and tied off.

Asp stepped back and ran a critical eye over his work. Yes, this would do. He sat down at the small wheel and lit a kerosene lamp. While he waited for Ricardo Castro de la Mata to wake up, he wet the stone and used his leg to pump the pedal making the stone turn. He pushed the blade at an angle against the wheel, drawing it in long, slow strokes against the stone. The edge sang against the wheel and soothed Asp's racing mind. A moan came from the man tied spread eagle between the support beams. He waited, quietly observing the bastard in front of him.

"What?" The man spoke in Spanish as he started to come to and then jerked awake.

Asp reached over and pushed the button on the device Duke had loaned him.

"What is this?" Ricardo pulled against the ropes, frantic and desperate. His eyes swiveled down to Asp. "Let me go! Do you not know who I am?"

Asp answered in the same language. "You are Ricardo Castro de la Mata and you are a murderer."

The man ceased his struggles, his eyes snapped to Asp with a laser-like stare. "I don't know what you are talking about."

Asp cocked his head and looked at the man. Did he really think he could pull off the innocent look?

"Why did you sneak into the Garcia house tonight with a rope and a gun?" Asp was suddenly tired. He needed to end this and go home. To Lyric.

"We had a report of a breaking and entering."

"Why did you kill the old man?" Asp lifted the machete, so Ricardo could see it.

"What are you going to do with that? You know the penalty for assaulting an officer of the National Police?"

"Oh, yes, I do. Do you know the penalty for murdering two innocent men in an effort to silence a woman you thought was making a report against you?"

The man choked before he blustered, "I have no idea what you are talking about." The man's eyes squinted. He stared down at Asp as if he was dirt on his shoes. A pretty cocky attitude for a man that was tied spread eagle. Asp stood up, and the man's eyes widened. He knew he was an intimidating bastard. His size had worked against him at times, but not today. Today he used every inch of his height and bulk. He took two steps forward, keeping his back to Duke's device.

"What I am talking about, Ricardo Castro de la Mata, Sergeant of the National Police, Identification number 23-97389451, is that you came in search of Lyric Gadson, to take her against her will." Asp didn't know that for sure, but all the pieces fell into line. He couldn't see Lyric enticing this asshole's attention, so he threw it in. "When she wasn't here, you freaked out and thought she might have gone to district headquarters and reported your unwanted attention to District Commander Jesus Garcia." Asp touched the tip of the machete to the top button of the man's uniform. A drop of sweat fell from Ricardo's brow onto the blade. Asp turned the steel and let the flat side of the weapon skim across the man's ribs, wiping away the sweat. Ricardo sucked wind and held his breath the entire time the steel swiped past his internal organs.

"I don't know..." Asp flicked the blade up and cut off the first button of the man's uniform and his words at the same time.

"Admit it to me now, and I won't make you suffer, too much." Asp wielded the knife in front of him. The reflection of the kerosene lamp flashed off steel that he'd polished for most of the afternoon.

"Admit what?"

"You know you killed those men. I know you killed them."

"I..." The tip of Asp's blade flicked up and pierced the skin under Ricardo's chin. Asp applied the smallest amount of pressure and blood traced along the metal in a tiny stream. "If you lie, I'll cut you." Asp trailed the tip of the blade down the man's throat, barely scratching the skin, but leaving a trail of blood.

"No, you'll kill me." Ricardo pulled belabored breaths into his lungs. His sweat was rolling off his forehead and down his neck.

"If you speak the truth, I won't kill you." Asp lifted his eyes and locked his stare with the terrified eyes of his prey. "I. Will. Not. Kill. You." Oh, but he would maim the mother-fucker. Asp had sworn an oath and had an allegiance to Guardian. As much as he wanted to slice the man into a million pieces...that was not who he was. It was not who he wanted to be for his future wife and their children.

Asp pulled the razor-sharp edge down the man's shirt easily popping every button. He slid the tip of the blade between the man's belt and his pants. A quick jerk severed the leather and dropped his utility belt to the ground with a silence shattering thud. "Admit what you did and live." Asp tilted the weapon, so the blade pointed down and slid it between Ricardo's shirt and uniform pants. He slid the weapon down cutting a perfect line from waistband to knee.

"Fuck you," Ricardo spit the words at Asp. It was expected.

Asp put the tip of the blade under the man's chin again. "Too bad." He let the blade trail down to the man's chest and sliced him from collarbone to belly button. The cut wasn't deep, but it damn well hurt. The blood loss would be minimal, but Ricardo wouldn't know that.

"Wait, stop! Don't!" The man started to tremble.

Ahh...he was finally absorbing this reality of his. *Yes, Ricardo, you are in a shit ton of trouble.*

"Why should I stop? Are you going to admit what you've done?" Asp lowered the tip of the blade and tucked it under the bulge of Ricardo's boxer briefs, bouncing his balls on the flat side of the blade.

"I haven't—oh, God, no!" Ricardo's falsetto rang high and clear through the empty expanse of the farm. Asp expertly split the man's underwear from the bottom of the leg to his waistband with one smooth motion. He really liked the edge on this machete. Maybe he'd look into using blades more while he was in the field.

Asp trailed the tip of the weapon from Ricardo's belly-button to the root of his very small and unsurprisingly flaccid cock. "You must be a grower and not a shower, hey Ricardo? Or are you just a three-inch twitcher?" Asp lifted the man's cock with the tip of the blade. "Make that two inches." He pressed the tip of the knife ever so slightly against the man's ball sack. Asp quickly stepped back as Ricardo pissed himself. Tears ran down his cheeks.

"Don't, man, I swear I'll tell the truth. Don't cut it off!" Ricardo babbled for a minute before he realized that Asp had removed the tip of the machete.

"Talk, bitch. Tell me exactly what happened." Asp tapped the bottom of the man's balls again.

"I came to talk with Lyric. She wasn't here. Her father wouldn't answer my questions. He acted like I was scum on his boots. The old man, he laughed. He said Lyric was free from me. He said she'd found her savior. I fucking told her not to go to my district commander. I told her what would happen if she did. The fucking bitch went anyway!"

"So, you killed her father and grandfather?"

"I wasn't going to kill them. The old man, he kept taunting me. Telling me I was nothing and that Lyric was safe from me. I told him to shut up. I screamed at him. He just laughed. I shoved him down and told him to shut the fuck up, but he didn't. The gun fired. I... I don't remember squeezing the trigger, I swear!"

"And her father?"

"He regained consciousness. I knocked him out so I could talk to the old man. I didn't know he'd come to. He attacked me. I fought him. We fought. The bastard slipped, and I got on top of him. I forced him to his knees, and I shot him."

"What weapon did you use to kill them?"

"My automatic." The man sniveled.

"What did you do with the gun?" Asp wanted to make sure when the man was prosecuted for his crimes, he'd be convicted.

"I threw it away in a dumpster in Cartagena. I reported it stolen to my supervisor." Real fear filled the man's eyes as he watched Asp move the machete.

"Why are you here tonight?" Asp ran the tip of the blade down the inside of the man's leg letting it scrape deep enough to cut the surface layers of skin. Ricardo whined, high pitched and pleading.

"Why?" Asp shouted.

"Lyric! I came for Lyric!"

"And what were you going to do with her?"

"Fuck her! Kill her, maybe? I don't know! I don't know!" Snot hung from the man's nose as he bawled uncontrollably. Blood from the shallow cut ran in small streaks down the man's thighs. Asp pulled a latex glove out of his pocket and put it on. He bent down and removed the man's new service weapon.

"Balls or knees?"

"What? What the fuck are you talking about? You said if I confessed you wouldn't kill me!"

"I did. And I'm not going to kill you. But you need to make a decision. Do you want your balls, or do you want your knees? Two balls or two knees for two lives. You're getting off easy."

Asp slapped the man's balls with the blade. He shrieked and pleaded, babbling incoherent words. "Balls or knees!" Asp shouted the question at the man. His patience had pegged in the red the minute the mother fucker had regained consciousness.

"No! No, no, no..." Ricardo screamed as Asp lifted the weapon and pointed it at his knees.

"So, you want to lose your balls?" Asp lifted the machete.

"No!" The shriek pierced the night.

"Which is it? You have ten seconds to decide." Asp started counting. "Ten, nine, eight..."

The man screamed and pulled at the ropes that secured him. "Five, four, three..."

"No! No!" Ricardo shrieked.

Asp dropped the weapon, pulled the man's ball sack down with his hand and sliced the entire package off. He looked up at the convulsing man. Unfortunately, he knew the bastard would live. Asp pulled his phone out and dialed. He told the emergency services team to dispatch an ambulance. He took the machete with him. He'd grown attached to it. Asp strode to the National Police Car and used his gloved hand to open the door. He got in, put the car into drive and left. He'd made the man pay. The confession was streamed from Duke's helmet camera to Guardian and from there to the district commander's personal IP address. He'd have the file on his computer in the morning when he logged in. Asp had honored his oath. He didn't kill the monster, but only because he didn't have clearance. He'd avenged Lyric's family. The bastard would go to jail and Asp could live with himself because justice was served.

He bumped down the pothole infested drive and turned left onto the paved road. Behind him, red lights crested a hill. The ambulance or other National Police officers no doubt. Asp turned on the radio and found a soft tune playing on one of the stations. He had a hell of a drive to get to Cartagena. He had a flight to catch. He was going home.

~

"**W**ait, what the fuck? There. Is someone else there?" Jared King pulled his brother's attention back to the video screen.

"Who?" Alpha barked across the room to Bengal. The video feed showed a man dressed in a hooded sweatshirt, the hood pulled over his head to hide his face, wearing baggy sweatpants and bulky gloves moving across the small space between the helmet cam and the man Asp had strung up.

"Not one of our assets. Can't be." Bengal picked up a landline and dialed Thanatos's number.

"Dude, I'm supposed to be on mandatory downtime. I'm kind of busy." Thanatos's voice crackled over the speaker.

"Where are you?"

"In bed, with a bonny lass." A woman's laugh popped all eyes up. They stared blankly at each other.

"Yeah, sorry for bothering you. I'll talk to you later." Bengal began to hang up.

"Wait, now you have me curious. Where did you think I was?"

"Never mind. Have a good night." Alpha gave Bengal the kill sign, and he cut the connection.

"Where's Lycos?" Archangel snapped.

Anubis answered from the video screen where he was patched into the conference from South Dakota. "He's here with us. I just saw him going into the mess hall. He was chasing after one of the new med techs not more than two hours ago."

Alpha's eyes hadn't left the screen. "Small. He's too small for one of our guys. Maybe he's a local?" The man stood in front of Ricardo. He lifted a gun from his side and put it under Ricardo's chin. The man was unconscious, so it wasn't...

Every man in the room jumped when the gun fired. Ricardo's head exploded, painting the small overhang with blood, skull, and brains. From the angle of the helmet cam, they could see flashing lights bouncing down the driveway. The killer side-stepped Ricardo's body and left as silently as he'd come.

"Jewell, tell me you can get a facial recognition on that man." Alpha snapped at his sister who was pounding the keyboard like it had offended her.

"No, in order to get a facial recognition, you need to see a face." She overlaid a grid onto a playback of the video. "Five-feet-five inches, if we use Asp's six-feet-five inches as a reference in this shot.

"So most likely Colombian? A local?"

"I couldn't say. The only thing I know for a fact is that guy is five-feet-five inches tall and is carrying a big ass weapon."

"Desert Eagle, forty-five caliber." Bengal nodded as he looked at the still of the weapon.

"An American weapon," Archangel mused.

Alpha waved that comment off. "Doesn't mean anything. They are highly sought after."

"But would a local have access to a weapon that expensive?" Jared stared at the gun. "That is not a Saturday Night Special or a Russian cast off."

"We know it isn't any of our assets. Our teams are out. Our Shadows are clear. Jewell, where did you cut off the video to the District Commander?"

She clicked on the file. "Here. When Asp drove away."

Archangel leaned back in his seat. "Pull the file."

Keystrokes sounded in rapid succession. "It's pulled."

"Delete it. All of it. We know Asp didn't violate protocol. We tried to play it on the up and up." Alpha interjected.

"Cutting off a man's balls is on the up and up?" Jared turned to his brother when he asked.

"Imagine if Christian's family...okay, wrong example, sorry. Imagine what I would do if someone killed Frank and Mom and went after Tori."

"You'd obliterate the bastard."

"I would. *Asp didn't*. Did he exact his pound of flesh?"

"More like a quarter pound." Jewell's unexpected sarcasm caused Alpha to blink. He held up a hand to her silencing her snark and continued to speak, "He notified us of what he'd found. He tracked down the evidence. We witnessed him leaving the man, alive. Granted, he was a bit worse for wear, but the son of a bitch was alive. Asp even fucking called emergency services in from the village. No, we are putting this in a can and sealing it. Whoever had a grudge against Ricardo killed that man. Not our monkey, not our zoo."

Archangel stood and took off his glasses, pinching the bridge of his nose. "I concur. That wasn't a Guardian asset. Shit can the video." He nodded at Bengal. "Tell me the second Asp touches American airspace. He's to stay at the ranch, and I want him evaluated." He placed his glasses back on his face and slid his hands into his slacks. "The man fucking cut the balls off another man." He gave a shudder and turned on his heel. "Tell Doc Wheeler I'm worried about this one."

Alpha acknowledged his older brother. When the door closed, he looked at Bengal. "I would have gutted the son of a bitch. I don't know how he restrained himself."

Bengal shrugged and shook his head. "I guess he's a better man than either of us."

CHAPTER 25

"**A**re you sure?" Lyric looked at the large tray of food that Miss Amanda set on the small counter of the cottage. "I don't think I can fit the platter in the refrigerator." Miss Amanda was the third person to drop off food. Lyric was happy to have visitors because the clock had been running backward ever since Kaeden had found her this morning and told her Isaac was on his way home. She was excited and scared at the same time. She didn't know which feeling to embrace and tried hard not to look at either. She pulled another deep breath in and let it out. Isaac would be here soon, and everything would be alright. She believed it. Almost.

"Honey, all of this can sit on the counter. Nothing needs to be refrigerated, and you won't have to take time away from welcoming him back to cook." Miss Amanda gave her a wide-eyed wink and laughed as Lyric choked in surprise.

"I'm old, honey, not dead."

Morbid embarrassment swamped Lyric. "Oh, no! I mean...it's just that..." Lyric dropped her head into her hands and groaned.

"What is it?" Miss Amanda put her hand on Lyric's shoulder and rubbed a small circle.

Lyric lifted her eyes to the matriarch of the ranch. She was such a kind woman. It wouldn't be fair to dump her fears and concerns on her. She smiled and shook her head. "Nothing, it's really nothing."

"Uh huh. Sweetheart, I've raised three girls, and I have three daughters-in-law and one more in the chute. I know when nothing *isn't* nothing. Let's sit down. Honestly, you can tell me anything. It goes no farther than this room. I promise." Amanda led her to the loveseat.

Lyric looked down at her entwined fingers. "I love Isaac with all my heart. It is a desperate kind of love, one that scares me because of the...I don't know, the magnitude of my feelings?" She shrugged, still looking down. "What if he doesn't feel that way? What if he doesn't love me the way I love him?" She glanced at Miss Amanda, swiping a tear away when it fell.

"Oh, honey. Have you told Isaac how you feel?" Amanda reached out and held her hand in hers.

Lyric nodded. "I have."

"And he told you that he loved you, right?"

"Yes, ma'am."

"And he sent you up here, to the one place he knew you'd be safe?"

Lyric nodded. "Yes, ma'am."

"And he's called you and told you why it was taking so long to come home?"

"He called." Lyric whispered in acknowledgement.

"Did he tell you he loved you on the call?"

"Yes, ma'am." She shook her head. "I'm just scared that he won't need me. That he won't feel what he felt for me now that we aren't in..." She glanced up at Miss Amanda and checked her words, "...the situation we were in."

"Don't borrow trouble, dear. You can 'what if ' yourself to death, and it won't change a single thing that is happening now. He said he loves you. Has he ever lied to you?"

"No, ma'am, he's always been honest." Lyric drew a deeper breath. "I'm stupid, aren't I?"

"Stupid? No. I think you're reacting the way anyone in your circumstances would react. You've been apart from the man you love for a while now. You're scared."

Lyric nodded. She was scared. It wasn't like her to be this way. She was a take the bull by the horns type of girl. Her dad always said...she stopped the thought when grief welled up inside her. She glanced at Miss Amanda and asked, "Do you think he could have the same kind of questions?"

Amanda smiled as she spoke, "Ah...well, I can't speak for Isaac, but I know the men that work here on the ranch and at the complex. To a person when they fall in love, they can become complete idiots." A surprised laugh burst from Lyric at Amanda's words. "Seriously! They are the best at what they do. Specialists, every one of them. They are elite, but when it comes to love, they're just like you and me. They don't have all the answers. These men are a special breed. They have demanding jobs that require the skill sets that most don't have. They think they know it all, but for the most part, they have no idea what we ladies need. So, we teach them."

"Thank you, for taking the time to talk with me and for bringing me more food than we can eat in a week."

Amanda laughed, slapped her hands against her thighs and stood up. "Girl, you are in for a rude awakening. Cooking for your man could be a full-time job. My sons can put some food away, but I have never seen anyone eat the way your Isaac does."

"That's what everyone says, but seriously, he barely ate when I was with him. We lived off of protein bars and fruit."

Amanda blinked at her and then smiled in a way that told

Lyric she was wrong, but Miss Amanda wasn't going to call her on it. "I should be going. I believe..." Amanda opened the door and nodded outside..."Yep, right on time."

"What?" Lyric glanced out the door. A truck was pulling up the long driveway.

"Kaeden called me when the plane was on approach. I came down to keep you distracted. Your man's home."

Lyric jolted at Miss Amanda's words. She stepped out of the door and watched as the black truck stopped by the big house across the clearing. The windows were tinted so she couldn't see inside the vehicle. The door opened and... *yes!* "Isaac!" Lyric shouted and launched herself at a dead run toward the man who exited the passenger side door. Somehow, she was in his arms and kissing him. He held her tight, so tight, and his arms felt like home.

"Shhh, babe. It's okay. I'm home." His words registered at the same time as she felt the tears on her cheeks. He lifted her, so her legs wrapped around his waist and he carried her into Drover's Cottage. Lyric folded around him, pulling herself so tightly against him that there was no space for air.

"I love you. I love you, so much." She repeated the words against his neck, still crying, but the tears were from happiness, not sorrow. He kicked the door to the cottage shut and squeezed her against him. His massive, rock-hard body, stood unwavering as he easily held her weight. He lifted her chin from his neck and smiled at her. "My beautiful Lyric. I love you."

Asp stared down at the woman in his arms. The flight home had been unusual for him. He couldn't stop his doubts from looping a narrative through his internal thinking. He knew Lyric was *it* for him, but she was young and so fucking beautiful. Her beauty shone from deep inside her as well the outside. Her radiance had become his guidepost in the darkness where he lived. He didn't have the right to have someone like her in his life, and that little fucker called doubt kept reminding him of that as he traveled home.

His worry was wiped away the second he opened the vehicle's door. Her expression told him everything. She hit him at a full-on run, and he absorbed her like the desert absorbs a raindrop. He managed to get them into the small cottage Anubis had told them they would be sharing until a permanent housing solution could be found. He didn't care if they lived in a tent. He just needed her.

She'd burrowed into him as he held her, and he fucking loved it. He smiled as he lifted her chin so he could see her face. Her whispered admissions of her love gave that fucker doubt a harsh kick in the ass. She loved *him*. She was in his arms and together they would figure out how to build a life. He smiled down at the perfection wrapped around his body. "My beautiful Lyric. I love you."

Something melted inside her. She relaxed and smiled at him before she pulled them down into a sweet kiss that quickly devolved into a need-filled, passionate, exchange. He pulled away to breathe and to find the bedroom...or bed. Damn the place was small, but it'd work. It only took four steps to rack his shins against the bed frame. He held her tight to his chest and laid them both on top of the feather soft mattress before he took possession of her lips again. He needed to devour her. He needed so damn much he was afraid to unleash the want and the desire.

Her hands gripped at his shirt. She broke free from the kiss. "Clothes off. Now."

Her wish was his command. He lost his shirt, boots, jeans, and briefs in the same time it took her to disrobe. He stood over her and admired the miles and miles of beautiful tan skin. Her dark hair fell over her breasts.

Asp dropped one knee onto the bed between her legs. He ran his fingers from her shin to her thigh. She shivered, and her skin prickled in anticipation of his touch. "What do you need from me?" He wanted her to lead. He was too hungry. He needed her to control his aggression, or he'd ravage her.

Her eyes traveled his chest, down his stomach to his cock. He'd circled his fist at the base and squeezed trying to control his desire, to harness the need.

"I need you to take that cock and fuck me. Hard. I want you to make me feel you. I want you to cum inside me, and I want it now. Don't make me wait and don't hold back." She trailed her finger to her sex and separated the folds, exposing herself to him. She dipped two fingers inside and slid them out, slick with her own juices. "See, I'm ready for you. I need you now, Isaac."

"I have condoms." Asp reached toward his pocket.

She reached out and stopped him. "No, I've taken care of that. I'm on the pill now. I want to feel you. Now, Isaac." Her hand reached for his cock and he lowered on top of her, took her lips with a possessive urgency that became as essential as breathing. He let her guide him home. Her legs circled his waist and tightened, urging him to go faster. He refused to hurt her. He slowly entered her and retreated, working his cock deeper. He paused once he was seated inside her. His lips slid from her mouth, down her jaw and onto her collarbone where he abused the sensitive skin, marking her as his.

"Take me. Isaac, for God's sake, stop teasing me," she panted and hit his shoulder. He lifted away from his mark and smiled at his efforts. A feeling of happiness washed over him when she cupped the back of his neck and made him look at her.

"You asked what I needed. I need you. Now. Don't make

me beg you, Isaac." She arched her hips against him as he pushed forward. "Harder."

Isaac lifted to his knees and pushed her legs over his forearms. "I don't want to hurt you."

"You can't hurt me." Her hands slid over his shoulders. "Show me how much you love me."

Those words ruined what little control he had. He snapped his hips forward and watched the sway of her breasts as he withdrew and thrust forward again. Her eyes closed and her back arched. He watched, mesmerized as she cupped her breasts and pinched her nipples. His orgasm lanced down his spine and pooled in his balls. Her back arched and she clenched, her shouts of ecstasy echoed around him, and he crashed inside her. A complete, catastrophic, annihilation. He dropped to his hands, his arms out straight supporting his weight over her. His body shook with the aftershocks of the best fucking orgasm he'd ever experienced. He knew the reason why he was obliterated right now. Love. What they shared was more than just physical. The emotional connection, hell, it magnified the pleasure they shared.

"Is it always this good with you?" She ran her hands up and down his shaking arms.

"Only with you." He pulled out of her and rolled onto his side, pulling her with him. "I missed you."

She smiled and caressed his brow and cheek with her fingers. "I missed you, so much. Did you finish your work in Colombia?"

"I did." He knew they'd go back to bury her family, but he also knew they'd make a life away from the Andes foothills. "Did Kaeden take care of you here?"

She nodded and tucked up against his chest. "They're all very nice, but I'm glad you're home."

"*You* are my home." Isaac closed his eyes and let his fingers caress her skin. He was home. Here, entwined in her arms, he was home. The logistics of where they'd live and how'd they'd manage his profession were just that. Logistics. As long as she was waiting for him, he'd be able to find his way home because Lyric was his lodestar to navigate through the darkness. Where ever she was would always be his home.

EPILOGUE

*L*ycos sat in the corner booth of his favorite D.C. bar. He enjoyed the atmosphere. The crowd, as usual, was diverse. Men with men, men with women, women with women, the dancers didn't give a fuck, and neither did he. Right now, the only thing he cared about was making her way through the grinding bodies on the small dance floor. Her tight ocean blue dress clung to every enticing curve of her holy-fuck-stop-all-traffic-accident-causing body. Her thick black hair would have fallen to her shoulders if she hadn't twisted it up and skewered it with long ornamental pins. Ornamental his ass.

Lycos leaned back in his seat and let her see his intimate regard. He had a reputation, one he didn't discourage, but one that he hadn't earned either. They'd been exclusive for years, except when the job required them to perform, and, as far as they knew, nobody else was aware of their sporadic domestic bliss. Their relationship started as one of convenience and had become one of stability for both of them. Were they in love? No. They'd had that talk often. He wasn't sure either one of them was capable of that particular emotion. What they had...worked. When it no longer did, they'd walk away. He'd be sad to see the end of it, but the only constant in life was change.

He stood as she approached and even in her four-inch heels, she barely reached his chin. She was his little China doll, although she wasn't fragile. In fact, Moriah was the deadliest woman on the face of the earth. He claimed her mouth as her arms circled his neck. If any of the bastards that were eye fucking her when she walked past them wanted her, they'd have to come through him first. Not that she needed him to protect her, but she allowed it, and that was some heady as fuck shit. She untangled herself from him with one last rub of her hips against his erection.

"Tease." He hissed as she slid into the booth.

"I don't think it's a tease if I'm a sure thing." She picked up his tumbler of Grey Goose and took a drink. She set the glass down and turned to him, leaning into his side, laying her head on his chest. "What's wrong?"

"Why do you think something's wrong?"

"Grey Goose. Your go to when you're stressed."

"They have you on video."

Moriah shrugged as if his concerns were nothing. He rolled his eyes at her cavalier attitude. She glanced up and caught him in the act. She huffed, moved away from him and flopped onto the backrest of the booth. "Look, they saw nothing. I watched. I saw what Asp set up, and I examined it when he was inside the house waiting for that bastard. I stole the clothes I wore from a stall in Cartagena, and I put stacks in the heels of my boots. Too tall, no face. Dead man tell no tales, right?"

"Desert Eagle?"

"What? I like *that* gun. Not like they can trace it or ammo to me or connect me to Colombia. I was in Egypt on assignment, remember?"

"You shouldn't have killed him. I wanted you there to back up Asp, not to take the Colombian fucker out. You should have left when Asp did." Lycos was livid when he'd learned that she'd popped a cap through that bastard's brain. This wasn't the first time she'd taken justice into her own hands. He sometimes wondered if the people doing her evaluations saw more than her beautiful face. The woman had deep, dark scars. He'd been with her for years, and he only knew the smallest details about her past.

"Don't tell me what to do, lover. I don't like it."

"I don't want to see you taken down. Stop with the vigilante justice, Miho, or sooner or later, it will come back and trap you."

Moriah blinked at the use of her given name. She took his Grey Goose and downed it in one swallow. "Stop worrying about me, Ryan. I'm not yours. I never will be. Perhaps it is time we said goodbye." She slid around the table and got out. Lycos stayed seated. She pulled down her skin-tight skirt and turned to face him. "I will always be there for you, my dear, sweet friend. Stay safe. Whatever it takes."

"As long as it takes, my beautiful China doll."

"I'm not a doll."

"I know," he said to her back as he watched the swing of eyes, both male and female, follow her out the door. He motioned to the waitress and ordered another Grey Goose. He knew he'd been pushing what she tolerated when he criticized her actions, but he'd never expected her to break off their arrangement. He watched the throng on the dance floor pulse and grind against each other while he tried to decide what he felt. He took his drink from the waitress and dropped a fifty on her tray. She smiled enticingly, but he ignored her. He took a long pull on his GG. Sad. He was sad the time with her was over. Wasn't that a shame. He should probably feel more, but...that wasn't him. Or her.

Moriah struggled to get to the exit before the first tear fell. Ending it with Ryan hurt so fucking bad. She jerked at the waist and caught a sob in her gut before it could escape. She'd developed intimate, powerful feelings for him years ago, and time had only deepened them. She'd killed that bastard because he'd taken a rope into that house. He would have taken Asp's woman, and he would have raped her. She knew it in the fiber of her DNA. She'd *been* that woman back when she'd been young…and fragile. She wasn't either of those things now. Now, she eradicated vermin like that bastard with the same lack of guilt she felt when stepping on a cockroach. Had Guardian sanctioned the hit? No. Did she regret it? Never.

The only thing she regretted right now was the feeling of being gutted when she walked away from Lycos. Lycos had meant well, but he couldn't know the reasons behind her actions. Nobody knew. Those reasons lay in her past, a past she'd buried as deep as the bodies of the men she killed to hide it. She lifted her hand and hailed a cab. Tonight, she'd grieve the loss of something that never should have been. At first light, she'd slip away, and become nobody until Guardian called her again.

After all, a Shadow was only an illusion, a lack of light cast upon the world for a short time.

The End.

ALSO BY KRIS MICHAELS

Other Titles by Kris Michaels:

Titles in the Kings of Guardian Series:

Jacob, The Kings of Guardian - Book One

Joseph, The Kings of Guardian - Book Two

Adam, The Kings of Guardian - Book Three

Jason, The Kings of Guardian - Book Four

Jared, The Kings of Guardian - Book Five

Jasmine, The Kings of Guardian - Book Six

Chief, The Kings of Guardian - Book Seven

Jewell, The Kings of Guardian - Book Eight

Jade, The Kings of Guardian - Book Nine

Justin, The Kings of Guardian - Book 10

Guardian Security Shadow World Series:

Anubis

The Everlight Series:

An Evidence of Magic

An Incident of Magic

Stand Alone Novel:

A Heart's Desire

96453220R00132

Made in the USA
Lexington, KY
21 August 2018